LOSING EVA

JENNIFER SIVEC

Edited by ROGENA MITCHELL-JONES

Edited by JC WING

Illustrated by BRENDA GONET

SOUL
SISTER
PRESS

To my Family, whom I love and adore with all of my heart. You are my promise, my possibility, and my everything .

PROLOGUE

It was a beautiful day.

Brynn couldn't ask for anything more perfect. The sun was shining and bright. The leaves on the trees and blades of grass were the greenest green, almost as if the ideal shade was painted on just for her. The weather had been dismal lately, but the beauty of the day was unsurpassed by any so far.

Brynn sat back in her lounge chair with a book, looking forward to getting lost in it for a few hours. She hadn't been able to enjoy the simplicity and beauty of their large backyard for a long time.

These days she needed it. Her doctor wanted her to take it easy, and as difficult as it was, she was trying.

She sat back and nestled deep into the Adirondack chair made comfortable with soft cushions and closed her eyes.

Suddenly, she felt the hairs on the back of her neck stand on end. Someone was there in the backyard watching her. Somehow, she knew that it was him. She looked around frantically trying to find him. *How did he find me? How did he know where I was?* She felt completely naked and exposed in the spaciousness of the grass and the trees.

Maxie, their 80-pound pet Lab lifted his head and looked around. He seemed to sense something, too—almost as though he could smell him in the air. He let out a few loud barks as a warning while being sure to stay close to Brynn.

Thomas was close, and he was watching her. Brynn knew it. She felt the saliva building in the back of her throat, nearly choking her. It was a familiar feeling, one that she hadn't felt for a long time. How can this be? How can he be here? He's dead, gone for almost two decades. How can he be here now?

Brynn frantically gathered her things and turned to go into the house. Suddenly he was there, standing in front of her, towering as he did when she was young.

He glared at her, ice blue eyes piercing through her soul, hatred, and resentment radiating dangerously. Brynn was in danger, and she felt it in every fiber of her being.

"W-w-what do you want?" she croaked, barely able to utter the words. Maxie stood next to her, alarmed. He was more of a lover than anything else, and Brynn knew that she couldn't count on him to protect her, despite his size.

Thomas didn't speak. He just stared at her. Brynn wanted to cry.

"You're supposed to be dead! Dead!" Brynn yelled, backing away from him cautiously, slowly. It felt like the house was a mile away from her as she tried to move her feet faster, yet keep her eyes on him. Thomas seemed to be getting closer and closer to her. "Oh my God, you're supposed to be dead."

Suddenly Brynn felt his hands around her throat, and before she knew it, she had fallen backwards onto the ground, and he was above her. He was squeezing slowly, tightening his grip, and Brynn felt her air supply cutting off.

"Please stop! P-p-please!" she cried, unable to raise her voice above barely a whisper.

She felt him release his grip on her, and she was grateful for a split second as she gasped for breath. Horrified, she watched him roll up his sleeve. What is he doing? It was an odd gesture, and she couldn't imagine why he would do that.

He opened his mouth to speak. His voice was different from the low, *gravelly voice that haunted Brynn's dreams from her childhood. His voice now was loud, booming, and clear like a bell. "You killed me. You were my daughter, and you killed me. How could you?"*

Brynn was stunned. He knows. How does he know?

"I know, because I know everything. And now, since you took something from me, I am going to take something from you."

Brynn was confused. What else can he take from me? He took my childhood, my ability to love openly and completely. He caused me to scar myself. What else can he do to me?

"This is what I am going to do to you." With one sudden movement, Thomas took his fist and shoved it violently into her belly. Brynn couldn't believe her eyes. Oh my God, what is he doing?

"I'm killing your baby, just like you killed me," Thomas sneered, his yellow teeth staring down at her as he grinned.

Brynn screamed. The pain was incredible as she watched him pulling his bloody arm in and out of her stomach, his fists squeezing the tiny life inside of her. She could feel that she was in pain, her little baby. She screamed, desperately, trapped beneath Thomas' massive body as he straddled her legs.

Suddenly she felt a sharp slap, then another. "Brynn! Brynn!"

Thomas was calling her name, but it wasn't his strange voice. It was someone else's. "Brynn! Brynn!"

Adam. She heard Adam's voice coming out of Thomas' mouth.

Brynn sat straight up, no longer trapped. "Where did Thomas go?" she screamed in horror.

"Brynn, it's me! It's Adam!" Adam held her with his strong hands, trying desperately to get her to see him. Her eyes were wide and frantic, her pupils huge and black. He knew that she was lost in her dream, as she was so many nights. "Brynn, sweetheart, it's me, honey. It's Adam. Wake up. It's just a bad dream."

Brynn stared straight ahead, her thick dark hair a tangled mess, tears running down her face. Maxie was sitting at her side, his big head lying next to her as he whimpered.

Slowly, her face started to relax a little, her hands flying to her belly, rubbing desperately. She shifted her gaze down to Maxie and then over to Adam, and then back to Maxie.

"Adam!" she cried. "Adam!" She was back, and Adam felt relief flood through him. This was a bad one, maybe even the worst one. He was afraid he wasn't going to get her back.

"It's okay Brynn. You're safe. It was just a bad dream."

"It was Thomas."

"I know it was Thomas. You screamed his name. It's always Thomas. But he's dead. He can't hurt you anymore." Adam took her hand and pulled her into his arms so that he could hold her close.

Brynn kept rubbing her stomach. She could feel the scars through her cotton nightshirt. Several of the deeper ones were pretty bumpy. She was sure those would never go away. Thomas was her father, and he was supposed to protect her. But instead, she had to protect herself. The cutting always allowed her to cocoon away into her own world for a bit so that she didn't have to feel the pain and the fear. If she didn't have the cutting, and then Adam, she knew that she never would have survived.

"Do you want to talk about it?" Adam asked gently. Sometimes she did, and sometimes she didn't. The shrink had told them that it was up to Brynn, so Adam always asked. He didn't want to pressure her.

"No. Yes...no." Brynn wasn't sure. She was trying to shut the dream out of her mind, but the sobs kept coming, and it was still difficult to breathe.

Adam looked at her cautiously. He had made the mistake once of leaving her behind. He was never going to do that again, but he wondered if they would ever be able to have a normal life. He wanted one, he needed one. He loved Brynn and he couldn't live without her.

"Let's go to sleep then, sweetheart. We need to rest. You need to rest." Adam turned off the bedside lamp, and they settled into the soft, comfortable sheets. They felt Maxie jump on to the end of the bed, which jostled as if an earthquake struck until they were all comfortable. Adam could tell that Brynn was smiling, and he smiled, too. Maxie had been good for both of them.

"I'm sorry, Adam," Brynn said in the dark, still sniffling.

"Don't be sorry. You can't help it," Adam said sleepily. "It'll be okay."

As they drifted off to sleep, Adam heard Brynn's voice.

"Adam, he was killing our baby."

1

JANE'S WEDDING DAY

Brynn was excited for the day.

Jane was finally getting married to a wonderful man, Andrew, and she had asked Brynn to be the Matron of Honor. Brynn had spent the last year dealing with ghosts and trying to put away the past, and Jane's wedding was the first time she had felt hopeful about anything for awhile.

Brynn's therapist helped her come to terms with her past. Most recently, they were working out her relationship with Rose, and the resentment she continued to feel toward her, even though she was dead. Theirs had been far from the ideal mother/daughter relationship. Brynn was finally beginning to understand, and to feel more at peace with just how much Rose had needed her, even when Brynn was just a child. Brynn missed Rose and had loved her, but the memory of how dependent Rose had been on her continued to plague her. It took a year for her to stop expecting the early morning phone calls or the constant text messaging, but Brynn felt herself finally able to relax rather than feel "on call" at all times.

The shrink also helped her come to terms with being abandoned, but the nightmares about running, hiding, and being terrified in the woods still tormented her. The nightmares were violent, intense, and brutally real, often leaving their imprint on Brynn for days.

Adam did his best to comfort her through the dreams when they happened, and he was glad when they began to occur less often. For awhile, it had stayed that way, but recently, they seemed to occur more often, almost nightly. The feelings of abandonment were strong, and they weren't going away, even though Brynn tried desperately to push them aside.

But with Jane's wedding and so many new things on the horizon, there was so much to look forward to now.

"Brynn, we have to go soon, sweetheart," Adam's voice called up from the bottom of the stairs. He was always the early riser, and Brynn knew that he was already up, dressed, and had breakfast waiting for her. She showered the night before and got up slowly. She was so tired and could use another hour or so of sleep, but she knew that Jane would kill her.

Jane's husband-to-be was a good man, and Jane credited Brynn with giving her the courage to date again. She wanted Brynn to stand up with them at the altar, and Brynn knew that she couldn't be late.

As Brynn applied her makeup, she took a long look at herself in the mirror. The woman looking back at her was finally happier and more at peace than she had been her entire life. Brynn was no longer obsessed with finding answers to the questions that had plagued her all of her life.

Why was I abandoned? Why did Thomas hurt me? Why didn't Rose stop him?

Brynn's shrink told her that there was nothing she could do about her past; she actually began to believe him. Brynn couldn't remember ever being happy, and it was a strange feeling.

She slowly brushed her thick dark hair in long strokes. It had taken her entire life, but Brynn was finally letting it grow. She knew that there was nobody in her life anymore, who would grab it and yank it or use it to hold her captive while he hit her as Thomas had. The fear slowly diminished with every passing day. As far as adopted fathers went, Thomas was the worst, but he was dead now, and she didn't have to be afraid any longer.

She sighed contentedly, and smiled into the mirror. Her cheeks were rounder now that she had gained some weight. She looked healthier, almost glowing.

The doorbell rang, startling Brynn. She waited to hear Adam answer it, but then it rang again.

Brynn padded down the stairs, moving a little slower than usual, her long, cotton nightgown flowing behind her. When she reached the front door, she hesitated for a moment and felt a shiver run down her spine.

Don't be silly, she told herself. *There's nothing to be afraid of...*

When she opened the door, she froze—her big coffee colored eyes opening wide in disbelief.

On the other side of the screen stood an almost exact replica of herself, aged about 15 years. Her hand instinctively went to her belly.

They stared at each other silently.

"Brynn, honey, who is it?" Adam called coming up behind her.

When he got close behind her, he put his hand on her shoulder and stared. Nobody moved.

The woman on the other side stared down at Brynn's swollen belly and smiled.

She spoke first, her voice husky, sounding eerily like Brynn's. "Eva? Eva? It's me. Do you recognize me, sweetheart?" She was petite like Brynn, with the same dark hair and beautiful brown eyes. But as much as she resembled Brynn, Adam could tell there was something different, almost absent, in this other woman.

She looked worn down, her skin thin and dull, and her hair unkempt. But there was more that unsettled him. While Brynn's eyes were bright and beautiful, this woman's eyes reflected something different, something darker, and Adam automatically felt anxious. He instinctively moved a step closer to Brynn.

Brynn was quiet. The moment stretched out in front of her in slow motion. She felt a chill run down her spine, and she shivered.

Ellie stared at Brynn with a mixture of curiosity and jealously.

"Eva. Are you okay? You don't look so good, honey. I'm your Momma. Can you let me in? I'd love to talk to you."

Brynn didn't want to let her in. She knew that she should want to, but she didn't. Against her better judgment, she reached out toward the door to unlock the screen. Brynn suddenly felt dizzy, the woman in front of her was making a strange face.

Brynn could hear Adam's voice call her name, and she wondered why he was yelling so loudly when she was standing right in front of him. The last thing Brynn saw was the distraught look on Adam's face as she fell to the floor.

2

BRYNN'S MOTHER

Brynn woke up, her head aching and heavy. She was in a curtained area. She could hear beeping and the quiet scuffle of feet and voices, but she was alone. Squinting, her eyes tried to adjust to the harsh impersonal lighting fixtures. Brynn looked around and realized she was in the hospital and wearing a gown that was two sizes too big. *Where are my clothes?*

The last thing that she remembered was opening the screen door and seeing...what? *What did I see? What made me faint?* Brynn's head felt fuzzy, and it hurt. A lot. Her tongue felt dry and thick, and too big for her mouth. She desperately wanted water. She reached up and pulled at her long thick hair, trying to make the headache stop.

She instinctively put her hand over her belly. Oh my God, the baby. *Is the baby okay?* Brynn's heart was starting to race. *How long have I been here? Is the baby alright? Adam, where are you? Why is this happening now that everything has been going so well? Why?*

Brynn still couldn't believe that she was pregnant. After all this time, she was finally ready to be a mother. Adam was ready to be a parent much sooner than she was, but now she was at peace with her past. And with everything they had been through together—they had endured a separation, but now they were repairing their marriage and their lives. With Rose gone for over a year, Brynn now had faith that she was capable of being a good mother.

She was done being afraid.

Adam said he was never going to leave again, and Brynn somehow believed that it was true. She was finally learning to open up and embrace life with him, and there was a connection between them that was stronger than ever before. She knew that he felt it every time she looked at him, and she could tell that he was happy. They were finally on common ground, and for the first time, she felt as if she were contributing to their relationship as much as he had since they were fifteen years old.

But now, her whole world felt as if it were crashing in, and there was no way to stop it. The baby isn't moving, oh God! The baby isn't moving!

She looked around and saw a plastic box by her side.

She pushed the red nurses call button frantically, terrified to be alone, and desperate for answers. I need Adam! I need someone!

"Yes, may I help you?" a distant voice came from nowhere, a subtle clicking sound accompanying it.

"Yes, I need my husband. Where is he? How is my baby?" Brynn said in one breath, talking to the air. She was lost. She needed Adam.

"We'll be right there," the voice said.

"Okay," she said weakly, to no one. She hated to be alone. What happened?

The moment came flooding back to her, almost overtaking her. Brynn remembered, and then her heart started to race. The woman! That woman who was at my front door... the woman who called me Eva!

The woman looked so much like Brynn—small, petite, with dark, pretty features, and big brown eyes that seemed too big for her face. She could have been Brynn's sister, only she wasn't. The woman said she was Brynn's Momma.

Brynn hadn't even gotten her name.

Could it really be my Mother? Why would she come into my life now, when I'm finally happy, when I have finally found some peace? Why would she bother to show up now when my life with Adam is starting to be really nice? Brynn's head was swimming with questions. How did my Mother even find me?

It didn't make sense. And then Brynn realized that the woman must have found her because years earlier, Brynn had put her name in with the adoption agency. She always thought that she wanted to connect with her parents someday, but now that the day had come, she wasn't as sure.

But why wouldn't someone have called her to give her some warning? How did this woman just show up at her door? It was the moment that Brynn had always dreamt about, her Mother coming to find her.

She thought back to when she was a little girl, kneeling beside her bed, earnestly folding her hands to pray. Dear God, please help my real Mommy to find me and take me and my Momma away from Daddy so he can't hurt me anymore." Brynn thought that her real Mommy would rescue her from Thomas' fist and feet, and protect her from his rage. Tiny brown-eyed Brynn, with her long hair and high-pitched little girl voice, prayed night after night to be saved.

Thomas blamed her for stealing all of Rose's love so that there was nothing left for him. Young Brynn would pray desperately that her birth Mommy would take her away. But she never came. So why now? Why did she show up now? It didn't make sense.

Brynn thought about the woman's face, even though she had only seen it for a fraction of a second. Brynn could tell that she had been beautiful at one time, but the beauty looked like it had slowly been erased. The woman looked like the shadow of someone else, someone that Brynn didn't know.

The nurse was taking so long, and Brynn worried about the baby. She saw that she had a strap, with what looked like a monitor of some sort, around her belly. The machine that the strap was connected to displayed a steady, green line that ran across the screen at a consistent pace, making the same up and down lines every time it went across. Brynn watched the monitor for a while feeling better. It was the same type of monitor she use to stare at as she sat by Rose's bedside for hours.

Brynn heard a noise, and turned from the monitor to see Adam racing into the room. His thick, brown hair was disheveled, and his beautiful blue eyes the color of the sea, wide with distress. "Brynn, you're awake!" he said, his voice full of concern. Brynn never tired of hearing him talk. She loved his voice and everything about him. To think that she nearly lost him forever still gravely chilled her. Living life without him in it for those long months was the worst time of her life. Even thinking about it made her want to cry, so she pushed the memory from her mind. She knew that if she thought about it, she would remain in a dark mood for the rest of the day. And there were too many other things to contend with right now.

Brynn couldn't blame Adam for leaving those months back. She had inexplicably withdrawn her love, leaving him alone even after he had always taken care of her. She knew he left without much of a choice.

"You've abandoned me, Brynn!" Adam would say to her time and again in total frustration. "You won't even discuss having a family with me! You just wallow! If I had known this is who you would become when I married you..." Adam never finished the sentence, but Brynn knew that he would never have married her in the first place.

They fell in love at fifteen and Adam was the only person to teach Brynn how to live, to laugh, and to smile. Even though Adam knew she had endured more than any one person should have ever had to, he wanted Brynn to want to be happy, with him. And as much as he loved her, he needed her to love him, too.

Adam needed her to let him love her, but Brynn refused, and so he left.

Those months without him were hell.

Now Brynn knew what life was without him, and she vowed to never lose him again. Adam returned with love, finally winning out over her anger and confusion.

Brynn sometimes wondered whether he would have come back if

Rose hadn't died. She knew it didn't matter, because her adopted mother did die, and Adam did come back, and she chastised herself for trying to over think it.

But it wasn't an easy road for either of them, and they had worked through much in the past year and a half since he moved home.

"I'm never leaving you again Brynn," Adam would say to her repeatedly. "I'll never hurt you again."

"I want to believe you, Adam." Brynn was stubborn and her heart had a hard time letting go of the fear. "I want to, but I just don't." Adam would try to hold her, and Brynn would stiffen up, pushing him away with her fear.

"Stop pushing me away. You don't have to push me away anymore." Adam won out, and he held her close, feeling her heart beating in her chest from the anxiety. "I'll never abandon you."

Brynn always felt herself give into the deep, low tone of his voice that she loved so much. She allowed herself to be enveloped in his strong, sturdy arms, but a tiny part of her still wanted to shrink away. She wondered if she would ever stop fighting the happiness he gave her.

She had experienced so much loss in life that she had come to expect it. First, her birth parents abandoning her. Then Stacy, her childhood friend who had been killed by her husband's lover. Then Rose. And now Adam. Brynn finally decided that she would give herself permission to accept Adam's love, no matter how long she was able to have it.

When she gave in, there was finally peace.

And now they were having a baby together. Brynn was five months along, and her belly was nice and round. When Brynn looked at her belly, naked in the mirror, she saw the scars from years of cutting stretched out wide. Some were still painfully visible while others were beginning to fade, but they all still served as a horrific reminder of her painful childhood. The first time she went to have her ultrasound done, Brynn was embarrassed. The technician didn't even blink twice, and proceeded with 'business as usual.' Brynn was grateful.

She knew that she needed to accept the pain from her past and move on in order to be a good mother.

Now she was enjoying every moment of her pregnancy. There was no morning sickness, and she loved how the growing baby was giving her an excuse to eat a little more. She finally looked healthy, and was actually glowing and radiant. Brynn looked so different from the sick, bony woman she had become when Adam was gone.

But now Brynn worried for her baby.

Jane! It's Jane's wedding day, and I am supposed to stand up with her. Brynn was horrified. Jane was her closest friend. She was the one who saw her through when Adam was gone, and Rose was dying. Jane helped pave the way for Adam to come home, and she took care of Brynn when Brynn couldn't take care of herself. And now it was Jane's day, and Brynn failed her... again.

Brynn was indebted to Jane in the same way that she was indebted to Adam. They both had brought her out of the darkness, and she loved her friend with all of her heart.

Before Jane, Brynn only had one friend in all of her life, but now Stacy was gone, murdered by her husband's lover. Now Jane was her very best friend, and only the second real friend she'd ever had.

"Oh, Adam! The baby!" she cried. "...and Jane!"

"Jane is fine sweetheart," Adam said smoothing her hair, which instantly calmed her. He knew just how to touch her to make her feel better. "She understands. She said she could postpone it, but I told her to just go ahead. This isn't our day. It's her day. She said it wouldn't be the same without you."

Brynn cried. She was looking forward to seeing her friend get married and finally find her happiness. Jane had come to work at Brynn's restaurant years before and was broke, overwhelmed, and grieving the loss of her husband from stomach cancer. Brynn helped her get on her feet and find hope again.

Now, Jane and her two girls were finally getting the happiness they deserved. Ryan was a great guy, and he loved them all so much. Brynn was so happy for her friend.

A nurse came into the room and started checking the monitors and wires efficiently. She smiled politely at Brynn and asked her how she was feeling. Brynn said she was fine. Brynn always said she was fine, even when she wasn't.

"How is my baby?" she asked, afraid of the answer. She was trying to live life unafraid for the first time ever, but this was a new kind of terror.

"Oh, the baby is fine. Don't worry, the doctor will talk to you when she gets in," the nurse smiled and patted Brynn's arm softly. Brynn sighed with relief.

When the nurse left, Brynn looked at Adam, her eyes filled with questions.

"She's in the waiting room," Adam said, answering her first, unspoken question. "She felt bad about shocking you the way that she did, but refused to leave."

Brynn was quiet. She didn't know what she would do with this woman in her life after all this time. Brynn didn't know this woman, and didn't know if she even wanted to... After all, this woman hadn't wanted her before, abandoning her as a toddler, leaving Brynn to fend for herself. Brynn broke her leg, and she had nearly starved to death trying to look for her mother.

Now that Brynn was about to have her own baby, she couldn't even imagine leaving a child. She had been terrified to become pregnant, but now that she was, she was terrified that harm would come to her baby. She couldn't even imagine a circumstance in which she would walk away from her child now.

Brynn looked down at her belly and smiled. She loved her baby with something inside of her that she hadn't even known existed. It was as though the moment she knew she was pregnant, a switch turned on. Now she thought it had been so silly to be afraid of motherhood. Protecting her child and caring for it seemed like the most natural thing in the world to do.

"What does she want?" Brynn asked even though she knew that Adam wouldn't know the answer.

"I don't know, sweetheart." Adam was asking himself the same question. While Ellie seemed concerned about Brynn, there was something in her demeanor that appeared detached. It made him uncomfortable.

His first impression of Ellie was unsettling, even though she was making every attempt to be friendly. Adam thought that he should give her a chance, but he couldn't shake the uneasiness. "Don't worry about that right now. I just want you to get some sleep. Please rest. The baby needs it, and so do you."

Suddenly Brynn felt a sharp pain, followed quickly by another.

The nurse was just about to leave the room when she noticed Brynn's face, grimaced in pain. "Are you okay?" She asked looking anxiously at the monitor, its lines jumping erratically. She quickly pushed the red button on Brynn's bed. "I need some assistance in room 210, Stat!"

Brynn felt pain. Sharp, stabbing pain and she yelped as she felt herself getting hot and starting to sweat. Oh God, no! No! You can't have my baby!

"Brynn, Brynn, can you hear me?"

Brynn could hear Adam's voice, but she couldn't answer. She was lost in pain, trying to gather herself, fearing for the tiny life growing inside. She felt pain, and then she felt wetness as a pool of red started to stain the crisp white sheet of the hospital bed. Adam and Brynn stared down in horror, and Brynn started to feel faint.

She felt the room growing dark, and she knew she was going to black out again.

The last thought she had was of the tiny baby inside fighting for life, and all she wanted was for her to live. She knew it was a girl, even though everyone else thought it was a boy. She knew with all of her heart that she was a girl. She even had a name picked out, even though she kept it to herself. She hadn't even told Adam. Not until it was time.

Please baby, fight. You have to live. I need you to live. Mommy needs you, and she wants you more than anything in the world. I have fought to have you, so don't leave me now.

Brynn felt herself getting weaker. She could still feel Adam in the distance holding her hand, calling her name. She knew that there was a flurry of excitement in the room, and that she was being hooked up to more monitors. She even thought that someone might have been pumping her chest, but she wasn't certain. Everything felt like a blur. She thought she saw the woman who claimed to be her mother at the door fighting with a nurse to get in. Her long hair was flying about as she yelled at the nurse, and Brynn could tell she was upset. But Brynn felt strangely calm, peaceful. Even though Adam looked like he was about to explode with fear and concern, and her birth mother fought desperately to get into the room. Still, Brynn felt at peace, so she talked to her baby and prayed.

Baby, fight! Mommy won't leave you. We will be together in this world, I promise. I won't abandon you like my mother abandoned me, and I will never hurt you. You will always be mine...mine and Daddy's. God, please let us live! Please! Amen.

Brynn prayed over and over, while the commotion in the room continued.

And then there was nothing.

3

GUILTY

The guilt was crushing Ellie from the inside out. She felt it as they had driven home from abandoning her child; she felt it in the morning when she woke up, and at night before she went to bed. She carried it with her like a sharp dagger not too far from her heart, wounding herself daily.

Jonas didn't understand it. He was a man, and he had never created life inside of his own body the way that she had. Ellie made sure to spend her entire pregnancy detached, but the moment Eva was born, she was in love.

But Jonas hated Eva. From the moment he found out Ellie was pregnant, he didn't want anything to do with her. Ellie couldn't believe how cold he could be, and how mean he was to his little girl. She could understand if Eva was an ugly child, but Ellie knew that she was beautiful, with big brown eyes and that cute little chin. Eva was the spitting image of her momma, and if nothing else, she thought Jonas should appreciate that.

Ellie wanted to leave him, but she loved him. She needed him. He was her drug, and she was addicted to him in a way that terrified her yet satisfied her all at once. But watching her baby lying on the cold ground crying as Jonas sped away was an image that was burned into Ellie's mind.

Ellie almost killed Jonas in his sleep that night.

When they arrived back at Jonas' dirty little apartment, Ellie was almost hysterical.

"Calm down, El. She'll be fine!" Jonas lit a cigarette and handed it to her. She took it, her hand shaking uncontrollably, her eyes unfocused. He was losing patience. She had cried and screamed for the entire two-hour drive back. She screamed for him to turn around. She pulled at her hair. She cursed him and herself. She was hysterical, and Jonas could do nothing to calm her down.

He thought about pushing her out of the car, *but even he wasn't that cruel.* "There were cars all up and down that road. The kid is going to be fine!"

Ellie looked at Jonas in a daze. What will Momma think? Daddy is going to hate me. What have I done? She felt something squeezing her heart, like a giant fist. Squeezing, squeezing. Her heart was going to explode. She knew that if it did, she would deserve it. She deserved a horrible death after what she had done to her baby girl.

Jonas looked at her in disgust. So young! He loved his little sweet Ellie, but she was so young and so dramatic. He didn't usually pick them this young, but Ellie had captivated him with her innocence. The twelve-year age difference didn't bother him, and it wasn't as though he planned to be with her forever. He got bored easily and didn't usually stay with his women very long. She had proven to be different, though. She tried to ditch him when she was pregnant with the kid, but he always made it a point to find her. It was an effort he wasn't used to making for a piece of ass, but for some reason, he couldn't seem to shake Ellie.

"My baby, my baby, my baby," Ellie had rocked back and forth on the floor, sobbing. Jonas had never seen anyone cry so much. And all over a snotty kid. He knew that he should feel bad, but Jonas' dad split when his mother was pregnant with him, and he turned out pretty good. Jonas didn't think that people should even have kids, and he certainly never wanted one. Not now, not ever.

He went to the drawer and pulled out a syringe. If he didn't quiet her down, he was never going to get any sleep, and he needed to sleep. He was tired from all the driving. And he needed to go out and move some product, or they weren't going to be able to eat. He pulled out the syringe and prepared it while she rocked and cried behind him.

"Ellie, shut the hell up. The kid is going to be fine! You'll see. We are going to be so much better off without her." Jonas used his sexy voice, the one that usually made her climb all over him. He knew that she liked it, but this time it didn't do anything to her.

He grabbed Ellie's arm and wrapped the stretchy band around it. She winced when he tightened it, but didn't move. Jonas watched Ellie's face when the needle went in, and her expression didn't change. Good, he thought. She'll be out of it for awhile, and I won't have to listen to her cry anymore. She will see how much better off we are now.

Ellie's body consumed the drug while Jonas watched her go limp. He knew that she needed it to cope, but he figured that after a few days she would forget, and things would be better. He had hoped anyway. For some reason he needed Ellie, and it was getting harder and harder to think about a life without her. He shook his head, trying to clear it. Don't get all sappy, you idiot. She's just like anyone else, take or leave her.

Ellie was lying peacefully on the ratty couch, and he laid a blanket over her and smoothed her hair. He sat next to her, careful not to jostle her too much. He thought about how young she looked, how innocent. He let his thumb run down her face and admired her perfect smooth skin and the long eyelashes that skimmed her cheeks. Five years after he met her, she still stopped his heart, even after everything they had been through. She did something to him that no one ever had before. He couldn't explain it.

The first time he saw her walking through town, Jonas was instantly drawn to her.

He had been driving with the windows of his beat up Mustang rolled all the way down. The car was his baby, and he was trying to pull in enough scratch to fix her up, but was far from doing anything yet. He saw Ellie on the other side of the street as he pulled up to the light, and Jonas felt his heart stop. She was young. Too young. But something about her made him forget all about her age. She had looked at Jonas and smiled—a beautiful smile with small perfect teeth, big brown eyes shining bright. He felt instantly blinded, not even realizing when he did a U-turn and pulled up next to her.

She looked unfazed.

"Hi," he said ignoring his heart in his throat. He hoped she wouldn't see his nervousness.

"Hi," she smiled, boldly, making him uneasy.

"I'm Jonas."

"I know who you are," she kept smiling, amused.

"You do?" he was curious. He had never seen this girl before in his life, and he would have remembered. She wasn't the kind of girl who lived on his side of town, or who would know the people that he knew. He could tell by looking at her that she was a little girl with money, and certainly not the kind of girl who usually hung out with the likes of him.

"Of course I do. You're Jonas Miles." She was having fun. He was much older than Ellie, but his reputation was big in town. All of the kids knew that he was the guy you could score dope from, or anything else you wanted. She had attended a few parties where her friends had gotten their "stuff" from him. He was legendary. She thought it was funny that he didn't know it.

"Yes," he looked surprised, his dark green eyes widening. He didn't think that someone like her would have any idea who he was. He looked at her tight cashmere sweater, and her nice expensive shoes and shook his head. She didn't make sense to him. "Where are you going?"

"Why?" she said coyly.

He cleared his throat. He knew she was toying with him. But why? "I thought I could give you a ride."

"Okay." She said matter-of-factly. He expected her to say "No" and was taken aback by how bold she was. Before he knew it, she hopped in the front seat, throwing her book bag in the back. It landed with a thud, and he thought it sounded too heavy for such a small girl like her to carry.

"Where are you going?" he repeated.

"Wherever," she said, smiling that blinding smile at him.

He smiled back, feeling his heart flutter with something he wasn't used to feeling. Excitement? Weird! He was confused. She was just a little rich girl who was way too young for him. But there was just something about her.

They spent the entire rest of the day together. And the following day he picked her up from school, and the day after that.

Jonas knew that Ellie was smitten with him, and he with her. He had been with a lot of girls, but he had never met anyone like her before. He was careful to keep his feelings hidden. He wasn't going to let some little rich girl take advantage of him. Jonas had seen it with his mother and her men, how they only used her for a little while and then left when they were done. All of his life he watched his mother's heart get broken, so much so that she abandoned love entirely and stayed high and loose most of the time. Jonas wasn't going to let anyone do that to him, ever.

But as Ellie lay in a drug-induced sleep, for a moment, Jonas let himself get lost in her. He stroked her cheek and kissed her forehead, and thought about how he would hate to ever lose her. She made him happy, even though she infuriated and frustrated him. He knew that he didn't want to ever be without her.

And now that the kid was gone, it would just be the two of them always.

4

ELLIE AND ADAM

Adam was frantic. He felt as though his head were about to explode. Everybody was ignoring him, and he just wanted to know what was happening to his wife. His purpose— nearly his entire life—had been to take care of Brynn, and not being in control of what was happening to her was unbearable.

"How is Brynn? What is going on? Someone needs to give me some answers, right NOW!" Adam was furious as he stood at the nurse's station, daring someone to make eye contact with him.

The nurses had kicked him out of Brynn's area, and had closed the curtain and the glass door so that he couldn't see in. No one would tell them what was going on. One moment he was holding Brynn's hand, and the next they were practically pushing him out of the room.

"Sir, Sir! Please, quiet down! I don't know anything yet, and as soon as I do, I will let you know. All that I know is that they are assessing her," a mousy little nurse with brown hair was trying not to show her frustration with him. "Please, go sit down. We will call you as soon as we know something!"

Ellie came up and stood behind him. "Adam," she said, startling him. She sounded so much like Brynn that it made him want to practically crawl out of his skin.

"What?" he turned on her angrily. If she had never shown up at the front door, none of this would have happened!

"Let's go sit down," Ellie said gently as she started to reach for his arm. She pulled back when she saw the look on his face.

Adam didn't want to sit with her. He couldn't sit right now. He needed to know what was happening. The last thing he saw before they closed the curtain was Brynn's face. It was as white as a sheet. His first thought was that she was dying. Only fifteen minutes had passed, but it felt like a lifetime.

Just then, the curtain to Brynn's room flew back and he saw the foot of her bed emerge as they quickly pushed it through the doorway.

Adam ran over to the room as the doctor stepped out and was following the bed.

"What's going on?" Adam said blocking his path. "I'm her husband. Tell me what is happening."

"The baby is in distress and your wife is in danger. We have to get the baby out immediately! We are going to do an emergency C-section." The doctor was clearly in a hurry, and Adam stepped quickly out of his way.

He was stunned. After everything that he and Brynn had been through, Adam couldn't bear the thought of losing her and their baby. He put his hands to his face and swallowed back a sob. One of the nurses appeared beside him and put her hand on his arm sympathetically. "I've called for one of our helpers to take you to the waiting room. They will come out and brief you as soon as the surgery is over."

The helper was an older gentleman, Henry, who was much chattier than Adam would have liked. Henry talked to Adam during the entire slow walk to the waiting room, up four floors and halfway across the hospital. Adam tried to tune him out, but the older gentleman kept talking, distracting him from his current mission, which was to get to the waiting room to see how Brynn and the baby were doing.

Ellie walked slowly behind them, careful to keep her distance. She could tell that Adam didn't like her, and she couldn't blame him.

She had shown up at the door, and now Brynn was in the hospital, though by no fault of her own. Ellie knew by the look in Adam's eyes that he blamed her. Ellie blamed herself, too. Trouble always seemed to gravitate toward her, and had all of her life. Why should this be any different? Ellie was feeling sorry for herself, and was trying to shake it off. She really needed something, anything, to calm her down.

Her hands were shaking and her nerves were a wreck, but Ellie knew that if she could make it through meeting her daughter, that she could make it through anything.

They finally made it to the quiet waiting room, and Ellie and Adam realized that Henry had stopped talking. "Here we are," he said, pleasantly pointing them to the small open room in front of them. "There is a television, some magazines, and there is coffee at the end of the hall."

Ellie couldn't get over the hospitality that he was showing them, and thought with irony that they must charge extra for Henry to show them around. She thought back to that night so long ago when she was just a young girl in the hospital, her belly swollen and awkward as she was about to give birth. There hadn't been anyone like Henry to show her around. She had been all alone and frightened. Ellie shook her head in awe at how much things had changed.

She snuck a peek at Adam, who had taken a seat across from her, and thought how lucky Eva must be to have someone like him. He clearly loved her deeply, his deep blue eyes awash in fear and pain. Ellie felt a twinge of jealousy and tried to shake it off. *How can I be so jealous of my own daughter? But she felt it deep in her bones. If it weren't for me, she wouldn't have him, so I must have done something right.* She must not have needed me as much as I thought she would!

Ellie and Adam were alone in the quiet little room, and she felt the weight of the awkwardness. They hadn't been completely alone yet. Ellie knew from the way he kept his distance that not only did Adam not like her, he didn't trust her. That made Ellie angry.

How dare he judge me? He doesn't know anything about me! Ellie peered at Adam through the corner of her eye. He was wearing a crisp button down shirt and dark gray slacks. They were getting ready to go somewhere nice, but were interrupted. By me? Or would this have happened anyway?

Adam cleared his throat, breaking the silence. Ellie realized that he was staring straight at her, and her heart stopped. She held her breath and waited for him to say something. His eyes were speaking, but she couldn't figure out what they were saying.

"Why are you here?" he said, his deep voice carrying a hard edge.

Ellie's eyes seemed to get bigger. She had been prepared to talk to Eva and explain herself, but she hadn't anticipated this. She was never good answering to men, and it was even more difficult for her now. She shrank down in her chair, looking even smaller than she already was.

"I..I don't think that this is something I can talk to you about," she said, her voice quiet and low. She fought the urge to run. He was bigger than she was, much bigger. Ellie knew that he wasn't like Jonas, but she was feeling the old familiar fear creeping up in her.

"If you can talk to Brynn, you can talk to me. I'm her husband. There is nothing that we don't share." Adam's jaw was set, and he stared hard at Ellie.

Ellie sat as still as possible. *I don't have to answer to him. I don't have to answer to any man! I'm here for my daughter, and that's it.* She fought the terror rising inside of her belly, fighting with the anger inside of her. She was nauseous.

Adam was getting impatient. He knew that he was making her uncomfortable, but he didn't care. This woman needed to answer for what she had done to Brynn!

"I just wanted to explain things to her. To. My. Daughter." Ellie was having a hard time speaking, her voice shaking almost as hard as her hands. She tried to sound confident but her voice gave her away.

Adam was quiet. He wanted to push her, to break her. He wanted her to answer for all of the pain she had caused Brynn. He stared at her, filled with disdain and overwhelming curiosity. She looked like Brynn, and sounded like Brynn, and she had probably even been as beautiful years ago. But Ellie's yellowed teeth and stringy hair painted an unfamiliar picture for Adam, and he could tell that this woman was nothing like his Love.

"You can talk to me," Adam said quietly, changing his tact. He knew that being aggressive with her was going nowhere. "You can...."

A nurse walked silently into the room. She looked at the woman and the man sitting opposite of one another and immediately wished that someone else had been sent to get them.

"Mr. Michael?" she said nervously.

Adam stood up immediately. "Yes, I'm Adam."

"The doctor wants to talk to you," she said, gathering herself.

"Where is he?" Adam asked, looking behind her for the doctor.

"You'll have to come into one of our private rooms, and the doctor will come in and talk to you."

Adam was confused. They couldn't have been in the surgery room for even an hour. How can he be done already?

Adam followed the nurse into the room without so much as a backward glance at Ellie and waited. He wasn't good at waiting, especially now that he and Brynn were back together. He had been waiting for years for her to decide that she trusted him. Adam had been patient with her, but now that Brynn was in jeopardy, the only thing that he cared about was making sure that she and the baby were safe.

He waited for the doctor to enter the private little room that felt more like a prison than a conference area. Five minutes felt like an hour. All that Adam could picture was Brynn's face when she passed out, and he fought back tears every time he let the image come to him.

The door opened and Adam stood up quickly. He was on edge, and every nerve in his body tingling with fear and anticipation.

The doctor was a young woman, tall, almost masculine, wearing clean, colorful hospital scrubs. She had a confident air about her that made Adam feel better.

"Please, sit," she said with a polite smile that didn't seem to reach her eyes.

Adam sat down quickly. He could tell that she had something serious to tell him.

The doctor started talking. Her words came out quickly and automatically, and Adam found himself confused. It seemed as though she were talking for an hour, when in reality it was only for a few minutes. She used words that weren't familiar, and he intentionally squinted his deep blue eyes as he tried to make sense of it all. At the end, he only understood when she said, "I'm sorry to be the one to tell you that you may have to make a choice."

"Choice? What choice?" Adam said, irritated. "I don't understand half of what you just said."

"Oh, I'm sorry." She said, taken aback. "I thought I was explaining it clearly."

"From what you just said, I have to choose what, the life of my wife, or my baby? How am I supposed to do that?" Adam ran his hands through his thick dark hair over and over, hoping to let the message sink in. How can she ask me to choose? How am I supposed to make a decision like that?

"I'm hoping it won't get to that. Dr. Emmett is very good at what she does. I'm hoping you don't have to make a choice. But Brynn has lost a lot of blood, and we want to prepare you for what may come if we can't stabilize her." The doctor looked at Adam sympathetically. Adam realized that he didn't even know her name—and that he didn't even care.

"So what do I do? Do I have to tell you now? What do I do?" Adam said, feeling on the edge of hysteria. Adam couldn't imagine needing to choose. He knew that he couldn't do it now. He knew that he needed help making the choice. He couldn't do it alone. "I need to call my parents."

She hated this part of her job. "If something happens, we won't be able to wait. We need you to make a decision about whose life you want us to save. Think about what your wife would want. We can't wait." She had been sitting across from Adam, and she stood up and rested her hand on his shoulder. "Think about what Brynn would want you to do."

"Save Brynn," Adam blurted out. "If you have to make a choice, save Brynn." Adam hated himself, feeling as though he just put a big X on his daughter's head. He felt like he was going to throw up.

Adam didn't look up as she left the room. She had asked him to do the impossible, and he hoped he would never have to see her again.

5

DIFFICULT ELLIE

Jonas Miles was used to compliant, cooperative women. But Ellie was different. She was stubborn and difficult, and even though there were times he hated her, he always had the uncontrollable urge to go back to her. He couldn't help himself.

When Jonas and Ellie got into a fight, he took it out on her as he usually did, by sleeping with another woman in their bed. He often punished her with the other girls, some younger and some older, all with dark hair and brown eyes like hers.

Ellie was tortured, but she loved Jonas, and needed him in ways she couldn't explain.

She hated how he flaunted the other women in front of her. Alcohol made him mean, and he had a venomous tongue that lashed out at her in his drunkenness. She wanted him to let her go, but he wouldn't, and she didn't know how to purge him completely. He was selfish, and she loathed herself for letting him treat her as if she were nothing, until she truly began to believe she really *was* nothing.

But Ellie really hated him for making her get rid of Eva. Ellie was weak and let him throw her baby out of the car. He cared so little about his own daughter that he threw her out as though she were little more than trash. Ellie despised him for it, and she let him know that every chance she got.

"Stop telling me that you hate me!" he said to her, exasperated. Two years had passed, then three, and five, and Ellie still told him how much she hated him. "The kid is gone. She has new parents and a new life, and I'm sure she's fine by now."

But Ellie couldn't believe him. She yearned for a simpler life. She had even tried to go back home, but her parents were gone. They moved and she had no way of finding them. All she knew was that the big house that she grew up in was empty. And she blamed him for that, too.

They fought viciously.

"You'll never change! You'll never let me go! I need to go home. I need to find my daughter. YOU'VE RUINED ME!" She slapped him and kicked at him. She scratched his beautiful face with her fingernails. She didn't care if he was scarred. She wanted him to be as ugly on the outside as she felt on the inside.

At only nineteen, Ellie had abandoned her daughter, her parents, and herself. She was living in a tiny apartment with a man who kept her drugged all of the time.

"It's the same fight, Ellie. The same damned fight!" He grabbed her and pulled her to him hard. He was crushing her with his arms until his face was only an inch from hers. His green eyes pierced her brown ones until she had to look away.

Ellie knew that as long as Jonas was alive, she would never get away from him. She imagined that he was dead. She daydreamed about it, dreamt about it. She didn't know if she could really ever survive his death, or if she could be the one to end him. But she did know that if she didn't, it would be the end of her.

Ellie considered ending it all for herself, but she dreamt of finding her Eva again. She knew that as long as Eva was out there, she would need to find her baby girl. She didn't care how long it took her. She just knew that she needed to be with her daughter.

There was hopelessness and futility in her life every day. When Ellie looked in the mirror, she hated what she saw—a disgusting reflection of a weak, desperate woman who allowed Jonas to take everything away. She had been too weak and too stoned to fight, but she was finally beginning to find clarity, and she realized that she wasn't happy.

When she met Jonas, she was a young, spoiled little girl flirting with danger. She was showing her parents that she could make her own choices and do what she wanted. She loved Amy and James, but she felt that they owed her. When they left for Europe, and Ellie had to fend for herself and Eva, she felt betrayed.

Looking back, Ellie realized that they were only trying to make her stronger. But it was too late. There was no going back to them now. She had made her choices and lost the only real love she had ever known in them. And there was no way she could return now without Eva.

She hated Jonas so much at times. She imagined the blood oozing out of him, thick and red. She thought of how it would look, and smell, and feel, and she pictured how she would make it flow. *Do I shoot him, or stab him? How do I kill him?*

She loved him, but she also hated him for what he had done to her, and what he had done to their baby. Ellie imagined Jonas' green eyes wide and staring up in disbelief. She knew he could never believe that she was strong enough to hurt him. Jonas thought she was weak. He used both drugs and words to keep her that way.

But life seemingly got better, and she forgot about it for awhile. They lived in a condo, which Jonas promised Ellie could decorate as she pleased.

"I told you that I would take care of you, baby," he said on moving day. "I always keep my word to you." He kissed Ellie full on the lips. It was important to him that he took care of her. He had never seen a man take care of his momma the way he was taking care of Ellie, and he was proud of himself. He had built a good business catering to wealthy kids and their parents, and had a reputation for being discreet.

But Ellie didn't care about the condo, or the beautiful clothes, or about decorating. She still dreamt about that night when she held Eva in her arms for the last time and had let her go.

"Mommeeeee, don't leave me!" Eva's tiny voice still echoed in her ears. She was clutching Betsy, wearing Jonas' oversized shirt for warmth. Ellie had preserved the picture of Eva in her mind, and nothing could steal it from her. When she needed it the most, she closed her eyes and pictured Eva with the pretty pink dress. Only in Ellie's mind, it was still clean and pretty and lacy. It wasn't soiled with urine and dirt like it had been on the night she last saw her.

"Mommeeeee, I need you. Don't leave me!" Eva's voice was small, like tiny tinkling bells, and Ellie couldn't get it out of her mind. She felt like her head would explode with the sound of it. Nothing she did could rid Eva's voice from her mind.

"Mommy, I peed. MOMMMEEEEE..." Ellie could see Eva disappearing as she watched through the back window of the car. Sometimes in her dreams, the car was the beater car that they had driven off in that night, and sometimes it was a limousine. Sometimes the car was a boat, but the dream was always the same. Ellie was leaving Eva behind, and Eva was running after her crying, her little face stained with dirt and tears.

Ellie woke up one day and decided that she had to do something to find some peace. She needed to try to find Eva, and find her parents. But she knew that Jonas would never let her go. She knew that she would need to do something to get away from Jonas before she could ever return to find her family.

6

PETEY SULLIVAN

Jonas' employees were like all of his women, except for Ellie. Easy, obedient, and stupid.

Petey Sullivan had always been loyal. Jonas knew that he could count on him for anything, but killing wasn't anything that Petey had bargained for.

"I'll do whatever you want me to, Jonas, but I can't kill nobody. I just can't do it." Petey was beside himself, shuffling his big body back and forth as he shifted his feet and looked down to the floor.

Jonas smiled at him with his girly lips. The guys secretly thought that Jonas looked like a girl with his big full lips and his pretty boy look. But for some strange reason, the girls seemed to dig him. Petey just didn't get it, and he didn't really like Jonas. But Petey's big brother, Mike, had hooked him up with the job, and would kick Petey's ass if he screwed it up. Petey wasn't sure who he was more scared of, Mike or Jonas. At the moment, it was Jonas.

Petey had heard the stories of what happened to people when Jonas got mad. They weren't ever seen again, or they were seen with missing digits, or unexplained scars. For as big as Petey was, he didn't like violence, and he didn't like getting hurt.

"Petey, you'll do whatever it is that I need you to do. And if that

involves, um, disposing of someone, then you'll just have to do it."
Jonas' voice had a hard edge to it as he stared Petey down.

Petey was uncomfortable. He didn't sign up for this. The money
that Jonas paid him over the past year was good, but Petey wasn't into
hurting nobody. Usually Jonas just had him take packages from place
to place, and pick stuff up for him. Jonas had other people to do the
"people thing." Petey had just wanted to handle the packages.

"It's simple really," Jonas said staring at him with his dark green
eyes. "You'll stop the car, you'll hold onto the Missus, and Sy will take
care of the rest. You think you can handle that?"

Petey could tell that Jonas was getting really frustrated with him.
It was best if he just agreed to whatever Jonas wanted him to do.
Jonas' reputation preceded itself, and Petey was just a small town kid
compared to him.

"I can do that," Petey said, his voice squeaking as he said it. He
was twenty-three, big and bulky, a small-time player most of the time,
and he was okay with that. He had been that way with football, and
in everything else in his life. He knew he wasn't that smart, and he
didn't want the responsibility. He just wanted to do what he was told.

But blood made him squeamish, and it made him upset when
girls cried. He never knew what to do when they cried. And with
what Jonas was asking him to do, he was sure to see a woman cry, and
it made him sick to his stomach.

He drove down that old road with Sy, and they cornered the rich
couple. It had all gone as planned. But then Petey couldn't take it no
more, and something inside of him, for the first time in his life, made
him act different from what he was told. He didn't want to do it, but
he couldn't watch the pretty lady cry no more. What Sy did to her
husband was bad enough, but what Sy was getting ready to do to her
next, Petey couldn't take it. He looked at her tiny face, her pretty eyes
staring at him, terrified and pleading.

Petey could never hurt a woman, and he couldn't let Sy. So he
stopped him, and then he disappeared, leaving Sy dead from the big
gash in his head.

Petey knew he had to hide. He couldn't face Jonas and lie to him.

Petey wasn't a good liar, and he knew that Jonas would see right through him. He didn't even care if he wasn't paid. He didn't want to be paid for this. So he hid at his cousin, Lily's house. He knew nobody would look for him there. Lily was the old maid of the family, and nobody even talked to her anymore, except Petey. He just didn't tell anyone.

He showed up at her door on foot. He had ditched the car that he and Sy drove in, after hiding the bodies as best as he could, and then he took off on foot. Him and the pretty woman. He didn't know what else to do with her, and he had to carry her every step of the way, keeping to the back roads and hiding in the woods. Sy had started to hurt her, started to tear her clothes off her, started to hit her, but then Petey stopped him. But not before Sy knocked her down, and she hit her head on a rock, blood gushing out freely and staining her pretty blonde hair.

He snuck up to Lily's door, exhausted. Her house was about five miles from the road they were on, isolated and quiet. She lived off money from her dead parents and rarely left the house.

"Petey!" Lily cried, her surprise obvious when she opened the door and saw him standing there. Her gray eyes widened in shock as she realized that he was covered in blood. She hadn't seen her cousin in a few months, but she would've recognized him anywhere. "Are you hurt?"

It was dark outside and when he stumbled in, she realized he was carrying something, someone.

"Petey! Are you hurt? Are you okay?" Lily was suddenly afraid, and she looked outside to see if anyone was out there. She shut the door quickly and locked it behind them.

"No, no. I'm okay. But I think she may be hurt." Petey was tired. The pretty lady didn't weigh much, but after carrying her for five miles at a pretty good clip, he was beat. "I just need some water."

Lily motioned to the couch where he set the woman down as gently as he could. The bleeding on her head had stopped a while ago, but she was still a mess, and needed cleaned up. She was unconscious but was starting to make little sounds, as if she wanted to wake up, but couldn't. Petey didn't want her to wake up. He didn't want her to look at him, remembering how he held onto her while Sy stabbed her husband. He shook his head at the memory of the blood. So much blood.

Lily's voice brought him out of his reverie. "Go get cleaned up, Petey!" she ordered him. "There are some of Daddy's old shirts upstairs. Those should fit you. Go get cleaned up, and I'll take care of her. Bring your clothes down with you and we'll burn them."

Lily looked down at the tiny woman lying on her couch. Her beautiful soft hair was coated in dried blood, but Lily was used to cleaning up blood. She had done it so many times, and had become used to it by now. Daddy used to come home covered in blood, and sometimes he brought home his guys who were covered in blood. Lily learned never to ask questions. She just cleaned them up, sometimes even stitching their wounds. She thought she could get away from it. She decided to go to college, become a veterinarian, get married and have her own babies. But Daddy had called her home when he said he was dying, and she ended up taking care of him and his cancer for a decade, all of her dreams fading away. So now she was alone, but she had the money he left her, which wasn't much comfort when she was all alone.

She took warm cloths and cleaned the woman up, careful not to reopen her wound. It wasn't as bad as it looked once she got the crusted blood off. It could use a stitch or two, but that was it.

She cleaned up the dirt from the pretty woman's face and admired how smooth and perfect her skin was. Lily wished she had been as pretty. All of her life, Lily knew just how plain she was. Not ugly, not hideous, just plain. Plain gray eyes, plain dishwater blonde hair, plain build. Nothing spectacular, nothing special, just plain. When she changed the woman into some of her own more sensible clothes, she saw that everything the woman wore was fine and expensive. Even her underwear.

Lily admired the woman's clothes. She had money to buy clothes like that, but nowhere to wear them, and nobody to wear them for, so she didn't. She just wore sensible clothes to fit her sensible, unremarkable life.

Lily could hear the shower running upstairs for what seemed like an hour. Petey must feel very dirty, she thought to herself. It was strange to hear the shower running when she wasn't in it.

Finally, he came out, and was fresh and clean smelling like the Irish Spring soap in her shower. She liked it. He was surprised when he saw her and the woman. Lily had done a good job cleaning her up, and the woman lay peacefully on her couch.

"How is she?" he asked, his voice in a low whisper.

"She's doing well. She only needed one stitch, and she didn't even flinch when I did it. I used a very small needle." Lily lifted up the woman's hair in the back of her head and showed him. The cut was barely visible now, and Petey breathed a sigh of relief.

"Is she going to be okay?" he was afraid of the answer.

"I don't know. We will have to see when she wakes up. What happened to her?" Lily was full of curiosity. She was disappointed that her beloved cousin had taken this track in life, but intrigued with him, just as she had always been. He had been the only one in the family not to shun her, for reasons that she didn't understand.

They left the woman sleeping on the couch and went into the kitchen.

Petey told her everything. He could always tell her everything. Ever since they were children, they had been close, until the families had divided over reasons that neither of them were completely clear about. But Petey refused to abandon her as the rest of her family had done.

She always admired him and thought how handsome and sweet he was. *I don't understand why nobody has ever snatched him up,* she found herself thinking often, and feeling slightly incestuous in her thoughts.

She listened as she poured him a drink and made him something to eat. She was happy to have some company for once. After he had eaten and was full, she told him to go upstairs to rest.

"What about her?" he said pointing to the couch. The woman was still in a deep sleep, though she cried out every now and then.

"I'll stay up with her. You can rest," Lily said graciously. She was happy to have a mission, to have a task.

Petey looked at Lily with gratitude. "Thank you," He said lumbering up the stairs. He was exhausted and needed to think of his next move. He didn't like thinking. He just wanted to do what he was told. Now he was stuck having to think about what to do. *I never should've taken that woman with me. I shoulda just left her there! Somebody would have found her! Now what the hell am I going to do with her?*

Lily stayed up all night, watching the woman sleep. As the sun came up, the woman slowly opened her eyes and looked around. She looked across the room and saw a weary looking woman in her forties, sitting in an old recliner across from her. Lily's eyes were closed as she leaned her head back, and the woman thought that she had a kind face. She looked up to the ceiling and tried to sit up, but the blinding pain in the back of her head told her to lie back down. The woman could tell that she was in an old house; it smelled old anyway.

She realized suddenly that the woman in the recliner was staring at her. "Hi, I'm Lily."

"Hello. I'm...I'm..." the woman on the couch was at a loss. Her mouth became dry and she felt herself panic. "I'm..." she couldn't remember. Her mind was a blank.

Lily looked at her evenly, and the woman couldn't read her. For a split second, Lily looked... grateful, but then she looked concerned. "It's okay. Don't push yourself. It's common in this type of situation to not remember."

"Situation?" the woman thought hard. "What kind of situation?"

"I mean, you just had a bad gash on your head. It would be a normal side effect to not remember." Lily's voice was comforting, and the woman felt a little better. Something about Lily made her feel safe.

The woman heard footsteps, and she looked up to see a large man coming toward her. Her big brown eyes grew wide in horror. She didn't know why, but she was suddenly very afraid.

7

ELLIE'S SINS

Ellie stared down at Jonas. His green eyes that seduced her time and time again, staring up at her were wide in disbelief. Blood was oozing out of the side of his mouth, and he was clutching his chest where the bullet went in and exploded.

Ellie's hands were shaking, and she was sweating uncontrollably. She wasn't sure if she could kill the man she had once loved so desperately. But right then, she felt nothing as she aimed the gun at him and pulled the trigger.

Even as the bullet ripped into him and she heard his blood-curdling scream, she felt nothing. Nothing, but relief. Only freedom. She had felt like a caged animal for so long that she knew this was her only escape from Jonas' prison. She had been *his* ever since she was a young girl, and now she was twenty-five, and now the only thing she needed was to find the baby she had abandoned so callously.

Jonas was on the ground writhing in pain. His long lean body stretched out, blood running down the marble tile of the beautiful foyer that he had chosen just for her.

"El...El, how could you?" his voice was barely above a whisper, and she leaned in to hear him, no longer afraid like before.

"I hate you. I hate you! You've ruined me, and I don't love you anymore!" Ellie snarled at him, her pupils were huge, turning her eyes nearly black as she glared at him with a complete absence of love. "I've dreamt of this moment, and now that it's here, I don't feel bad for you. This is what you deserve."

Ellie had given shooting him a lot of thought, but she wasn't sure if she could really do it. She had never even shot a gun at a real person before, but she knew that if she aimed it at him she had better be able to do it, or she would never have another chance.

Jonas was in shock.

When he walked in the door, the last thing he expected to see was his Ellie pointing a gun at him. Today was supposed to be a special day. He was going to ask Ellie to be his wife at dinner that night. Business was good and he knew that he needed to change. Ellie had stood by his side for years now, and he was finally ready to make the commitment. He had never wanted to get married before, but it was starting to look like a good idea now. He was done with the other women. Even though he often used them to punish her for misbehaving, he was starting to regret it, something he had never done before.

He figured that must mean something.

"What the..." Jonas hadn't finished his sentence when he heard the crack of the gun and saw the smoke. He felt the bullet tear into his chest, fast and sharp, and he fell to his knees as the blood started pouring out. "Ellie, Ellie."

She had been the only woman he had ever loved, except for his mother. His mother who taught him that he should never stay in one place too long, or love only one person. Jonas had watched a string of men come in and out of her life—some stayed for a month or two, none of them ever paying much attention to him. When he met Ellie, Jonas knew that she was special, and he fell for her right away. He was careful to keep her in line, though.

Now he didn't want to just keep her in line, he just wanted to marry her. He wanted to have a real life with her, a legitimate life with her. He was in disbelief now as he lay on the ground, his lifeblood flowing out of him, his body growing weaker.

Her face was inches from his, and the venom of her words spewed hatred. *I can't believe this is my Ellie. My Ellie who I've loved more than anyone else in my life.*

"You've hit me, you've drugged me, and you stole my innocence and my life. Because of you, my parents left me. But most of all, you stole my baby. How could you ever think that I would ever forgive you for making me abandon my baby?" Ellie was fighting back tears as she spit the words at him. "I loved you, but you betrayed me with your selfishness, and I let you. If you would have just let me go, I wouldn't have to do this."

"Ellie, Ellie," Jonas was getting weaker. His body was turning cold, his mind was racing, and his thoughts were becoming mush. *Do I tell her that I killed her parents? I'm dead already, so what does it matter now? She already hates me. She already....* The pain of her hatred made the physical pain from the gunshot seem insignificant. "Ellie, Ellie, listen to me..."

"You have nothing to say that I want to hear. I am going to be free from you once and for all." Ellie shook her head back and forth trying to block out the sound of his voice. Jonas thought that Ellie was just as pretty now as she was the first time that he saw her.

"You want to hear this..." His voice was barely audible and she leaned in close. "I love you. I've always loved you and I'm sorry."

She shook her head, the hatred starting to dissipate as the adrenaline started to fade. The reality of what she had done was starting to hit her as she saw the life flowing out of Jonas.

"Come closer," he was barely breathing, "I... had... your... parents killed."

Ellie watched his head roll over to the side, his dull green eyes opened, staring into nothingness, and she screamed as she heard the sirens coming for her.

8

ROSE

Brynn couldn't believe that she was seeing Rose. It didn't make any sense. She looked down at her belly and was relieved to see that it was still swollen, full of her growing baby. She was still wearing her nightgown, her long flowing white nightgown that made her feel so pretty and feminine.

And now, out of nowhere, there was Rose coming toward her, almost floating.

Where am I? She thought, confused. She had never been in a place like this before, and it was nothing that she recognized. It was like a place in a dream where there were no ceilings, floors, or walls. There was just space, and Brynn felt like she was dreaming.

You're nowhere. Rose answered her wordlessly, and Brynn was surprised that Rose could read her thoughts. *Don't think about where you are. You are here with me, and that's all you need to know.*

Brynn had a thought. *Am I dead? Are my baby and I both dead?*

No! Rose's voice in Brynn's head seemed to laugh a musical, pretty laugh that Brynn had never heard before. *You aren't dead. I'm just looking out for you for the time being. Your body is going through a great ordeal right now. Don't worry. You'll be fine.*

Brynn felt better, relieved. She put her hand on her belly and rubbed it gently as though to tell her baby that it was going to be okay. *Are you okay, Momma? I'm sorry for abandoning you before you died.*

Oh, baby girl, don't worry about that. I was fine. Jane was wonderful to me. Rose was always forgiving, and Brynn wasn't surprised that she forgave her so easily.

But Momma, I left you when you needed me the most. And I'm so sorry for what I did to you. I didn't know how sick you were. Brynn was so ashamed. She had been living with the guilt for abandoning Rose for over a year. Rose had loved her too much, and Brynn was suffocating under the weight of her neediness. And when Adam left her, Brynn couldn't deal with Rose any longer. She was fighting her own battles, and she couldn't deal with Rose's anymore. *If I had known...*

I know, baby girl. I know. Brynn felt Rose's forgiveness flowing through her, like a tingling feeling from the inside out. Rose was different here. She made sense and was motherly; unlike how she was all of Brynn's life. Brynn wished Rose had been this way while she was alive.

I wish that I had been different, too. I know that I needed you too much. I know that I wasn't much of a mother to you. But I couldn't be that person to you. I didn't know how. And by the time I figured it out, it was far too late.

Brynn was ashamed of herself. How could she let Rose know her thoughts? She had to be more careful. *I know that it wasn't your fault, Momma. I know now that you did protect me from him. You did try to keep him from hurting me.*

I didn't do everything that I could have, Brynn. You know that. I should have left. That was the only sure way to protect you. Brynn felt Rose's sadness, and it made her want to cry.

Oh, Momma, why weren't you like this when you were alive with me? Why now? Why are you so different now? Brynn's heart was filled with longing for a life that she could've lived with this Rose.

I was afraid. But I'm not afraid any longer. I was a coward, and I failed at my most important and only job. And I'm sorry. But you'll be different. You'll be a much better mother than I ever was.

Will I? How will I? Brynn was curious how this Rose could know.

Suddenly it got blindingly bright, and Rose disappeared with a flash. Brynn felt as though she were flying at a high rate of speed, controlled and even.

She realized that she wasn't afraid anymore.

She was finally ready to be a mother.

9

THE LONG ROAD HOME

The sounds of the sirens were distant, but audible. She knew that the sirens were coming, because someone had heard the gunshot. She knew they would come for her, looking for her.

Ellie did what she always did best. She ran.

Everyone knew that she was Jonas' main girl, and would be looking for her. She was careful to wipe the gun off, and shove it in her purse after she took out the remaining bullets. She was careful to have an alibi.

She was careful not to let anyone see her go into the house, and she was careful to write a "Dear John" letter to Jonas explaining that she was sorry, and that she no longer loved him. She told him that she was going far, far away. And she left it in a place that the cops would easily find it. She planned everything out, hoping to get away. She knew she would run. She had to find Eva. He had so many enemies that it wouldn't be hard to imagine that one of them did it. She knew where she needed to go, and she wasn't going to let anyone stop her from getting there.

Momma, Daddy. Ellie tried hard not to let her grief overcome her as she took off on foot. She wanted to crumble on the ground. She wanted to pummel his newly dead body with her small fists. *How could he do that? How could he take them from me forever? Why? Why?* Ellie pushed the thoughts from her head as she ran as fast as she could. The sirens were getting louder, even as she ran further away. She took the back way and ran the two miles where she hid her car and stashed her bags. She ran as if her life depended on it, her body ragged and worn from the drugs that he had filled her with over the years.

It felt as if she had been running forever, and when she finally got to the car, she let out a sob. She jumped in and started the car, careful not to pull out too fast. She didn't want to get pulled over for something stupid. She just wanted to get away.

I'm going home. Now I'm going home to nothing. NOTHING. They are dead. Who knows how long they've been dead! God Dammit, why didn't he die before he told me what he did? Why? Ellie gripped the wheel as tight as she could, her knuckles white, tears running down her face uncontrollably. Slow down! Slow down! Ellie looked at the speedometer. Fifty-five in a forty-five. Slow down, you idiot!

Ellie tried to get a hold of herself. She knew that anyone looking in at her through the car windows would think that she was a mess. She wanted to look normal. You needed to look normal. Ellie couldn't be caught now. There were too many questions. Too many questions that needed answered. But she knew that she couldn't get those answers alone. She had been gone from home for seven long years. Eva would be ten now. *How long have Momma and Daddy been gone? Oh, Momma!*

Ellie pictured Amy in her mind, petite, pretty. Ellie was the spitting image of her, only with dark hair instead of the pretty blonde hair that Amy wore so well. Ellie had been proud of her beautiful mother, and now Amy was dead. Ellie couldn't stop the picture of Amy's rotting corpse full of worms from entering her mind.

Her chest felt heavy, and Ellie felt as if she were going to drive off the road. She held the wheel tight, praying for control.

She knew that she had to get away from Jonas. He hadn't given her a choice.

"Jonas, do you ever want to have a baby with me?" It wasn't the first time Ellie had ever brought it up. She wanted a child. She wanted someone in her life who loved her unconditionally, who looked up to her and admired her. She wanted to re-create her time with Eva. She wanted to redeem herself for what she had done to Eva. She wanted the nightmares to go away.

"Jesus, Ellie. Do we have to go through this again and again and again? We've been talking about it for seven years. You've been bringing it up since we ditched the first kid. NO! I. Do. Not. Want. A. Child. Ever." Jonas couldn't believe how thick she could be sometimes. He knew that she was still haunted by losing the first one, but he definitely didn't want another one.

Ellie knew that was the last time that she would ever ask him. She was only about six weeks along, but she knew that she couldn't afford to have him shoot her up again, or have her abandon this one, too. She knew he would make her. He would make her leave it as a newborn. He would've made her leave Eva as a newborn if she had been with him then. But she hadn't. She had been smart then, and had left him. But then she went back, because she was blinded by love.

Not this time. He won't take my child away from me again this time! Ellie knew where he kept his gun, and knew where he kept his bullets. He taught her how to shoot it in order to protect herself, because he had a lot of enemies. Little did he know that she would use it on him. *I was protecting myself, and my baby.*

Ellie looked down at her tight small stomach that would soon be swelling with the growth of new life, and she was excited. Jonas hadn't shot her up for at least three weeks, and she knew that if she were strong, she could stay off the drugs and keep her baby strong and safe. Her body hurt, and her back and legs ached. She craved the drug, wanted it bad.

But she knew that she needed to stay away. She had already gone through a lot of the ups and the downs that the withdrawal took her through, but usually she didn't have to go through an entire cycle. Jonas always made sure that he shot her up just before she started to go too crazy. But she didn't let him do it to her every day, just often enough to keep her from crashing too hard. This was the longest she had gone in a long time, but she was doing it for her baby. She didn't want to screw it up this time.

She didn't want to lose the baby as she had lost Eva. And she didn't want to hurt him. Somehow, she knew that it was a boy, though she couldn't explain how. She was going to name him after her daddy, James. But now Daddy was gone, and it didn't feel right to name him after a dead man.

Ellie felt her heart breaking. She hated feeling this way. She missed the euphoria of the drug. She missed being happy.

STOP IT! STOP IT! You need to stay straight for your son! You need to find Eva! You can live without it. You can live without the drugs! Go home! You'll figure it out.

Ellie forgot about the police and recklessly drove about five more miles. She stopped the car in front of a familiar apartment building.

The door to her car opened suddenly, making her jump.

"Shit! Don't do that to me!" she said angrily.

"I'm sorry, babe. I thought you saw me." The young man leaned over and kissed her tenderly on the lips. She felt herself melting into him, her whole body leaning in, inviting him as she had already done so many times before.

"I'm sorry. You just scared me." Ellie smiled. She was so taken with him. He was tall, handsome, with light sandy hair and hazel eyes. He was so different from Jonas, so much kinder to her, so much gentler. When she met him by chance three months ago when he was fixing her car, she knew that he would never treat her the way that Jonas had. She also knew that she wanted him, possibly even needed him.

"Where are we going?" he asked, tossing the duffel bag that he had been holding on his lap in the back seat.

Ellie paused. She needed a solution now that her parents were gone. *John! John will know what to do! John Palmer was Daddy's Vice President, the man that Daddy had been grooming to be his second in command.* John and his wife, Tricia were always so nice to her, though

Ellie had not always returned their kindness. *I wonder if he will help me. He has to help me. Daddy would want him to help me!*

Ellie was excited. She knew what she would do.

"We're going home, babe. We're going home." Ellie turned the car toward a familiar road that she hadn't travelled in nearly a decade.

10

PETEY AND CARLY

"It's okay," Lily said to the woman. The woman saw Petey coming toward her and fear gripped her for no obvious reason.

"Lily, who is that?" the woman asked, fearful.

"That's my cousin, Petey. He saved you." Lily was studying her carefully. The woman seemed delicate, timid.

"Saved me? Saved me from what?" the woman was surprised. She couldn't imagine that she would ever be in danger. But she couldn't imagine anything at this point. Her head was still pounding and fuzzy, and she couldn't focus well on anything.

Lily didn't want to tell her who she was. It wasn't her place. Petey had detoured into the kitchen, and he was making his way back to the living room, awkwardly carrying three glasses of orange juice.

"Here ya go," he said holding one out for Lily and the other one out for the woman. He saw that she was finally awake and figured that she was probably thirsty. The woman took it from him tentatively, almost as though it were a snake. Her fear wasn't lost on Petey. He had tossed and turned all night trying to figure out what to do. He had brought her back to the house, but had no idea what he was going to do with Amy Harper now.

Lily looked at Petey evenly, her gray eyes cool and steely. "She wants to know who she is Petey, and what you saved her from."

Petey looked surprised. He wasn't sure what Amy was going to remember, but he hadn't expected that her memory would be completely gone. He was comfortable leaving her overnight with Lily, because he knew that his cousin knew how to handle herself. With a father like hers, she was far more capable than she looked.

"Um, uh, she doesn't remember anything?" Petey was talking to his cousin, ignoring the pretty woman sitting on the couch staring up at him.

"I don't," Amy said bewildered that he was talking about her, yet ignoring her at the same time.

"I'm sorry, Ma'am." Petey said, embarrassed by his rudeness. His Momma wouldn't be very happy with him right now.

Petey was confused. How can she have no memory of what happened? How can she not remember watching Sy stab her husband, and watching Sy and I fight? How can she forget me killing Sy, trying to defend her? Petey was out of his league.

"I think we should have breakfast," Lily said breaking the uncomfortable silence that was starting to fill the room. "And then we need to figure out what to call you," she said looking pointedly at Amy.

"Okay," Amy said miserably. "Maybe you should take me to a doctor?" she said hopeful.

"Well, um... Lily is kind of a doctor," Petey said shyly. He had been watching Amy for some time and was taken with her beauty. Those long days staking her out so that they would know when to pounce on them had him watching her for hours, sometimes days. It didn't matter to him that she was in her late thirties. Petey was in his mid-twenties, but he knew a beautiful woman when he saw one. Even after everything she had been through, she was just a natural beauty.

"Kind of a doctor?" Amy said tilting her head at him. "What does that mean?"

"She's an animal doctor, but a doctor nonetheless." Petey was getting frustrated. He felt like Amy was making fun of him.

"Oh," Amy said blankly. She looked at Petey with curiosity. He looked familiar to her, yet she was afraid of him. He stood tall and awkward in front of her, avoiding her eyes. He looked strong and capable but strangely shy, and she was confused by him. "Well, what is my name?"

Lily ducked out of the room, careful to stay close by in case Petey needed her. She wanted to protect him as she always had, but she knew that he would need to face Amy alone.

Petey looked at her blankly, his palms starting to sweat. He knew that this moment was coming, and he still didn't know what to tell her. "Uh, I don't know. Let's call you... uh, let's call you Jessica."

"Is that my name?" Amy said stubbornly.

"I don't know. But I have to call you something!" Petey said nervously.

"Why Jessica? Does my name start with a 'J'?"

"I don't know! I don't know if your name starts with a 'J'. If you don't like it, then you can choose something else." Petey hated facing Amy alone. He looked around desperately for Lily. "What do you want me to call you?"

"Jessica? That doesn't sound like it fits me." Amy said thoughtfully. "What about...Carly? I like the name Carly."

"Fine. We can call you Carly." Petey was ready for the conversation to be over. He never liked talking to women, and this one in particular made him very nervous.

"I want to leave. Do you know where I live? Do you know who I am? I just want to go home," Amy said, her voice low but demanding. She didn't want to be in this house anymore. She wanted to go wherever she belonged, and she knew that she didn't belong here.

"I don't know who you are or where you live." Petey lied, avoiding her gaze. "You just need to stay here for now, and that's final."

Amy stared up at him defiantly. He towered over her, but she glared at him. She was angry. She knew from the way he was refusing to look at her that he knew more than what he was telling. She stood up quickly, determined to make him look at her. Suddenly, the floor gave way beneath her and she felt herself fall to the floor.

Before she knew it, Lily was by her side, grabbing her arm gently, but sturdily.

"It's okay," Lily said in a soothing voice. "You're okay. You just need to take it easy and not be in such a hurry. It's going to take you some time."

Amy nodded very slowly. She was dizzy, and her head was pounding. It felt like someone was hitting her in the back of the head with an axe, and she was starting to feel nauseous.

"She don't look so good, Lily," Petey said concerned.

"Let's take you upstairs to the spare room so that you can have some peace and quiet," Lily said taking her by the arm and leading her toward the stairway.

Amy went with her slowly, dragging her feet. She hated feeling so helpless, but she had no choice and nowhere else to go. She looked at Petey, her eyes turning hard for one second. He refused to look at her, but he could feel her growing resentment bouncing off him. It made him uncomfortable, and he looked down at the ground until she was out of sight.

A few moments later, Lily came silently down the stairs. She sat in the chair across from where Petey had settled on the old couch. They sat and stared at each other, exhausted.

"What are we going to do with her?" Lily finally asked, breaking the silence.

"I don't know," Petey said quietly. "I don't know. Their disappearance is all over the news. We can't let her know. She can't know."

"I'll do whatever you need me to," Lily said looking him directly in the eye.

"You've always been there for me, Lily," Petey said staring at her. *Why is she all alone here? Why hasn't she found a good man yet?* Petey always thought the world of her and couldn't imagine why she lived by herself.

"Yes," Lily said smiling. "I always will be. You are my only family now."

They sat in silence, lost in their own thoughts.

"Can she stay here for a little while?" Petey asked slowly. "I know it's a lot to ask, but..."

"Of course, she can stay," Lily said quickly. She was relieved that he finally asked. She knew that he would. After all, he had no one else and no where else to turn.

11

SOMETHING TERRIBLY WRONG

The lights in the room were blinding.

Brynn felt as if she were still in a dream, only Rose had disappeared, and she could hear the echo of metal and the hurried hushed voices of people in masks surrounding her. Her brain was working in slow motion, and every movement reverberated slowly.

"Brynn, can you hear me?" Brynn knew it was her doctor, but she couldn't remember her name. Her doctor was a small woman who moved and talked quickly. Brynn liked her confidence, but right now, she didn't care who her doctor was. She felt her eyelids fluttering and she was fighting to stay awake.

"Brynn!" The doctor was talking to her, and Brynn could see dark brown eyes above the green hospital mask. "I need you to stay strong and stay with me."

Brynn was trying to nod, but her head felt like it weighed a hundred pounds. *Where is Rose? Momma?*

Brynn squinted and closed her eyes. She just wanted to fall asleep. She felt herself fading as the din of the room became silent.

She awoke in another room. It was quiet and not as bright. She was nauseous. She needed to throw up. She looked around desperately for someone to help her, and then felt her stomach heave violently. She opened her mouth and watched helplessly as she threw up all over the side of the bed, all over the floor. It landed with a loud splat, and she felt the warmth of the liquid on her skin and on her side. She wretched and heaved violently for what seemed like forever, though she knew it must only have been a few minutes.

Every time she heaved, she felt a sharp pain in her stomach. When she was done, she looked around desperately for her call button. She pushed it relentlessly until she heard the familiar click of the speaker.

"Yes, can I help you?" the voice said sounding a little bored.

"I need help, now," Brynn said her voice hoarse and barely audible.

"I'm sorry, can you repeat that?" the voice said, this time irritated.

"Help me, NOW," Brynn was angry. "NOW!'

"Someone will be there right away, Miss." The voice said hurriedly.

Brynn was soaked in her own vomit. She looked around for Adam. *Where is Adam? Why am I alone?* Brynn was still nauseated, gulping and gasping for air. She fought the waves that threatened to overcome her. She didn't want to throw up anymore. Every time she heaved, the sharp pain in her gut returned. She felt dehydrated, and her head was pounding.

Where is my baby? Why am I alone?

Brynn waited for long moments staring at the door.

When the nurse came in, she looked at Brynn and her eyes immediately widened. She pushed the call button and asked for help. Another nurse came in and they both cleaned her up quickly. The nurse kept looking at Brynn apologetically, and Brynn knew that she must be the nurse who had been so short with her.

When Brynn was dry and clean, the first nurse started to walk away, and Brynn grabbed her by the arm. "Where is my baby? Where is my husband?"

The nurse looked startled. "Hasn't anyone spoken to you?"

"No, nobody." Brynn's heart was pounding, and she felt her breath catch in her throat. "Why? What's going on?"

The nurse pulled away. "I can't talk to you. You need to talk to a doctor." She started backing out of the room, trying to maintain her composure.

"Why can't you talk to me?" Brynn was starting to panic. "Why can't you tell me what is happening?"

"I just can't," the nurse said apologetically. "I'm not allowed. I could get fired." The nurse looked like she was barely twenty-five and Brynn felt bad for her for a split second, but then the anger returned.

"I don't care. I want to know!" Brynn was desperate. "Get me a doctor. Where is my husband? Find my husband! I need answers. Oh my God, what is happening? Tell me now! Tell me now!" The nurse raced out of the room and returned quickly with an orderly.

"Miss, Miss. You have to calm down. You have to calm down now!" the orderly said.

Brynn felt desperate. She was alone, and she knew that something must have gone terribly wrong or Adam would be with her. *Adam would be here.* She knew that Adam would never leave her, never abandon her when she needed him the most. Not now. Not after everything they had been through.

She looked at the familiar monitor above her and knew that her heart rate was off the charts as she watched the line spiking one after another after another.

She felt something sharp going into her arm. "What are you... doing?" she said feeling her body starting to relax. "Why? Why?"

The nurse looked at her with a small, sad smile. "It's going to be okay, Brynn. Just try to relax."

Brynn felt her mind start to drift, and she felt her body go limp. Her hands felt numb, and she felt as if she were floating.

Why would they do this? Something must be terribly wrong.

12

ELLIE AND DYLAN

Ellie met Dylan by accident when he was working on her car. There was an immediate, undeniable attraction, and she felt drawn to him in a way that she had never felt before, not even with Jonas. She knew he felt that same. When they spoke, it was as though there was no one else around, and she couldn't help staring in his eyes when he was around. It was like a moth to a flame, uncontrollable and hot. And she knew that if Jonas found out, something bad would happen. Something horrible.

Ellie knew that Dylan felt the same way about her. Again, those eyes. The way his beautiful, hazel eyes lit up when she was around told her so. She started making excuses to have him look at her car, and eventually, she asked him to go have coffee with her in the next town over. She could tell that Dylan was equally as smitten with her.

He had never met anyone like her before in all of his life, so beautiful and confident. He wasn't used to girls like her.

Dylan had barely graduated from high school, but found that he knew his way around cars. He had taken vocational classes and landed a job in the garage, much to his surprise. He was young, but wanted to get out of his little town. He couldn't wait to grow up so that he could move, and now that he was growing up, it didn't look like he was going anywhere. His story was typical, and he didn't like where it was headed.

"But, you have so much potential!" Ellie said to him, peering over her coffee cup. She had gotten fancy coffee and ordered him just a black coffee since he couldn't decide. He would have just as soon had a beer, but she insisted on going to a fancy coffee place instead. She missed fancy coffee, and he couldn't believe it when their check was almost ten dollars.

"Potential for what?" Dylan asked, his tone as dark as the blackness in his eyes.

Ellie shrugged. "I just think you could do so much more than change oil and work in a little garage."

Dylan was offended. "I work hard, and I make good money. I don't know who you think you are, but I'm doing pretty good on my own considering that nobody handed me anything."

Ellie immediately regretted her words. "I didn't mean it like that." She knew that she had a tendency to speak too quickly at times.

"Well, how did you mean it?" he said, glaring at her, his mood shifting noticeably.

"Uh, I just meant that you could go to college, or do something else. You seem smart," Ellie said staring down at the froth in her cup.

"What if I don't want to do anything else?" he said, lightening his tone to almost teasing.

"Well, then..." her cheeks turned bright red, and Dylan found himself enjoying her discomfort immensely. "I guess you just have to be happy doing what you're doing."

"Well, I'm not," Dylan said, finally letting her off the hook. "I would love to go to college. I would love to get out of this town. I would love to do a million things that don't involve ever seeing this shitty place ever again."

Ellie smiled a big bright smile, and he was hooked.

He didn't know why, but after having coffee with her, he couldn't stop thinking about Ellie. Everyone in town knew that she was hooked up with the drug dealer, but it didn't stop him from thinking and fantasizing about her.

"I just don't know what I want," she said to him one night, months after their coffee date. They had been meeting secretly a few times a week for months when Jonas was "working."

"It's simple," Dylan said sighing, tracing her jawline with his fingers. He didn't want to keep having the same conversation with her. "Either you leave him, or you don't. Do you want to be happy?"

"It's not that easy," Ellie said exasperated. "It seems that easy, but it's not."

Dylan was beside himself. "It really is that simple. You just make it more difficult than it is."

Dylan made choices and never looked back, not even for a moment. When he decided to enroll in college after their first coffee date, he knew that it was the right decision. He knew he would graduate and not look back.

Growing up without a father made him bitter, but realistic. Dylan knew what he needed to do in life. He knew that he was in control of his own destiny and that nobody could do it for him. Not his alcoholic mother, and not even a confused little girl that was involved with the wrong people. Dylan was smitten with Ellie, but he felt like she wasn't quite what she seemed, so he was cautious.

"I don't get you," he said one afternoon a few months later as he was tracing her slender, naked back with his index finger. It was a beautiful summer day, and they had stolen away for a couple of hours.

"What don't you get?" she asked, her eyes closed enjoying the hot sun and the feel of his fingertips on her skin.

"You don't seem like you belong with him. You seem more, I don't know. Independent. Maybe the word is stubborn." He struggled with the words. He had always used his mouth and hands to speak for him with the girls he had been with, but Ellie made him talk to her. She made him want to talk. "I don't know why you would want to be with him."

"I don't know," Ellie said, annoyed. She didn't know why Dylan always wanted to talk about Jonas. She didn't want to talk about Jonas when she was with Dylan. She had only agreed to be with Dylan on the condition that he knew she wasn't leaving her life with Jonas. "Why do you always want to talk about it?"

He shrugged, his handsome face wincing from the sting of her words. She pretended not to notice.

She looked at him out of the corner of her eye. When she looked at him, he astounded her. Ellie loved how she could see his muscles through his t-shirts. She could feel the strength in his back when she hugged him, and it made her heart beat quicker.

She loved the feel of his fingers on her skin. His hands were rough and hard from his years of manual labor, and she loved the feel of them on her body.

She had only ever been with Jonas, and occasionally one of his other girls, but she dared not to tell Dylan. She didn't want him to know the power that he had over her. Once he knew, she figured he would end up treating her just like Jonas treated her, and she couldn't bear it.

She rolled over on her back, reveling in her nakedness. She never felt this free with Jonas. Dylan's eyes got big as he looked down at her, enjoying the view. "I really like you," Ellie said pulling his face close to hers. "I want to spend time with you. But I don't want to talk about Jonas when we are together. I just want to enjoy us, our time. If you can't do that then we can't be together. You are ruining this for me."

He was quiet as he looked into her eyes, searching. He liked that she never looked away. He knew that she was missing something inside, but he had fallen for her, and he didn't want to give her up.

He nodded ever so slightly. He had never been asked to share anyone before, and never imagined that he could even consider it. However, he knew that if he wanted to be with her, that this was his only option.

For now.

I'll do this for her. But not always. I'll make her love me. I'll make her want only me. Dylan knew he would never allow her to stay with Jonas forever. *I have to get her away from him.*

"What are you thinking?" she said, smiling at him.

"I'm thinking about how I can't believe what you do to me." He said nuzzling her neck, tasting her saltiness.

"Mmmm," she sighed, smiling as she felt his hot breath on her neck. "I know. You do the same thing to me. You make me forget my life. You make me..." Ellie paused. *Be careful not to tell him too much!*

Dylan waited for her to finish. He had been waiting for months for her to say how she felt about him.

"...want to have a cheeseburger. Ellie jumped up suddenly and threw her shirt on laughing. "Let's go. I've got to get going!"

Dylan sighed and got up after her. He knew he would have to continue to wait. But he knew he wouldn't wait much longer before he took matters into his own hands.

13

SOPHIE

Brynn was on the verge of hysteria. She was still nauseated, but the medicine they gave her was starting to kick in and she was feeling better.

"Where is my baby?! Where is my baby?! Is my baby alive? Somebody please, please, help me!" Brynn cried helplessly, burying her face in her hands, trying to block out the fear and pain that grew inside.

"Brynn, Brynn. Calm down." A familiar voice was by her side.

"Dr. Nguyen! Oh my God, where is my baby?" Brynn looked up at the doctor, desperation pouring from her big brown eyes. The doctor was beautiful, middle aged, exotic looking, and typically very poised and calm. But today, she looked different. Today she looked slightly disheveled and messy, and Brynn had never recalled seeing her look quite this way.

"Brynn. I need you to calm down and breathe. Everything is going to be okay, but I need you to calm down and breathe first." Patricia Nguyen had been Brynn's obstetrician during her pregnancy, and though she never asked Brynn about her scars, she knew that they told a horrific story. From Brynn's visits and the scars, Patricia knew that she needed to be careful with Brynn.

Brynn could tell that the doctor was biding time. She tried to take deep breaths and calm herself down. But the anxiety was swelling over her like the tide, and she felt like an elephant was sitting on her chest.

Just then, Adam flew into the room, eyes wet and red. Brynn was alarmed, and immediately felt her heart start to race. He stood next to Brynn and held her hand, gripping it tightly and looking into her eyes.

"Brynn," Dr. Nguyen took a deep breath. "Your baby was premature. When you came in, we found you and the baby in distress. We acted as quickly as we could..."

The room was silent and Brynn felt the roar of quiet resounding in her ears. All she was aware of was that she was not breathing, not thinking. It was as though the moment had stopped, waiting for the doctor's next words to move it forward in whatever direction it was meant to go.

Brynn dared not breathe, waiting for what Dr. Nguyen was going to say next.

"Your baby is in the NICU. Her lungs are still not fully developed, and with the loss of oxygen to her brain..."

Brynn faded out. She could see Dr. Nguyen's lips moving and see the sadness on her face that she was trying to mask with her professionalism, but Brynn could see. She could see Adam out of the corner of her eye, and feel his hand gripping hers tightly.

She could make our words like *ventilator, lung function, brain damage,* but the rest of the words jumbled together into nothingness. She could tell by her expression that the message wasn't good, but the words ran together into incomprehensible sounds, and Brynn was silent.

Dr. Nguyen finished talking and looked at Brynn expectantly, not realizing that she hadn't been listening the entire time.

Adam looked at Brynn, waiting.

After what felt like a lifetime of silence, Brynn turned to Adam, her eyes overflowing with tears as she smiled. "A girl, Adam. We have a baby girl. We have our baby Sophie."

Adam was dumbfounded. It was as though Brynn hadn't heard a word the doctor had said.

"Brynn, Brynn. Do you understand? Do you understand what Dr. Nguyen said?" Adam was beside himself. He had expected many different reactions, but this wasn't one of them.

BRYNN LOOKED AT DR. NGUYEN, her eyes pleading. "Can I see my baby girl? When can I see her? I want to see her now. Now!"

The doctor looked at Brynn, tears welling in her own eyes. "We can go see her now if you would like."

"Yes, I would like to go see her now," Brynn said her voice strong and resolute.

After fifteen minutes, they made their way to the elevator, Brynn secure in a wheelchair with an escort, and Adam, and the beautiful doctor leading the way. Brynn was excited, although Adam had warned her about the incubator and the tubes, but Brynn didn't seem to hear him. She didn't hear anything. As they got closer, she was flush with anticipation, and was oblivious to everyone around her.

They made their way into the NICU, and Adam stayed as close to Brynn as possible. He knew that she was not prepared for what she was about to see. Dr. Nguyen led them to a single room and held her breath as the reached for the handle. "Brynn, are you okay? Are you ready?"

Brynn didn't look at her. She looked around her through the glass of the room. "I'm ready. Just open the door," she said, a hint of frustration in her voice. She was anxious to meet her daughter.

Dr. Nguyen opened the door and they wheeled Brynn into a room full of monitors and a mini bed enclosed in plastic. Brynn was confused. *Where is my baby?*

She looked frantically around the room and couldn't find the crib. *Where is my baby?*

Her big brown eyes settled on the mini bed encased in hard plastic. She peered inside.

Her breath caught as she saw the tiny arms and legs inside. *She's so small, how can she even be alive? Oh my God, how is she alive?*

She looked at Adam helplessly.

"Honey, we've been trying to tell you..." Adam said, his voice trailing off.

The room was silent as Brynn took it all in, looking but not seeing.

"Can I touch her?" Brynn finally said, quietly. "I want to touch her."

Dr. Nguyen started to speak, and then cleared her throat. "You can reach in through here," she said pointing to two holes that were big enough for Brynn's hands to reach through. "But for right now, she needs to be isolated. She can't be exposed to any germs."

Brynn looked at the baby, her eyes wide and her face glowing against the incandescent light of the incubator. She was in awe. The tiny body was full of tubes. Brynn couldn't believe there were so many.

Dr. Nguyen showed her where to put her hands and how to touch the baby, and Brynn put her hands in eagerly. The gloves frustrated her, and she hated not being able to feel her with her own skin. Dr. Nguyen explained that it was to protect the baby.

Brynn needed to touch her baby.

"Sophie," she said in a singsong voice that she had never heard come out of her before. "Sophie, it's Momma."

Adam watched silently as Brynn talked to her. He had listened to every word that Dr. Nguyen said, and he doubted that Sophie would make it past week two. But he loved her in spite of himself. He was worried about Brynn. He knew that Brynn would love her even if they said she wouldn't make it for another day. He knew his Brynn, and he knew how deeply she loved.

Brynn looked at the tiny body in the incubator. Barely four pounds, the tiny body was nothing but skin and bones. She couldn't believe how small the body was. Sophie's arms were so little, and Brynn stared hard at her spindly arms and legs. She had never seen anyone so frail.

"Sophie," Brynn said, putting her face as close to the baby's head as she could. "Sophie, Mommy's here. We love you. I love you so much."

The baby lay still, her tiny chest moving up and down ever so slightly with each labored breath. Brynn watched, fascinated with her tiny body, wanting so desperately to touch her hands, to feel her skin with her fingers. She looked at Adam with an expression that he had never seen before. Brynn had known deep sadness in her life, but this was something more than she had ever felt before. Even in the depths of her misery, after an especially harsh beating from Thomas, she had never felt as desolate as she felt now—separated from her baby by a thick plastic enclosure.

It was torture to be so near her, but not be able to pick her up and hold her. She ached from somewhere deep within a part of her soul that she never knew existed, when she looked at Sophie.

"Oh my God, Adam," she said turning to him, her big brown eyes bigger than he had ever seen them before, "Oh my God."

Adam stood behind her and held her tight. He could feel the frailness of her body, and he got as close to her as he could to try to give her some of his strength. He had been down in the NICU while Brynn was sleeping and had come to terms with the inevitable. He knew that Sophie wouldn't make it, and he was preparing himself. But he didn't know how he could prepare Brynn.

Tragedy seemed to separate them, and he was terrified of what losing Sophie would do to her. He prayed that Dr. Nguyen was wrong and that Sophie would come out of it strong and well.

"What do we do?" Brynn whispered to no one in particular, as she stared down at Sophie's tiny body. She marveled at her dark fluff of hair, much like her own. She imagined what it would be like if Sophie were a little girl, and she could brush and braid her hair.

Dr. Nguyen's voice came from beside them, low and quiet. "She's suffered a lot, Brynn, and she isn't doing well. I don't know how much longer she will have. You have to decide how and when to let her go when the time comes."

Brynn felt her heart stop.

"You can't ask me to do this! You can't ask me to let her go!" she said angrily. "I can't, and I won't."

"I hope you don't have to," Dr. Nguyen said slowly, looking at Brynn sympathetically. "But you and Adam need to talk about what is realistic, and what may happen."

Brynn stared at Sophie. Brynn's heart beat loudly in her chest. She hadn't imagined when she woke up this morning that this would be the conversation she would have with her doctor. She imagined a beautiful day watching her friend get married, not this. *How does it come to this? How can my life become this, after everything I have gone through?*

"We don't have to do anything now, honey," Adam said holding Brynn close to him. Brynn stared over his shoulder at the incubator, her eyes dark. "We can take our time."

The room was silent with only the sound of the machines working to keep Sophie alive, humming and swooshing quietly.

Brynn closed her eyes and tried to clear her mind. She ignored the voices echoing through the room, telling her that everything was going to be alright.

14

ELLIE'S RETURN

J ohn Palmer opened the door and stared. He couldn't believe his eyes.

"Ellie!" He yelled, reaching out and engulfing her in a hug before she could step away. He was so excited to see her that he didn't notice when she didn't hug him back. "Where have you been? Where's Eva?"

Ellie looked at him coldly. John realized that he was still holding her, and he let her go abruptly. Caught up in his excitement, he had forgotten how Ellie was. John could just feel James' disapproval in his mind. James would never have approved of John losing his composure the way that he did.

"Where is Eva?" John repeated looking around.

Ellie knew that this would be the first question that he asked her, but she still didn't feel prepared to answer him.

Ellie said the first thing that came to her mind. "Eva's dead."

John stepped back, his deep hazel eyes wide with grief. He had imagined the worst, but now that it was reality, he was saddened beyond expectation. "How? How?" he whispered motionless.

Ellie didn't answer. She put her head down and pretended to cry, loud, wailing sobs that shook her entire body. *Shit! Shit! Shit! Why did I say she was dead? Shit! Now I am going to have to figure out an answer!*

Just then, John realized that there was a young man on the porch behind her. "Who...who is this?" he said to Ellie.

"This is my friend, Dylan." Ellie sniffed loudly, keeping her head down and avoiding John's gaze.

John knew that he should have felt more sympathetic toward her, but he didn't. Something just didn't feel right. Realizing that they were still on the porch, he stepped aside, even though he didn't feel comfortable letting them in.

"John, who is it?" Tricia's voice startled him from behind. She appeared and gasped when she saw Ellie. "Oh my God! Ellie! Where is Eva?"

Ellie was annoyed. *Why is it always about Eva? Why can't she just ask me how I am? Jesus!*

John turned around and looked at Tricia, his eyes big, and Tricia froze. She could read her husband like an open book, and she knew what that look meant.

Tears immediately sprung up in her blue eyes, and she turned away, stifling a sob. She had been hoping and praying for so long that everything was going to turn out well, and that they would find Ellie and Eva safe and sound. *How can God do this?*

"Do you want to come in?" John said slowly, opening the massive oak door just a little wider.

"Um, sure," Dylan said awkwardly, pushing Ellie toward the door, her head still down.

He was beginning to question why he was even there. He had agreed to go to Ellie's hometown with her, but he didn't know what they were doing at this stiff's home. *What the hell is she doing?*

They stepped into the foyer and paused.

"Have you been home?" John asked Ellie, looking only at her and ignoring the young man behind her.

"No," Ellie said quietly.

"Then why are you here?" John was confused.

"I heard. I heard they were missing. I heard they were possibly even dead. I knew you would know," Ellie spoke mechanically, coldly, almost as though she had no feelings whatsoever.

"How did you hear?" John said, trying not to sound annoyed. He wanted to know where she had been. He wanted to know what happened to Eva. She wasn't volunteering any information, and he wanted desperately to know what happened to her over the past decade.

"I just did." Ellie avoided his gaze.

He should have known that Ellie wouldn't offer more than she wanted to. She was straight to the point, and never gave more information than she needed. This infuriated James, but John had never dealt with Ellie before, and now he felt frustrated. How can she go missing for nearly ten years, and then reappear with no explanation?

John turned around and looked for Tricia. She had been his rock, helping him to grow in confidence so that he could run the company that James was no longer there to run. They had their difficulties, but overall, the company was solid, and John knew that his mentor would be proud of him. John felt lost without Tricia. She was his confidante and the person who knew all of the right things to say. Aside from being at work, she was never too far from him, and that is the way he liked it.

She came around the corner and he breathed a sigh of relief. At not even forty, she had barely aged a day as far as he was concerned. He smiled at her and she smiled back. Everything is going to be okay, he could almost hear her telling him.

"Ellie," Tricia said warmly. "Come with me, you look tired, sweetheart. Let's get you some tea, and then you and your friend can stay here for the night if you'd like."

John was struck with how warm and wonderful Tricia was, even though she had never liked Ellie.

"We don't want to impose," Ellie hesitated, and John realized that her eyes were dry, even after all of the crying.

"We can stay," Dylan's deep voice surprised them all. He hadn't spoken at all, and they had forgotten that he was even there.

Ellie gave him a sharp look, but then smiled sheepishly at Tricia.

"Sure," she said following her slowly down the long hallway toward the kitchen.

When James and Dylan were alone, John gestured toward the great room, and Dylan walked in, slowly looking around as he went.

Money. Money. Money. Dylan thought, shaking his head.

"Do you want a cigar?" John asked him, pulling one out and cutting it for himself.

"Uh, sure." Dylan said, surprised by the gesture.

John pulled another one out and cut it, giving it to him slowly.

They smoked their cigars in silence, each lost in their own thoughts.

"So, what happened to Eva?" John said finally, breaking the uncomfortable silence.

"I don't know. It was before me, and she won't talk about it." Dylan said hesitantly. Ellie had warned him about what to say. He didn't want to say something he wasn't supposed to.

"I'm sure you know," John was challenging him, and Dylan could tell. *Dammit, Ellie.*

"I don't know. I really don't." Dylan was desperately puffing on his cigar, hoping to escape the conversation.

"How can you not know? Did you just meet Ellie? How can you not know what happened to her daughter? Where has she been? God dammit, give me something!" John was frustrated. He couldn't imagine how this idiot standing in front of him could have no knowledge of Ellie's child whatsoever.

"I don't know. I don't know." Dylan was looking for somewhere to stub out his cigar. "I don't know anything. We've only been together for a few months. She hasn't told me anything!"

"I don't believe you. I can tell you are lying." John was angry.

"What's going on?" Ellie's voice was angry and strong as she entered the room. Dylan looked at her, grateful that she had appeared.

"I want to know what happened to Eva. You don't understand, there is a lot at stake here," John said, directing his attention toward her.

"Like what?" Ellie said, curious.

"I can't tell you that."

"You're grilling Dylan about something that he knows nothing about. So what is at stake?" Ellie glared at John angrily, feeling a strange sensation of power coming over her. Shooting Jonas had awakened something in her that she hadn't realized she possessed. She wasn't about to let John bully her now. "I have a right to know."

"Everything, Ellie! Everything is at stake." John looked at her, searching her face for something honest and real. "Your parents were missing. And when you didn't appear, and then we couldn't find you, we had no choice but declare them dead. Your father left control of the company to me and to the shareholders, but he left everything else to Eva. The house, his fortune, everything!"

The room was silent and nobody moved. Ellie couldn't believe her ears. *How could he have left everything to Eva? What about me? What did he leave for me?*

"He left you as guardian of Eva. You benefit as a result of being her mother and having control over his estate," John said, almost as though he could hear her thoughts. "He wanted it that way on purpose to make sure that you remained her mother. He wanted to make sure that you still took care of her the way that he wanted you to."

Nobody moved. Ellie hadn't realized that she wasn't breathing.

"I'm pregnant."

Tricia gasped. She had been standing behind Ellie, silently watching the conversation.

"What?" John asked, not believing his ears.

"I'm pregnant," Ellie repeated. "So what does that mean?"

She looked at John who had turned white, and then she turned and gave Dylan a small smile.

15

HELPLESS

The NICU reminded Brynn of a church, quiet and reverent, where healing was happening slowly and silently. She couldn't wait to have Sophie out of the NICU and onto the regular floor so that she could eventually take her home. Brynn hated being in the NICU. She just wanted to have Sophie to herself in their nursery at home, caring for her there.

"Sophie, it's Mommy. I'm here," Brynn said quietly, her hand grasping the tiny hand in the incubator. "I'm here, baby girl."

Brynn looked at Sophie's tiny body covered with tubes and tape, trying to stifle a sob. She had never felt so helpless in all of her life. Even when Thomas was beating her, Brynn knew in her mind that she could escape. She knew that her adopted father would eventually stop, and that she could hide in her room and escape when she would cut herself. *But this—this was torturous and with no apparent end in sight.*

"Oh, baby girl, I'm so sorry that this had to happen to you," Brynn choked back a sob. She didn't want her tiny baby to hear her cry. She stepped out often to cry in the hallway or in the bathroom, but she refused to let her baby girl hear the sound of her crying. *If there is a small possibility that she can feel my sadness, I won't allow her to. I will be strong for her.*

Brynn marveled at how small her daughter was, her tiny chest moving up and down with the ventilator. Her hair was dark like Brynn's, but the tape obstructed Sophie's face, and Brynn couldn't clearly see the rest of her features. *Does she look like Adam, or does she look like me?*

"Baby Sophie. You have to wake up. You have to be strong. I know that you've been through a lot, but you can make it. You can do this. I know that you can." Brynn felt her voice wavering. *No, no, no. I have to sound strong. She has to know that I believe in her.*

Brynn sent Adam home to sleep. He had been up for three days straight, and he needed to sleep. Brynn knew that he couldn't continue on this way. He fought her, but she won. He was too exhausted and he knew that he needed to sleep.

Sophie was silent. She lay motionless in her plastic enclosure, her tiny chest moving up and down with the ventilator that was taped gently to her mouth. Brynn felt the familiar heaviness on her own chest. The heaviness she felt when Adam left her, when she was completely alone. She tried so hard to forget it, but the familiarity of that feeling now terrified her.

I can't lose you, Sophie. I can't! You have to pull through this. You have to be able to breathe on your own. You have to!

Brynn knew that Sophie couldn't hear her well, but the nurses told her to talk to Sophie as much as she could. They said that Brynn's voice could soothe her. She sat and watched Sophie for hours, marveling at her smallness, at how vulnerable she was.

Jane called on her way to the airport. She and her new husband had delayed their honeymoon until she knew that Brynn's baby was safe and out of the woods. "I'll stay with you until Sophie is in the clear," Jane said to her friend. She had always been there when Brynn needed her most.

"No Jane! No. You deserve your happiness!" Brynn was grateful for Jane, but she couldn't let her put off her honeymoon. Jane left the restaurant prepared for her absence, putting Lucia in charge. Lucia was an Assistant Manager now, making money while she went to school. Both Brynn and Jane were confident having her in charge.

"Are you okay, honey?" Jane asked her voice full of concern. She knew what happened to Brynn when Adam left. She couldn't imagine how she may react if Sophie didn't survive.

Brynn was silent. She couldn't talk. Expressing her sadness was still so difficult for her. The words always wanted to come out, but stopped right before they could come out.

"I... I... don't know. I don't know," was all that Brynn could muster. *I want to tell her that I'm dying inside. I want to tell her that my heart is breaking with every breath. I want to tell her that I don't know how I will go on if Sophie dies.*

Silent tears burned hot down Brynn's face as she sat silently on the phone.

"Don't shut down on me, Brynn. I'm here if you need to talk. I'm here for everything. I'll only be gone for a week, and then I will be back, and you can call me anytime you want. Oh shit, I shouldn't even go. Brynn..." Jane battled with herself. She didn't want to leave her friend. They had been through so much together.

"I'll be okay. Please go. I couldn't live with myself if you didn't enjoy your honeymoon. I don't think that Andrew would ever forgive me if you put your honeymoon off." Brynn tried to smile as she spoke because she knew that she would sound stronger to her friend that way. "I have to go now, but I need you to go on your honeymoon. I need you to have the happiness you deserve."

Jane was quiet. She knew that Andrew would understand, but she couldn't ask him to put their honeymoon off. It was the only time he was going to have off for the remainder of the year, and with their hectic lives, she doubted they could reschedule it.

"I'll go, but if something happens you have to call me, and I will be on the first flight back!"

"I will. You are my best friend, and I love you. I'll call you if I need you." Brynn was just getting comfortable telling Jane how much she cared about her. She had only ever told three people in her life that she loved them, with Jane being the fourth.

Brynn turned her attention back to Sophie. The nurses bustled in and out, checking monitors, hanging bags of fluid. Brynn hardly noticed them.

She stared at Sophie and willed her to move, to breathe, and to do something that would let Brynn know that she was going to survive. She pictured Sophie bigger, older, with Adam's blue eyes, and her own brown hair. She pictured Sophie's small sweet cheeks, and she imagined kissing them, and snuggling her face. She envisioned herself holding her, and singing to her, and doing all of the things that Brynn's own mother had never done for her—or at least imagined that she had never done for her.

After all, how could she have done all of those things to me and then let me go? Brynn's thoughts went to Ellie. She hadn't seen her since she arrived at the front door of Brynn and Adam's house. Adam said that he hadn't seen her since the waiting room, and Brynn wondered briefly where she had gone. *What does she want? Why is she even here?*

Brynn couldn't help but feel anger when she thought about Ellie. She was curious and excited, but the anger won out. She couldn't imagine what Ellie would want with her.

Brynn looked at Sophie and felt a strange sensation of fullness in her heart that she had never known before. "I will never leave you, baby. I will never let anyone hurt you. I will always protect you."

They sat in silence for a few moments, and then Brynn realized that Sophie's color had changed. *Oh my God, she's turning blue.* Brynn screamed for help, desperately punching the nurses red call button. Suddenly, two nurses flew into the room, and before Brynn knew it, one of them had her on her feet as they pushed her to the door.

"What's going on?" Brynn demanded, startled. The nurse looked at Brynn, trying to suppress her own panic.

"You're baby isn't breathing," the nurse said, grabbing Brynn's arm and pulling her to the side as three other people entered the room. They pulled the curtain and Brynn couldn't see. She could hear the flurry of activity, and felt her heart pounding loudly in her ears. There was bile coming up in her throat, and suddenly she felt faint.

"I have to call Adam! Someone has to call Adam!" Brynn cried desperately.

"We called him, honey. He's already on the way." The nurse's knew to call him immediately if anything happened.

The nurse led Brynn to a well-lit, comfortable looking lounge where Brynn waited. Moments passed slowly, and every minute felt like an hour. She felt like she was dying inside, waiting to hear something as she paced the lounge like a caged animal.

Brynn was anxious for Adam to get there. She couldn't stand to be alone, not knowing what was going on with her baby. Brynn heard the sound of footsteps running down the hall and saw Adam race into the lounge. He frantically searched the room until he met her gaze, and he rushed toward her, engulfing her in a hug. Only in his arms did she feel safe, as though he could take away all the pain of the world and protect her in his embrace.

"Adam, S-S-S-Sophie..." Brynn couldn't speak. She had only known her tiny daughter for a day, but already she was so in love with her that she could barely breathe with the thought of losing her.

"I know, sweetheart. I know." Adam held her close, smoothing her hair and kissing her over and over. Brynn could tell that he had been crying, his beautiful blue eyes rimmed in red, bloodshot from lack of sleep.

They sat in silence, holding onto one another tightly. Minutes turned into an hour, and they sat waiting, their hearts fragile and worn.

They looked up expectantly when Dr. Nguyen walked into the lounge, her expression sober.

"How is Sophie?" Brynn and Adam said in unison, standing together quickly.

"Please sit," Dr. Nguyen said, motioning them to sit back down. "I'm afraid that the news isn't good."

Brynn listened half-heartedly, and could tell that Adam was absorbing everything. She only heard "...the news isn't good."

Brynn watched Dr. Nguyen hand Adam something to sign, and he scribbled his name without even looking at the paper. Adam's eyes filled with tears, and she could feel the tears filling up her own, even though she hadn't heard a word the doctor had said. She could tell from Adam's face that whatever she was saying was terrible, and Brynn could hear Thomas' awful dream voice in her head saying over and over, "I'm killing your baby like you killed me."

Brynn stared at Dr. Nguyen, but didn't say a word. It was clear that Brynn wasn't listening, as the doctor looked at Adam anxiously. Brynn heard Adam talking and saw Dr. Nguyen nodding and attempting a sad smile. Dr. Nguyen squeezed Brynn's arm and walked out of the room.

Adam looked at Brynn and sat her down on the couch.

"Brynn, are you listening?" Adam said gently, but firmly. "I need you to listen to what I am going to tell you."

Brynn felt like a small child. She nodded, unable to speak.

"Brynn."

Again, Brynn nodded.

"Sophie suffered a stroke and almost died. She's not doing well. Brynn... we have to say good-bye to Sophie. We have to let her go."

Brynn looked at Adam blankly, tears streaming down her face.

"We have to say good-bye to our baby."

16

MOTHER OF THE YEAR

Ellie walked up the steps of the big house she had lived in with her parents. She hadn't been there in over ten years, and everything looked old, worn, cracked. Nothing like it had looked when they all lived in it. She tried to remember what her parents looked like, what they sounded like. It had been so long since she thought of them.

Ellie sniffed. The house smelled. But looking at it made her feel... sad. And now here she was with Dylan and her infant son. She wanted to make it work with Dylan. The infatuation had worn away, but she still really liked him, and he took care of the baby.

Dylan had stood by her, taking care of her, even when she gave birth, even knowing their son might not be his but may have belonged to Jonas. And even now that they knew that the child was... different. Dylan said he would always be there for Ellie, and as they walked into the big house, Ellie tried to believe that he would.

John Palmer had come through and taken care of everything. He had been able to get her back into house, and to get her the money that was rightfully hers. He had done everything she had asked him to do. *He and Tricia had even let them live in their home even though that stupid cow hates me,* Ellie thought bitterly.

Stupid Mother of the Year, Little Miss Know-it-All, Fake Bitch. Ellie hated Tricia and tried not to let it show too much, but Ellie was never good at being fake. She loathed how domesticated and subservient Tricia was to her husband. *She disgusts me.*

John had taken care of it all, which Ellie found extremely appealing. She knew now why Daddy had made him his successor. Ellie owed everything to John, and made it a point to tell him so every chance she got. She even offered to show him how grateful he was, but after that, he made it a point to avoid her like the plague. Ellie pouted, but then got over it. After all, Dylan may not be all that bright, but he was pretty.

Ellie thought that her baby boy was going to be her redemption. "Noah will make everything right—for me, for this family."

But when he wasn't developing the way he should, the tests showed that there was something wrong with his brain.

"This can't be!" Ellie raged at Dylan. "You gave me a retarded son!"

"Hey, I don't even know if he's mine." Dylan said defensively. Dylan didn't know the first thing about kids, but for some reason, this baby tugged at him.

"Maybe it was all of the drugs that you did when you were pregnant," Dylan said angrily. Dylan had fallen hard for Ellie, and he knew that he could make it work with her if she would just let him. If only she would stop pushing at him.

He thought how lucky he was to find her, and the fact that she had all of the money now was just an added bonus.

But the kid was special. Not just mentally special, but special in a way that Dylan didn't understand.

"I didn't grow up with a dad, so I'm not gonna leave this kid ever," Dylan said to Ellie. He didn't understand why Ellie was acting so indifferently to her son. Dylan was thankful for the nannies that Ellie had hired, because when the baby cried, the nannies took care of him. They were even teaching Dylan how to bathe, change, feed, and take care of him. And as Noah got older, they taught Dylan how to adjust to his changing needs.

Ellie was happy to settle into the house, replacing all of the old furniture with new. She had the house repainted and cleaned from top to bottom. She even had her old room made into a suite for Dylan and the baby. "Sometimes I just need to be alone, so we are going to have separate rooms," she explained to him. Dylan didn't care, as long as he got to be near her, and close to Noah.

The nannies adored Dylan. They thought he was such a good daddy, and couldn't understand what he saw in Ellie. Nanny Lisa was tiny, blonde, and pretty. She enjoyed teaching Dylan about his baby. She loved Noah from the moment she set her eyes on him, and knew that he would need special attention. Nanny Lisa was glad that Dylan was so committed to his son, and thought about both of them long after she went home for the evening.

John Palmer stopped by every so often to check on them, but Ellie was over him almost as quickly as she became infatuated with him. She only cared that the money kept coming in. John told her that as long as Noah was with her, she would continue to be taken care of. She knew that it didn't matter if she loved her son, it only mattered that they lived under the same roof. When she saw how much Dylan truly loved him, she knew that she could be free to live as she wanted, keeping Dylan captive under her own roof.

Noah had beautiful green eyes, but his features were growing to be slightly asymmetrical. Ellie was embarrassed when she took him out in public and people stared. She tried to hide him in hats, but people still stared. He made weird noises and didn't respond when she talked to him. He only seemed to respond to Dylan and after a while, Ellie stopped taking him out altogether. "You can take him out from now on," Ellie said to Dylan angrily. "It's embarrassing. Everyone stares, he drools and it's disgusting. I hate it."

Dylan didn't understand Ellie, but he never said anything. But when Noah was three, he couldn't take it anymore.

"Ellie, he's your son! He's beautiful!" Dylan said exasperated. "How can you be such a bitch about your own child?"

Ellie narrowed her dark eyes and glared at him. "I can say whatever I want about him, because he is my son. And you live in my house, so you have no right to judge me."

"What if I didn't live in your house any longer?" Dylan said angrily. He had been thinking about leaving for quite some time. He didn't love Ellie, and she never even let him touch her anymore. He couldn't stand watching how Noah tried to communicate with Ellie, and how Ellie shunned him time after time. He had special needs, but Ellie didn't want to take care of even one of them.

Ellie froze. "What do you mean, Dylan? Do you want to move out?"

Dylan was silent. "I dunno. But I don't want to be with you any longer. I'm not happy."

Ellie smiled. "Fine, then go. But Noah doesn't go with you. Noah stays with me. And you'll never see him again." She watched him flinch. She knew how much he loved Noah.

"You can't do that! I love him!" Dylan knew he shouldn't be surprised by anything she did, but he didn't think she would use Noah to trap him.

"I can, and I will," Ellie said looking deep into his eyes. She tried to remember what she found so appealing about him in the first place. She missed Jonas as she often did, and she wished that she had thought things through more clearly.

Dylan was such a disappointment.

"I'll stay," Dylan said, defeated, looking at the floor. In the old days he would have cut and run. He was always the one in control, and now Ellie clearly had all the power. Ellie was the one who called the shots, and they both knew it. Dylan hated himself for giving in so quickly.

"Good," Ellie said patting him on the chest. She felt his muscles through his shirt, and she found herself remembering what she liked so much about him. She pulled him close and breathed him in like she used to. She closed her eyes and thought about how he tried to take care of her, and how she tried to let him. She paused with her hands splayed out on his chest and felt him catch his breath.

She pulled away from him quickly.

"Okay, good," She said turning away from him.

The next morning she woke up and the house felt unusually quiet.

She went to the suite and found that Dylan and Noah were both gone.

17

THE LONG GOOD-BYE

Adam knew that the moment was coming, and he knew that it would be up to him to convince Brynn.

"I can't! I can't say good-bye! I'm not giving up on Sophie." Brynn said angrily, refusing to look at him.

"Brynn, she's suffering. She's not breathing on her own and her brain has too much damage. We need to do what's right and let her go." Adam's voice was deep and hoarse. He was in pain, more than any pain he had ever experienced before. He knew that he was going to have to talk to Brynn. He knew that she could never let Sophie go on her own. *I wish that just for once Brynn could see things for what they are, and not what she wants them to be! If she could only see this is the right thing to do.*

"I can't leave her to die. I can't just let her go. I can't! How can you ask me to let my child die? How dare you?"

"Your child? How about my child? Brynn, she's ours!" Adam couldn't believe what he was hearing. She's doing what she always does, making it about her and not about us, or about me. Adam was trying not to get frustrated. The marriage Counselor had warned them that they had to remain united, and that they couldn't think independently all of the time, or else they wouldn't make it.

"She needs a chance. She needs a chance to live. She can live," Brynn was desperately pleading her case.

"She's already dead, Brynn. She's brain dead. Her brain went too long without oxygen. We have to let her go," Adam's tone was final.

Brynn dropped to her knees. This was worse than anything she had ever experienced, or imagined in her worst nightmares. It was worse than when Adam left her. It was worse than the ferocious beatings, and it was worse than wondering what was so wrong with her that her parents just discarded her like garbage. This... this was far worse.

She thought of Sophie's tiny body growing inside of her own. And then she pictured her struggling, fighting for every breath, ever since she was born. *How can this be? How is this fair? I can't say good-bye to her, I've barely even gotten to meet her. I haven't even held her. How can I let her go?* Brynn felt her throat closing in. Something was squeezing her so tight she was gasping for air.

"Breathe, Brynn. Just breathe. Slowly, in and out. Breathe," Adam said, his voice full of concern, but something else that Brynn couldn't put her finger on. "Please, sweetheart..."

"Adam, I need to hold her," Brynn said looking at him, terrified that he would say "no."

"The doctor said we could hold her. We can spend as much time with her as we need to. But then it's only right to let her go. She can't go on like this. It's just too hard, and it's not right to put her through it." Adam was amazed at how little Brynn heard, almost as though she wasn't even in the room.

Brynn nodded slowly. *I need to call Jane. I can't call Jane! I can't ruin her honeymoon. I have no one else to call. There is only Jane.* For a brief moment, she thought about Ellie. But she knew that she would never confide in Ellie, or go to her for anything. Brynn felt very alone.

Adam wanted desperately to call his parents, but they were overseas on a mission trip with their church, and there was no way to get a hold of them. He watched Brynn carefully trying to gauge her reaction, but as usual, he couldn't read her.

He just didn't know which way she was going to go with the news, and he wanted desperately to be there for her, but he didn't think she would let him. They had made so much progress over the past few months, but Adam felt as though he was instantaneously watching them slide backwards.

Brynn already felt like she was slipping away.

"Sweetheart," he said gently. "What do you want to do? Do you want to go in?"

Brynn was still sitting on the floor, her chin resting on her knees, her arms encircling them. She looked like a child, and Adam felt strangely annoyed with her. He wanted her to make him feel better. He needed her to make him feel better.

Almost as though she read Adam's mind, she suddenly stood up and wrapped her arms around him tightly.

"I'm sorry," Brynn whispered. "I got lost for a moment, and I'm sorry."

Adam kissed the top of her head. "It's okay. Don't worry about it." This is the Brynn I want and need. He paused. "What do we do? Do we want to say 'good-bye' now?"

Brynn's heart sunk. She nodded. She wanted to shake her head and run away, but she nodded instead, her heart feeling as though it were being stabbed with a thousand jagged knives.

They walked slowly, hand in hand, down the long corridor into the locked maternity ward. They stood outside and waited to be let in. As they walked to their room, they knew that the nurses knew, everyone knew, what they were about to do. The nurses all looked at them with sad, teary eyes. Brynn hid her face in Adam's shoulder so that she wouldn't have to look at them.

They paused at the doorway of the room and looked at each other silently. Brynn knew that he was waiting for her to let him know she was ready. She took a deep breath and stepped into the room.

The room was different. Quiet. There was only one machine on, the one keeping Sophie breathing, the one keeping her alive. But all of the other machines were gone. They looked around the room and realized that her plastic enclosure was missing too. The only thing left in the room was a standard hospital bassinet. The nurses had dressed Sophie in a pretty pink onesie, and Brynn stared down at her daughter and sighed.

"She's beautiful," she breathed. Brynn was caught off guard by how beautiful her baby was, how amazingly small and beautiful and perfect. And Brynn was horrified by what she was there to do, her heart caught in her throat, unable to utter another word.

A nurse appeared out of nowhere. "Would you like to hold her?"

Brynn looked at Adam, her eyes frantic with fear, but he was lost in his own grief. She hadn't gotten to hold her yet, and now that she could, she wasn't sure if she would be able to let her go when the time came.

Brynn looked at the nurse and nodded her head, slowly.

The nurse gestured to the nearby chair and picked Sophie up, wrapping her quickly in a blanket. She handed her gently to Brynn who felt like she was being handed a secret prize, an invaluable token. She felt nervous and awkward as she looked up to Adam for reassurance. He smiled at her sadly, and Brynn realized that this was going to be the one and only time she was going to get to hold her baby.

"She's so light!" Brynn said with wonder, amazed at how Sophie felt like air in her arms. She closed her eyes and imagined herself getting to hold her every day, waking her up in the morning, and putting her to bed at night. She felt her heart start to swell almost uncontrollably. It was so full of despair. She held her for what felt like forever, time frozen, the room still.

Brynn felt Adam's hand on her shoulder and it startled her. She looked up and saw tears in his blue eyes. "You hold her, honey," Brynn offered, her voice a small whisper.

"Keep her a little while longer," Adam said, smiling down at her, blinded, barely able to see. He wiped the tears away and looked deep into her eyes. "Keep her as long as you want."

Brynn held Sophie, talking to her, rocking her in her arms. She was careful not to talk about sad things. *I doubt she can understand but I'm not going to take the chance.*

Adam watched her, mesmerized by the sound of Brynn's voice. He loved watching her talk to Sophie. It confirmed what he had always known about her—Brynn was going to be a wonderful mother, even though she had no one to teach her, and no role models of her own. He felt his heart cracking, but he tried to stay strong just a little while longer. He knew that he would need to for Brynn.

She eventually handed Sophie over to Adam, and they took turns gently passing her back and forth. The nurse watched carefully from a distance, trying not to cry. This part never got any easier, no matter how many times she saw it, and this young couple was no exception.

"I love you, Sophie. I didn't know if I could be a good Mommy, but here you are. And now I know that I can be. And I have you to thank for that," Brynn fought back the sobs that were beginning to engulf her. Her heart felt like a raw open wound. Even Adam's abandonment felt minimal compared to the pain she was feeling trying to let her daughter go.

Adam held her and Sophie tight, enveloping them with his arms. "Oh God, I wish I could just protect you from this, but I can't!"

Brynn wasn't for sure if he was talking to Sophie or if he was talking to her.

"I can't do this. I can't. Let. Her. Go." Brynn was crying hard, her entire body shaking as she tried not to let herself scream. "I can't say good-bye. I just can't. I can't!"

Adam held Brynn and Sophie tight. He didn't want the moment to get past him. He didn't know how he was going to survive. He looked at his small, beautiful daughter in the arms of the only woman he had ever loved, and he wanted to keep them like this, with him always. He couldn't imagine how he was ever going to get Brynn past this, or how he was going to get past this.

Adam held Brynn through her sobs, tortured and raw, wishing that he could ease her pain. Brynn tried desperately to stop crying. She didn't want Sophie to go without her realizing it, and she knew that if she kept crying that she would miss her last moments. She summoned her strength and quieted herself as best as she could.

Brynn held Sophie close, breathing in her sweet scent, and feeling the slight rise and fall of her chest as it moved slower and slower. They had given the doctor permission to stop the machines, knowing that it would mean an end to her suffering. Brynn didn't know what to expect. She didn't know if Sophie would float away, or if she would cry. She just knew that she couldn't let her go. She stared at her face. *Will I know when she's gone?*

Brynn held her breath, waiting.

The doctor had said that after they stopped 'taking measures,' it wouldn't be long. Brynn wanted it to last forever. She couldn't bear the thought of letting her go.

They sat for an hour, and Brynn felt every minute as though it were a lifetime. She touched every tiny finger and toe, tracing them with her own fingers, enjoying the softness and the newness. She nuzzled Sophie, enjoying her smell, knowing that she would never get to smell her again, and praying that she would always remember what she smelled like.

Finally, Sophie was still, her tiny chest no longer moving and Brynn marveled at how she simply looked as though she were sleeping. Brynn gasped, realizing that Sophie didn't move at all, as she looked at Adam helplessly. Adam blindly fumbled for the nurses call button, not seeing it through the tears that were flowing down his face. He stood up, unable to look at Brynn, unable to look at his daughter.

"Did we do the right thing? Adam? Oh God, did we do the right thing?" Brynn's voice cracked as she begged Adam for an answer.

Adam nodded, his blue eyes dark and somber. "She's not suffering anymore, Brynn. She isn't in pain anymore."

"But she never knew us. She never knew that we loved her." Brynn held Sophie close to her chest, desperately searching her mind for a way she could be with her forever. She refused to believe that she was truly gone.

"She knew us, Brynn. She knew us before she was ever born. She knew we loved her. She loved us, even if only for a brief time. She knew, Brynn." Adam couldn't believe anything different. He knew that if it weren't true, that nothing else in the world could ever make sense again.

Brynn nodded. She couldn't see Adam or Sophie. She could only see the tears that kept coming no matter how hard she tried to make them stop.

Brynn handed the still bundle to Adam, and Adam took her, carefully. Adam held her and rocked her back and forth in his arms, humming quietly. Adam kissed Sophie's cheek, taking in its softness and knowing he would always remember how it felt on his lips.

When he started to hand her back, Brynn shook her head. She didn't want to hold her dead child any longer. She wanted the moment to be over. She wanted to stop looking at the tiny beautiful face that would have been her daughter. She just wanted to go home, and she didn't want to feel the pain anymore.

The nurse had been waiting respectfully, silently. She looked at Brynn who sat with her head in her hands on the bed. She refused to look at the nurse even though she could feel the heaviness of her eyes.

"Do you want to hold her one last time, and say good-bye?" the nurse said gently to Brynn.

Brynn was silent. The nurse waited.

Brynn stood up and walked toward the nurse. She walked as though she was in a daze, and the nurse recognized the glazed look in her eyes. Brynn took Sophie slowly and nuzzled her against her neck, knowing that this would be the last time that she would ever hold her.

"I love you more than you will ever know, and I will never forget you. Never." Brynn kissed her on the cheek and then on the forehead, hating the coldness that was starting to settle into Sophie's skin. She took one last look at Sophie's face and couldn't believe that she was going to have to live her life without her.

The nurse entered the room, quietly. Brynn handed Sophie to the nurse and immediately turned away unable to believe what she had just done The nurse quickly left the room, and the room fell eerily silent.

Neither Brynn nor Adam touched one another or spoke. Each was lost in their own pain oblivious to the other as they sat isolated and surrounded by a deep shroud of impenetrable sorrow. Without speaking, they both knew that absolutely nothing in their lives would ever be the same again.

18

CARLY'S LIFE

Carly smiled at Petey. She had been living with them for several years now, and after the initial first year, found that as time went on, she smiled more and more often. The biggest black spot in her life now were the headaches, the terrible headaches that always came, and then stayed for days.

Other than that, she had learned to be content with her life. The doctor told her that she may never get her memory back, and she was coming to terms with that. She wanted to know who she was and what her life was like before coming to live with Petey and Lily, but with every passing year, she found that it didn't bother her quite as much.

"What are you smiling at, honey?" Petey said smiling back. He remained stunned by Amy's beauty, as he was from the first moment that he saw her. He was careful to call her 'Carly' now, instead of 'Amy'. *Carly, Carly, Carly. Don't ever mess it up, Petey.* He had been calling her Carly for several years, but he was still afraid that he would forget and call her Amy one day. Amy didn't know that he knew who she was. She thought he just found her wandering somewhere, and he had saved her from some terrible men who were trying to hurt her.

"You," she said leaning her chin on her hands. "You're so handsome and serious all of the time." She pretended to pout.

"I just want you to be happy," Petey said trying not to sound nervous. He leaned over and kissed her, feeling that familiar rush as he did so. He had never cared about anyone like he cared about her. For the first time in his life, he felt as though he had a lot to lose.

"I am," Carly sighed happily. She busied herself making breakfast, knowing that Lily would be leaving for work soon at the veterinarian clinic.

"Why are you so happy?" Petey asked, curious.

"I don't know. I woke up this morning and I felt... happy. I can't explain it. I just felt at peace." Carly shook her short blonde hair, mussing it up, and Petey felt his heart thump in his chest. He thought she was beautiful from the moment he saw her, which is why he couldn't let Sy kill her as he had killed her husband. They met with such violence, Petey didn't believe she would ever be able to let that go had she remembered what he did to her. He never believe she could have come to love him. *But she doesn't remember!* Petey reminded himself.

Lily came into the kitchen silently. "Good morning," she said brightly.

"Lily, I made breakfast," Carly said proudly. She loved Lily like a sister and wanted her to be pleased. Lily had taken care of her, taught her how to cook, how to sew, and how to clean. Carly was ashamed of how much she didn't know how to do, but Lily had taught her to be useful around the house.

"It looks wonderful," Lily said, smiling at Carly with approval. Lily was surprised at what a quick learner Carly was. It was evident that Carly hadn't cooked or cleaned in a long time, and Lily needed her to be able to help around the house. She was pleased and surprised at how eager Carly was, and was even more surprised that she wanted to learn how to sew. When Lily was offered a job, she and Petey were hesitant about leaving Carly alone, but she had already been with them for a couple of years, and there was no sign of her memory returning.

"I'm glad you found a job," Carly said, looking at Lily. "You seem so much happier."

"I am. Thank you." Lily didn't realize that it was so evident.

"I just wish that I could do more," Carly said, a trace of sadness in her voice.

"You don't need to work, honey. Not with your headaches. We will take care of you," Petey said quickly. "I don't want you to hurt yourself."

Carly was quiet, busying herself with pouring coffee and juice and buttering the toast. "I haven't had a headache in a month now," she said quietly.

The room was silent, with only the sound of thoughtful chewing.

"You do a lot around here," Lily said breaking the silence. "I honestly don't know what I would do without you."

Carly smiled as she looked around the room. She had sewn the new curtains on the windows and repaired the tablecloth. She would do the laundry, clean the house, and had been cooking more and more of the meals. But she felt like she was missing something. She was happy, but she fought the feeling that she should be doing more.

"Don't worry about it, sweetheart," Petey said, his mouth full of eggs. It pained him to think that Carly could be unhappy. "You do plenty. If you're bored, then I can get you a dog or..."

"I'm not bored," Carly said quickly. "I'm happy. I'm just talking."

Lily and Petey exchanged quick glances, each looking away quickly. Carly knew they were cousins, she knew that they looked out for her, but she didn't really know who they were, or that they lived in fear every day that she would find out. They both loved her. She fulfilled a need in them that neither recognized until Petey inadvertently moved her in with Lily.

"Why don't we do some online shopping when I get home?" Lily said, smiling. She knew how much Carly loved to shop online. She shopped for everything online with a small budget, and she enjoyed it.

"Okay. Or..." Carly paused, "Or... we could go into town and shop there."

Carly didn't miss the look that passed between the two people she loved the most. She had posed this question on numerous occasions, and every time she was denied.

"You know what we've said, Carly. It's just not safe," Lily said slowly. "We don't know who was after you or why. We don't want anything bad to happen to you, or for anyone to know where you are."

"The men who were after you were bad men. We can't protect you if they find out where you are," Petey added.

Carly nodded. She knew what they would say. She knew that it didn't matter how many times she asked, she knew that the answer would still be the same. She wanted to be safe, but she didn't feel like she was in danger. She couldn't imagine who would ever try to hurt her, or why anyone would ever want to, but then again, she couldn't remember. She couldn't remember anything, and she was trying to find happiness in her current state, but sometimes it was just too hard.

"Okay," Carly said with a small smile. "I'm ruining breakfast."

"I know it's hard, but it will be okay. You'll see," Lily said getting up and hugging her tight. "I hate to see you sad. Try to be happy. You are with people who love you."

"I can stay with you for a while," Petey said, wiping his mouth as he finished the last of his breakfast. "If you want."

Carly smiled. "I'd like that."

Lily went to work, and Carly and Petey sat on the couch, sitting close together in silence.

"I wish I knew who I was, and where I came from," Carly said after a little while. "I am happy with you and with Lily, but I feel like I'm missing something."

"I know." Petey never knew what to say when she started talking like this. He didn't want to discourage her, but he had never spent much time talking to girls before. He wasn't much for talking. He was a better listener.

"I wonder if I had a family. I wonder if...if...," Carly hesitated.

"If what?" Petey asked, not sure that he wanted to hear the question.

"I wonder if I had any children. If I have any children," Carly said, her voice barely audible. "I always dream of a beautiful little girl with big brown eyes. She's holding out her arms to me and..."

Petey felt a knot in the pit of his stomach. He knew that he didn't want to hear the rest.

"I just feel like I know her, and I can't get her out of my mind."

Petey held her tight, pushing away his own fear. *When she figures out who she is, she'll hate me. I can't let that happen.*

Carly snuggled up against his big, strong frame losing herself in the only comfort she knew.

19

NOAH

"Lee-uh," Noah lifted his arms up begging to be picked up.

"No, no, no. Noah sleep. Sleep!" Lisa ordered gently.

"Lee-uh, Pick up!"

"Noah. No. Sleep." Lisa said firmly. "It's nap time. Sleep."

They had driven for hours all through the night, and Lisa was exhausted. She wanted to sleep, and she knew that she couldn't sleep until Dylan did. She didn't want to lose patience with Noah, she knew that would just make it worse. He's just a special little boy. He didn't ask for this. He didn't ask for his mother to be a complete and useless bitch. It's not his fault. *Patience, Lisa, patience.*

The door to the hotel room opened. Dylan walked in—tall, lean, and handsome, breathtakingly so...

"He's not asleep yet?" Dylan asked, his voice tired and aggravated.

"No, not yet," Lisa said trying not to cry.

"Lay him on the bed." Dylan said sharply.

Lisa picked Noah up out of the pack and play she was trying to get him to sleep in. She laid him carefully in the middle of the bed. At three he was getting heavy, almost too heavy for Lisa to pick him up.

Noah looked at her with big brown eyes. His brow was furrowed and he was confused. Lisa looked at his little face, at his eyes that were too close together and his forehead that seemed oddly large for his size, and she thought that he was beautiful.

"Lay next to him." Dylan said gesturing to the bed. "He can't sleep when he's alone."

Lisa lay down next to Noah, covering Noah gently with the blanket. She smoothed his dark brown hair over his brow and watched him close his eyes. He fell asleep instantaneously, and Lisa sighed with relief.

"It's going to be okay," Dylan smiled at Lisa. "We have each other. We are away from that bitch, and we can start over. We can start a family without her."

Lisa smiled sleepily. She loved Noah and wanted him to be happy. She had been dreaming of the three of them being a family for a long time. She just never believed it could happen. Finally, after three years of flirting, and talking, and pretending like they weren't in love, they decided that they couldn't deny it anymore.

And now here she was.

She drifted off to sleep with her arm protectively wrapped around Noah. "Goodnight, Noah bug," she whispered as she did every night.

Dylan watched them sleeping, his whole world wrapped up in them. *I thought that Ellie would make me happy, but she's nothing but a selfish, drug-addicted whore. I can't let Noah know who his mother really is.*

Dylan imagined a world where the three of them could be happy, but he knew they would have to get further away. He knew that as soon as Ellie realized they were gone, she would call John, and that they would call the police.

He drifted off in the chair, watching over them.

The next thing he knew, the world sounded as if it were crashing in, and he jumped up as the door flew open. He then found himself staring down the barrel of several guns in his face, and he was being thrown to the ground.

"Police! Don't move! Don't move!" Dylan felt a boot on the back of his neck and the sound of Lisa's screams.

Noah was moaning, and Dylan felt tears running down his face. "Noah! Noah!" He cried out.

"Don't move, I said!" A strong angry voice was shouting down at him. "You're under arrest for kidnapping."

"He's my son!" Dylan screamed. "He's my son!"

"We'll see what the court says," the voice said hand cuffing him roughly and picking him up. He looked around desperately for Lisa, but she was already gone. All he caught was a glimpse of Noah on the bed.

My poor baby boy. Daddy loves you! Daddy loves you!

20

THE MEETING

The table was large. Dark. Cherry.

The room was massive. Cold. A place where hopes were dashed and dreams were destroyed. It was a large room that didn't care about the tears that were shed, or the hearts that were broken. It was created for sadness and misery and devastation.

Brynn stepped into the room first.

She was ushered into the room by the secretary, a young, serious woman with black rimmed glasses who gestured toward one of the large leather chairs. "Mr. Black will be right with you," she said in a no-nonsense tone. Her tone was very business-like, and lacked any warmth or compassion.

Brynn sat down, the chair swallowing her instantly, making her feel very small. She shifted in the chair trying to get comfortable. Her feet barely touched the floor, and she immediately questioned whether she should be there.

A few moments later, a heavyset man in his late fifties entered the room carrying a heavy leather bag filled with files, and sweating profusely. "I'm sorry, Mrs. Michael, traffic was terrible and..."

Brynn wasn't listening. Her eyes were large and panicked as she looked around the room. She kept smoothing her dark hair behind her ears as she squirmed in her chair.

He could tell that she was nervous, and she looked like she was going to throw up. He had warned her that it wasn't going to be easy. He warned her that this was going to be a difficult day. "You can back out any time you want. This isn't going to be pleasant," he told her at their last meeting. "If you aren't sure you want to go through with it, then maybe you're just not ready. You have to be sure that this is what you want to do. This is permanent."

Brynn had nodded at him. She was sure. She knew that this is what she wanted to do. She knew that there was no other choice.

Mr. Black unloaded his bag. He set the files on the table and poured himself a big glass of water from the crystal pitcher on the table.

"Would you like some?" he asked, gesturing to Brynn.

Brynn shook her head. She was afraid that if she opened her mouth she would vomit all over the beautifully polished table.

"You should have some," Mr. Black said pouring her a glass of water and setting it clumsily in front of her, some of it spilling out onto the table.

Brynn watched the water spilling on the table and looked around for a napkin. She didn't want water all over the table in front of her. She grabbed a tissue from the box in front of her and wiped the table down.

"Are you sure you want to do this? Is this what you really want?" he said, some of the redness from his face disappearing, the sweat still dripping from his double chin.

"Yes." Brynn said, offering nothing else.

Mr. Black busied himself with pulling out his papers and his legal pad, making notes as he thumbed through the pages. Brynn could see her bank statements, papers from the restaurant, and various pages that she had given him over the past few months. It made her sad to see her entire life reduced to pages in a manila folder in the hands of a balding, middle-aged stranger, who she was going to owe a lot of money to when it was all said and done.

The big glass door to the room opened and a masculine looking woman who must have been at least six feet tall entered the room with Adam trailing behind her. Brynn's breath caught in her throat.

She hadn't seen Adam in months, and now here he was walking around the large table avoiding her eyes. It had been so long since she had seen him, even longer since she had touched him. She suddenly fought a strong urge to run up to him and grab him, but after Sophie's death, things between them had steadily declined. He wanted nothing to do with her now.

Oh, God. What are we doing? Brynn suddenly realized that she had been holding her breath.

Adam and his lawyer sat down on the other side of the table, neither of them saying a word.

"Mr. Black," the mannish looking woman said curtly, her voice oddly deep.

"Ms. St. George," Mr. Black said with a trace of contempt.

Brynn sensed that this wasn't their first meeting, and it made her uneasy.

She tried to catch Adam's eye, but he refused to look at her. She finally gave up and looked down at the table, fighting the tears that threatened to spring up.

"Well," Ms. St. George said, her low voice resonating in the large room. "I think we know why we are all here."

"Yes," Brynn and Adam said at the same time. Adam glanced up quickly, his blue eyes flashing toward Brynn and then looking away.

"It would be nice if we could get through this quickly, civilly. If anyone needs a break, please say so. We will try to get through the division of property as quickly as possible." Ms. St. George wasted no time getting to the point. "There will simply be the matter of going to court to stand in front of the judge after this, and then everything will be final."

Adam nodded, and Brynn felt the lump in her throat getting bigger. She had been dreading this meeting all week, and now that it was finally here, she couldn't believe it. She hadn't spoken to Adam in months, and she longed just to hear the sound of his voice. She wondered if he missed her as much as she missed him. *It doesn't matter now.*

The lawyers started talking, dividing assets as Brynn and Adam nodded in agreement. There was nothing that either of them wanted to fight over. The beautiful Victorian was going to be put on the market, with the profit of the sale being divided equally; the dishes, the cars, even the candle holders they had received for a wedding gift, everything. The only thing left to determine was the fate of the restaurant.

"I want her to have it. She can have it all, " Adam said looking directly at Brynn for the first time.

"Are you sure that you want to do that?" Ms. St. George said skeptically. The profit of the restaurant had quadrupled over the past few years.

"I do. I want her to have it. She's worked for it. It's hers." Adam's tone was firm. He had given it a lot of thought. He didn't feel as though he was owed anything from the restaurant.

"No. No," Brynn said, shaking her head. "He deserves half. He should get half."

Mr. Black and Ms. St. George looked at each other.

Nobody spoke as the lawyers communicated silently with one another.

"If that is what you want, Adam, but I strongly advise against it," Ms. St. George said finally.

"That is what I want," Adam said never taking his eyes off Brynn.

Brynn's eyes filled with tears, and she couldn't stop it. Adam knew how much the restaurant meant to her, but she didn't expect him to leave it to her completely. Not after he had blamed her for everything else. Not after he had blamed her for Sophie. She blamed herself for losing Sophie, so they at least agreed upon that.

His words came back to her. "You never wanted a child! You never even wanted to be a mother! Your selfishness is the reason Sophie is dead. If you had wanted her more, if you had loved her more, maybe she would still be here!" Brynn felt the venom of his words cutting through her like they did the first time that he said them. He blamed her for the loss of their beautiful daughter, and nothing that she could say or do could make him think differently.

She didn't want him to think differently.

But she resented him for forcing her to decide to get pregnant in the first place. Even after he knew how afraid she was to be a mother, he still wanted to have a baby, and she knew that in order to keep him, she would have to concede.

And now Sophie was gone, dead, buried over a year ago. And here they were, dividing their lives together as though it never even existed, as though it never mattered.

Brynn agreed to everything that Ms. St. George proposed after that, and within an hour and a half, they were done.

"Thank you, Ms. Michael. I know how difficult this must be for you." Ms. St. George said smiling sympathetically. It was the first show of emotion that Brynn had seen from her.

Mr. Black stood up, pushing his chair back from the table, and Brynn stood up next to him. Ms. St. George stood up and, even though they were some distance apart, Brynn could tell that she towered over her. Adam stood up slowly, his shoulders slumped, his eyes red from lack of sleep. Brynn knew that he was miserable, but there was nothing she could do for him anymore.

"Mr. Black," Ms. St. George said, nodding to him respectfully and putting her hand on Adam's shoulder.

"Ms. St. George, Mr. Michael." Mr. Black nodded back.

Adam looked slowly at Brynn. He missed her. But he couldn't look at her any longer. She reminded him too much of Sophie, and he knew that if he stayed married to her that she would continue to remind him of his precious daughter that he lost, every day.

They locked eyes for a moment, both of them fighting back tears. The sorrow in the room was evident. The room was use to hatred, anger, and resentment, but sorrow and love in this room were rare. Even the lawyers, who orchestrated these deals daily, squirmed. They could tell that there was still a great deal of love between Brynn and Adam, even if they were completely unaware.

Adam and Ms. St. George walked out of the room slowly. Brynn avoided his eyes. She looked down at the floor and knew that she would only see him once more, in court. She realized that after that, she might never see her beautiful Adam ever again. There were no children to tie them together, and they just divided everything that had ever been between them.

At least they were trying to keep it civil between them. The last night before Brynn left, Adam agreed to let her keep Maxie before the lawyers got involved. He had gotten Maxie for Brynn as a gift, and he wasn't going to take him now. He knew that Brynn would need him for security since Adam was no longer going to be sleeping next to her.

She had protested as he had expected her to. "I can't keep Maxie. He's our dog. Can't we just... I don't know, share custody of him?"

"No. He's yours. He was a gift." Adam said in that strange monotone voice he had been using for months now. Brynn hadn't grown accustomed to his lack of emotion, and it still cut her deeply.

"But you love him, too. He loves you. He needs both of us." Brynn argued.

"He's just a dog, Brynn. He'll be fine," Adam said as a matter of fact. "He'll be fine. And besides..."

Adam stopped.

"Besides what?" Brynn said, prodding gently.

"Besides, if we share custody, I'll have to see you. I don't want to see you anymore."

Brynn felt like she had been punched in the stomach.

"I... I... didn't realize..." Brynn was speechless.

"I've tried to forgive you. I've tried to love you again, but I just can't." Adam said as he turned around and continued to pack his bags. "Part of me knows that it may not really be your fault, but I can't change how I feel. I hate that I just don't love you anymore."

Adam's words cut through her, but the look on his face hurt her more. There was a complete absence of love, almost as though she were looking at someone completely different. Sophie's death had changed him, and the old, sweet, hopeful Adam had been buried with their beautiful baby.

Brynn had no defense.

She knew that Adam was partly right. "I'm sorry," was all Brynn could say.

Adam was leaving her for the second time, and this time she knew he wouldn't be back. She could tell by the look in his eyes. He was a changed man, and there was no trace left of the boy that she had fallen in love with.

But then again, the old Brynn had been dead and buried, too.

21

BRYNN AND ELLIE

The doorbell rang, startling Brynn.

Maxie took off toward the door, his nails clicking on the hardwood floors as he let out a deep bark and growl. He stood by the door waiting for Brynn to get there.

Shit! She thought looking out. It's her. What does she want?

She hadn't seen Ellie since the first time she saw her, standing at her door. *When I was pregnant... with Sophie.*

Brynn pushed down the sadness as she did hundreds of times a day. She turned around and looked at the house, the hallway littered with boxes.

Ellie stood, waiting patiently for Brynn to open the door.

"It's okay, boy," Brynn said to Maxie, patting him on the head. "Maybe if you're good, I'll let you bite her."

She opened the screen door a few inches. "What do you want?"

"Brynn," Ellie paused. She was shuffling her feet back and forth. "I uh... was hoping, that we could... uh, talk."

"Talk about what?" Brynn's voice had a hard edge to it.

Ellie peered hard at Brynn through the screen door. "I just want to talk to you, if you would let me."

Brynn hesitated. What does she want from me now?

She looked down at Maxie who looked at her blankly. "You're no help," she muttered.

She opened the door and stood to the side. Ellie walked by her and Brynn was surprised at how small she was. She was actually a few inches shorter than Brynn, and about ten pounds lighter. Brynn knew that she looked like Ellie, but not completely. What did my father look like?

Brynn walked in front of Ellie and led her to the living room. Brynn moved boxes off the couch and gestured for Ellie to sit.

"I'd offer you a drink, but I'm kind of busy. So if you could just tell me what you want, I would appreciate it." Brynn got straight to the point.

Ellie was tapping her foot.

"I, uh, am so sorry about your baby," Ellie said slowly.

"Okay. Thanks." Brynn said, impatiently. Brynn didn't think about Sophie, she couldn't think about Sophie. She knew that if she did, she would die. She blocked her out of her mind and refused to talk about her with anyone. "What else? That's not what you came here to say."

"No, but I wanted to say it." Ellie looked around the room. Everything was disheveled as Brynn was starting to pack, and Adam had already taken his belongings. "You're moving?"

"Yes. That's what happens when your husband no longer loves you, because he thinks you killed your baby."

Ellie took a sharp breath. "Oh, Brynn, I'm sorry."

"Don't be. You have nothing to do with it. But really, what do you want?" Brynn's face was hard, her brown eyes as black as coal.

"You're not making this easy, are you?" Ellie said, clearly getting frustrated.

"Why would I make it easy for you? Did you make it easy for me?" Brynn's anger was palpable.

"No. No, I didn't. I'm trying to fix things, though. I'm trying to make it right, now." Ellie's voice was weak, and Brynn felt an awkward surge of strength.

"Why now? I don't understand why you would bother, NOW?"

"Because, there is a lot at stake," Ellie said quietly.

Brynn looked at her suspiciously. Ellie's clothes were nice enough, Designer, Brynn thought. But it didn't fit with her dark teeth and her sallow skin. It didn't make sense. She wants something. But what?

Ellie took a deep breath. "I have a son. You have a brother."

Brynn froze. A brother? Oh my God, I have a brother?!

Brynn was silent. She looked at Ellie, her mouth open. She knew that she looked shocked, but she didn't care. "How... I mean, what happened? Where is he now?"

The mood of the room shifted, and Ellie knew that she had the advantage. Brynn had been playing hard to get, but now Ellie had something that Brynn wanted. Family.

"His name is Noah. And he can't wait to meet his sister," Ellie said, smiling at Brynn. "I know that I wasn't a mother to you, but I've done what I could do for him."

Brynn looked at Ellie and narrowed her eyes.

"Why? Why did you leave me?" Brynn sat next to her on the couch and stared evenly at her. She held her breath. She had always imagined herself asking the questions, but had never been able to imagine the answers.

"Do you really want to know?" Ellie hesitated. She knew that she was going to have to tell her, but she dreaded it. She wanted to cleanse herself of the truth, but she knew that it meant that Brynn might never want to see her again. She had been dreaming of this moment for almost thirty years, but now she wasn't sure that she could go through with it. "You will hate me."

"I already hate you," Brynn said instantly wishing she could take back the words when she saw Ellie's face fall instantly. "I'm sorry, I don't hate you. I hate myself."

Ellie's eyes filled with tears. She wanted to be high. She wanted to fade away and not to have to face Brynn. She realized that this is what she had been running from her entire life.

"I left you on the side of the road." Ellie went on to tell Brynn every detail that she could remember about the horrible night she had abandoned her, and of the years that followed. She talked without stopping for what felt like hours.

Brynn sat quietly, wringing her hands in her lap as she listened. She cried out in pain when Ellie told her about how little Eva ran after the car screaming for Ellie not to leave. But Ellie kept talking, almost as if she were in a trance. Ellie told Brynn about her life, about Noah, and about Dylan.

"What happened to my father?" Brynn asked when Ellie paused.

"He died. He was a bad man, and he died." Ellie said quietly. "I was messed up on every drug he could give me, and he died."

"What about now? Are you on drugs now?" Brynn asked angrily.

"No. I'm clean. I've been clean for five years," Ellie said, wincing from Brynn's anger. "I never meant to hurt you. I never wanted to hurt you. But I know that I did. I was a terrible mother. I know."

"How were you a mother to Noah if you've only been clean for five years? Surely he is older than five!" Brynn was confused.

"He's been in a home, getting the best of care. I've been able to visit him. It was the best place for him. Truly!" Ellie spoke quickly trying to convince Brynn with every breath.

There was silence as Ellie stopped talking. Brynn was taking it all in, replaying the information repeatedly in her mind. It doesn't make sense that she was coming to her now after all of this time. "Why are you here?" Brynn asked, refusing to let go of her suspicion.

"I'm here for you," Ellie said attempting to smile.

"But why now? How long have you known how to find me?"

Ellie stopped talking. "I've known for a long time."

"Then why, NOW?"

Ellie sighed. She knew that this part was going to be the hardest. Brynn will just think that I am using her, and she wouldn't be entirely wrong. "Noah and I are going to lose everything. But now that I've found you, it'll be okay. I can take care of him again, and everything is going to be fine."

"Why? Why are you going to lose everything?" Brynn asked curious.

"There are rules to the estate. Rules to the money. They thought you were dead, and now they know that you are alive, and so you have a right to some of the money." Ellie knew that she wasn't making sense. She was trying to explain it the best way that she could, but she knew that John was going to have to tell her about it.

"Estate? What estate are you talking about?" Brynn was getting frustrated. Ellie isn't what she appears after all! I knew it!

"My parent's estate. They were very wealthy. They've been gone for a very long time, and you are entitled to some of the money. Noah and I need you. Without you, we lose everything." Elli was trying not to sound desperate.

"How much money are we talking about?" Brynn said slowly, her mouth very dry.

Ellie paused. "Millions. Millions."

22

CARLY'S NEW HOME

Petey's heart was broken.

After loving Carly for ten years, one day she woke up and something inside of her brain had changed. The doctor said she must have been experiencing mini strokes for years. Carly had been deteriorating for a long time, but now she was beyond the place where Lily could continue to take care of her.

Carly still looked the same on the outside, beautiful, tiny and fragile, her hair only slightly gray. But her brain was a scrambled mess of scattered memories from a different life, and the inability to retain anything from her current life.

"She needs to be in a home where she can be cared for properly," the doctor, a family friend of Petey's who never asked questions, told Petey and Lily when they called him to look at her. "Whatever happened to her is only going to get worse and not better. I can get her into a place a few towns over where nobody will question where she came from, or whom she is. But it's a couple of hours away."

Petey nodded. He knew that his life with her was never meant to be permanent, but she was the only woman he knew how to love. *I don't know how I'm going to let her go.*

After the doctor left, Lily looked at Petey, her gray eyes full of concern. Petey was closer than a brother, and his pain hurt her. "Are you okay?" she hesitated to ask him, she knew that he wouldn't want to talk about it.

"I'll be fine. I just need her to be taken care of," Petey said sadly. "This home that the doc is talking about is expensive. And she needs to go now. I don't know what to do, Lily. She needs more than what I can do. I ain't got that kind of money."

"I do," Lily said without hesitation.

"No you don't," Petey said. "You can't afford it any more than I can."

Lily's expression was one that he hadn't seen before.

"I can," Lily said her tone firm. "Daddy left me a lot of money. A lot. I've never told anyone, because I didn't want anyone to come after it. But I can afford it, and I'm going to."

Petey's eyes filled with tears. "But why? Why would you?"

"Why would I?" Lily couldn't believe that he didn't see it. "Before you brought her here, I was completely alone. But then she came and suddenly, I had a family. YOU became my brother, and she became my sister, and I haven't been lonely since. So I would do anything for her. And I would do anything for you."

Petey started to cry, and Lily realized that she had never seen this giant man cry before.

"It'll be okay. We will take turns visiting her, but it will be okay." Lily's heart was broken. Somehow, Lily knew that she would never get married, but having Carly with her made her not care anymore. She didn't want to go back to the solitary life she had before Carly and Petey came into her life.

"Its a few hours away, Lil. How often am I going to get to see her? And she may not even know me. So then what?" Petey was beginning to realize what it all meant.

"I don't know, Petey. But maybe this will mean that..." Lily hesitated. She never should have said anything. She knew Petey would be angry, and she wanted to kick herself for opening her mouth.

"What?" Petey asked, curious at Lily's expression.

"Nothing. I shouldn't have said anything."

"Maybe it will mean that I can have a family? I can get married? I can have a wife? Is that what you were going to say?" Petey asked quietly, almost guiltily. As much as he loved Carly, he knew that he could never have those things with her. It wouldn't be right after what he helped do to her husband. He wouldn't have felt right.

"Yes," Lily said. "That is what I was going to say. I'm sorry."

"Don't be sorry, Lil. I thought the same thing lots of times. I always wanted a family, kids to call me Daddy. I knew it wasn't going to be happy with Carly, but I just didn't care. I was trying to make up for what I did to her."

"But you loved her, and you took care of her, and she's been happy. You did make up for it," Lily put her hand on Petey's massive arm. "We need to get her packed."

Carly had been lying in the bed, half-awake, half-asleep. She stretched out her arms and looked at Petey.

"What are you doing?" she asked, yawning.

"I'm packing for you, sweetheart." Petey said trying to smile.

"Why? Where am I going?" Carly asked trying to sit up. Her head hurt, and she winced in pain.

"You're going to a hospital. You're going to live there where they can take care of you better," Lily said gently.

"Oh, James. What is wrong with me?"

Petey looked at Lily, his eyes wide. *Oh God. She thinks I'm James.* "James? Who is James?" Petey asked trying not to reveal the panic in his voice.

"My husband, of course, silly." Carly said smiling. "I don't want to go to the hospital. I want to stay here with my sister. I don't want to leave Lily."

Lily felt the tears welling up in her eyes. "This will be best for all of us, Carly. The hospital will be able to take care of you best. I don't want you to leave, either."

"Carly? Who is Carly? I'm Ellie."

23

ADAM'S MESS

Adam was hung over. Again.

The day in court to finalize the divorce was hard. It was much harder than he thought it would be. He almost didn't go. *If I don't go, maybe it won't be real. If I don't go, I can still change my mind. If I don't go, maybe I will wake up tomorrow and it'll all be a dream and Sophie won't be dead.*

When he finally did arrive in court, he was fifteen minutes late and smelled like gin and beer. The judge shook her head, but the process was short and painless. And then they were divorced.

It was easier than Adam thought it would be. No sobbing, no tearful good-byes. It was simple and short, and when it was over, it was over. It was very anticlimactic. And Adam felt let down, disappointed. He wanted Brynn to cry, he wanted Brynn to throw herself on the ground and beg him to reconsider. He wanted to see her suffer as he was suffering.

When it was done, he glared hard at her and left the courthouse, walking right into the closest bar. He didn't care that it was eleven in the morning. He didn't care that he was wearing the same clothes he had worn the night before.

After six Beefeater and tonics with lime, he felt much better. He felt clearer. The bartender was getting ready to cut him off, but Adam was tipping so well, he thought a few more might be fine.

A pretty young redhead sat down on the bar stool next to Adam, and he pretended not to notice.

"I'll have a Bloody Mary, spicy, top shelf," she said smiling at the bartender.

"Sure," The bartender said, smiling back.

"Bloody Mary? Have sssome gin," Adam slurred, grinning at her.

"No, thank you," she said, wrinkling her nose. He was handsome enough, but he was already drunk, and it was still light outside. Experience told her to stay away from men like him.

"Why? You got something against gin?" Adam said, slightly offended by her expression. "Or me?"

"No, no. You're fine," she said quickly, wishing she had sat down at a different place in the empty bar.

"Sssorry. Bad day," he said hanging his head.

She took pity on him. "It's okay," she said smiling sympathetically. "Let's start all over. I'm Jessie."

"Adam," he said putting out his hand to shake and accidentally hitting her in the head. "Oh God, I'm sorry."

Much to Adam's surprise, Jessie laughed.

"It's okay. You're a mess. Are you always this bad?" she said, resting her pretty face on her hand, gazing at him with sincere interest.

"No." Adam laughed for the first time since he could remember. "I got divorced today."

"Oh, I'm sorry," Jessie said, immediately sorry for dismissing him so fast. "That must be difficult."

"Yeahhhh," Adam said taking a drink of gin & tonic number seven. "It sucked."

They talked for a while, and by five p.m. Adam was drinking water and messily eating a greasy Rueben. Jessie found herself drawn to him. At first, she thought it was because he reminded her of a stray puppy, but then she started to think that it was because she really may like him. She didn't usually drink so early in the day, but she was supposed to be meeting a guy from the night before who was a no show.

"Can I see you again?" Adam said, not sure of what he was doing. *You just got divorced today. What in the hell are you doing?*

"I don't know," Jessie said, smiling a beautiful toothy smile. "I think you have a lot to work out, with the divorce and all. You may not even want to talk to me when you are sober."

"I haven't been sober for months. So it won't really matter," Adam said, a little embarrassed.

"Oh, great. In that case, we're definitely meant to just be friends." Jessie smiled again, and Adam thought that he hadn't ever met anyone who smiled so much.

The bar was getting crowded with the after work crowd, and their daytime bartender had ended his shift a couple of hours prior. There was a young girl with a short skirt and tight top running the length of the bar, missing half of the people in front of her who needed drinks. Adam only cared that his and Jessie's drinks were full as they talked well into the night.

THE NEXT MORNING, Adam woke up face down on the bathroom floor. The tile was cool on his cheek, but the pounding in his head made him want to kill himself. "Shit!" he said groggily, his voice hoarse.

He looked in the toilet. Fuck. That sucks. Adam hated throwing up.

He washed off his face letting the cool water revive him a little. Thank God, I took a couple of days off work to get my shit together.

He stumbled into the kitchen, his dry throat begging for something wet. But his stomach promised him that it wouldn't keep much down. Adam tried to remember the night before. There was a girl. There wasn't usually a girl. No matter how drunk he was, he didn't usually mess with the girls. The only girl he had ever been with had been Brynn, but since he couldn't love her anymore, he couldn't imagine himself with anyone else.

He chugged a glass of cold water and immediately regretted it as it came up as quickly as it went down. *SHIT!*

Adam was angry. He felt angry often. All of the time, actually. He didn't want to be angry, but there was no other emotion he felt at home in anymore. He wanted a family with Brynn for so long, and when the time finally came, it was taken from him far too quickly. He blamed Brynn. He knew that it wasn't right, but he blamed her anyway, and no matter how hard he tried, he couldn't stop.

He splashed cold water on his face, over and over.

He stumbled around his apartment. He hated it. He missed his big house. He stared at the bare walls. He hated it.

Shit.

Suddenly he heard a sound. A groan?

What the hell? He froze. *Where was I last night? How did I get home?*

He heard it again. A small, almost imperceptible groan. *Shit! Who is that? What did I do?*

He stumbled into the bedroom, trying to focus his eyes. The room was dark. There was nothing in his bedroom except for his bed and a bunch of boxes. He hadn't even bothered to unpack. He had been living there for months, but he couldn't bring himself to take anything out of the boxes. All he had unpacked were his clothes, as he needed them, which were mostly all over the floor.

The room was dark and he squinted trying to find the source of the noise.

There!

He stared at the bed and saw a perfectly naked girl laying there, twisted in the blankets, red hair spilling over her beautiful ivory skin.

Oh, shit. What did I do?

He looked down at himself and realized for the first time that he was naked.

He looked up and saw a big pair of beautiful green eyes staring at him.

"Hi," the pretty red head said bashfully.

"Hi." he said feeling embarrassed.

"How are you feeling?" the pretty girl said, her voice hoarse, sounding concerned.

"Like Shit," he said, smiling wryly.

"Me, too," she said smiling back at him, her pretty teeth perfect and white.

They stared at each other, both unsure of what to say.

"Do you remember anything?" the girl said, pulling the sheet up around her naked chest.

"Not really. You?" Adam said wishing he could disappear, his head feeling as if it were going to explode.

"Some," the girl said, her cheeks turning red.

"Um... what is your name?" Adam hated asking. He didn't know what else to say.

"Jessie."

"I'm Adam."

"I know," Jessie said, knowing that he didn't remember who she was. She looked at Adam's naked body and remembered how he had cried in her arms. They had just lain together in their nakedness; neither of them able to do anything more than just hold tightly onto one another. She loved lying next to him, staring at him.

Adam felt ashamed. He had never done anything like this before and wasn't sure what to do next. She looked like a perfectly nice girl —too young for him, but beautiful.

"I don't remember much from last night. I had a bad day, yesterday."

"I know. It's okay. I've had a lot of bad yesterdays," Jessie said smiling again. "Come, lay with me."

Adam hesitated. He wanted to be alone. But something about her made him want to lie next to her, too.

"Come. I won't bite you," she said pulling the sheet around her, covering her body up. "Besides, you need to sleep and so do I. I promise I won't do anything to you."

I have never been in bed next to anyone but Brynn. But Brynn is gone now, forever. She will never be with me again.

Adam felt the tears welling in his eyes.

He walked slowly to the bed and laid down, his head pounding, his body stiff from lying on the hard bathroom floor. He needed sleep.

He laid down, pulling the sheet over him. Jessie snuggled up next to him, and he could feel her warm flesh against his. Her even breathing made him relax as he felt her warm breasts on his back, her arms wrapped around him. Her body was nestled against him, and he felt immediately at ease.

For the first time in a long time, Adam didn't feel completely alone.

He closed his eyes, and he drifted off to sleep, his mind deliciously blank.

24

MILLION DOLLAR BABY

"Millions? Millions?" Brynn was beside herself.

"Yes, millions. Actually, more than millions," Ellie said matter of factly.

"Who are you that you have that kind of money?" Brynn asked, completely stunned.

"The question you should be asking is 'Who am *I*?'" Ellie said, almost as though she had rehearsed this.

"Okay. Then who am *I*?" Brynn asked, not sure that she wanted to know the answer.

"You are Eva. Granddaughter of James and Amy Harper. Harper Enterprises? I think you know about Harper Enterprises," Ellie said as Brynn noticed a trace of pride in her voice. "Of course, you'll need a DNA test, but I've assured them that you are the real deal."

Brynn stared at Ellie, her big brown eyes much larger than usual. "How can this be?"

"It's easy," Ellie sighed as she hated explaining the details. "I am their daughter. You are the granddaughter. They went missing years ago, presumed dead. I have a son who is you're half-brother, Noah. Noah needs constant care and can't be on his own. He has the mental capacity of a five year old, though you will clearly see that he is much older than that."

"So why did you even bother to tell me about the money? You could have pretended like I didn't even exist and kept it all to yourself." Brynn wondered what Ellie wanted from her.

Ellie paused.

"You're right. I could have just pretended that you didn't exist. But I have more money than I need. And when I'm gone, Noah will need someone to look out for him, to visit him, to explain things to him, and help take care of him. I'm the only family he has now, and he needs someone else in his life."

"What do you mean? He needs someone else in his life?" Brynn was confused.

"He needs family. A mother. A sister. People who understand him, who will take care of him. The money provides for his physical needs, but he needs more. God knows I've been a shitty mother, but this is the one thing I can do for him." Ellie was tired of all of the explaining. She just wanted to go home and medicate so that she didn't have to think of anything else.

"You're young so you'll be around for a while. Why now? Why not wait?" Brynn felt like she was being set up. She couldn't figure out what Ellie wanted no matter how hard she tried.

"You never know what will happen in life," Ellie said, her voice low and distant. "Like I said, I haven't done much right in this world. This is the only thing I can think of to do that can possibly buy me some decent karma."

"So you just assumed that I would do it? That I would step in for you after what you did to me? Why would I take care of a brother I have never met when YOU abandoned me?" Brynn's voice was rising, and Ellie took a step backwards.

"I-I-I just thought you would want to know your family," Ellie stuttered.

"Why would I want my family when my family didn't want me? Why in the hell would I want you when you dropped me off on the side of the road like a piece of garbage?" Brynn was furious, her hands clenching uncontrollably.

"It wasn't like that Eva... I mean Brynn. It wasn't like that. I didn't mean to... I was just really messed up at the time. I'm just not a good person. I've made horrible, horrible choices." Ellie was pleading with her.

"You are not a good person! You're not even a person. I don't know how you can even live with yourself. What kind of person leaves their child by the side of the road?" Brynn felt her face getting hot. She had dreamed of this moment her entire life, and now that it was here, she wasn't sure if she would be able to find the words. "You left me! And then you left your son in a home for other people to take care of! You're not even a mother at all! You don't even take care of him. I can't even imagine what happened to my father, or to Noah's father, but neither of them are obviously in the picture anymore."

"You don't want to know, and you're right." Ellie stood up to leave. "I know that it's a lot to take in, Brynn. I know that you hate me, and you have every right to, but I'm just thinking of what's best for Noah now. And that will be you, his sister, one day."

Brynn turned around and refused to look at her birth mother. She had been staring at Ellie in shock and disbelief. But mostly Brynn was stunned by how much she resembled Ellie. She was even more surprised by how secretly pleased she was by the resemblance. Brynn hated that even after everything Ellie had done and how so much time had passed, she still wanted this woman to love and need her. And now, here she was telling her that she needed her, and Brynn needed to fight it. Fight Ellie.

"I'm leaving my number for you. I'll wait for you to call me. I want you to meet Noah." Brynn heard Ellie set something on the end table, and then she heard the sound of her footsteps walking away, and the sound of the door opening and closing behind her. She didn't turn around until she knew that she was gone. She didn't want Ellie to see the tears cascading down her face.

Brynn picked up the card with her name and phone number on

it. She took a picture of it with her phone and slowly tore the card up, piece by piece.

A brother! Family!

She thought about Noah. *How old is he? What does he look like? Would he even care that I'm his sister?*

I wish I could tell Adam! Adam would know what to do. Adam would help me.

Brynn felt a pain deep in her chest. It didn't matter how many times a day she thought about Adam, it was never going to change for her. Adam was gone and so was her baby, Sophie.

Brynn had enough for the day. She took a sleeping pill that her doctor had prescribed and laid down in her bed. Maxie was happy for any excuse to be on the bed, and snuggled as close to her as he could. Brynn closed her eyes praying desperately that sleep would overtake her as quickly as possible.

25

NOAH'S NEW FRIEND

"Noah! It's time for lunch!" Kelly the pretty caregiver called out for him.

Noah liked this time of day. Lunch was his favorite time, and they were having his favorite food—hot dogs and macaroni and cheese. He had been looking forward to today's lunch all week.

"Lunch!!" Noah cried out, enthusiastically as he ran to his chair throwing his tall, lean body into it.

"What do we say about running, Noah?" Kelly said chiding him with a smile.

"No running! Sorry," Noah said, hanging his head. His dark brown hair falling into his glittering green eyes.

"It's okay. I just don't want you to get hurt, silly!" Kelly smiled. Noah was her favorite patient, and she loved working with him every day. Noah reminded her of her younger brother whom she missed terribly and who was away at college. *I wish that Noah had a normal life so that he could be away at college now, too.*

"Okay, Kelly!" Noah's smile reappeared instantly as he stared down at his hot dog. "Ketchup, please!"

"Ketchup?" Kelly said giving him a funny look. "You don't like ketchup!"

"I know, I was just teasing!" Noah smiled at her again and then took a big bite of his plain hot dog. "Is my Mommy coming today?" he asked with his mouth full.

"I don't know, Noah. Please don't talk with your mouth full," Kelly said, dreading having to answer the same question every day. "I haven't heard anything, and she usually calls when she is coming. I'm sorry, buddy, but I don't think she will be here today."

Noah's face fell. It had been forty-seven days since he saw his mommy last, and he missed her. He was keeping count on the calendar even though Kelly told him that he shouldn't.

Kelly shook her head, trying to mask her annoyance. *Why wouldn't she come see him? He doesn't even need to be here! She could take care of him at home with help, if she ever wanted to. He's such a joy!* Kelly knew that when she had children of her own one day, she would never abandon them or leave them, as Noah's mother had. She was raised in a close-knit family, and she couldn't imagine not being with her own child when the time came.

"Okay," Noah said, chewing slowly, trying to remember not to talk with his mouth full. He took a sip of his drink and swallowed carefully. "It's been forty-seven days since I've seen Mommy, Kelly. That's a long time."

"I know, buddy." Kelly said smiling warmly at him, her pretty face making him forget his sadness. "Let's finish lunch, and we will go make a new friend."

Noah liked this game. Kelly would take him around and introduce him to people that he didn't know yet. People were always coming and going there. When someone left, someone always took their place. Noah liked where he lived. He always got to make new friends.

When Noah was done eating, he cleaned up his tray like Kelly had taught him and washed his hands carefully. He didn't want to spread germs and make people sick, so he was always careful to wash his hands, and he did so lots of time during the day.

"I'm ready," He said cheerfully. "Where are we going?"

"Let's just go for a walk, and we'll see who we find." Kelly said happily. She loved watching Noah meet new people. He was so friendly and easy to talk to, and the older residents loved meeting him, even the grumpy ones.

They walked down a long walkway for a while past the beautiful green lawn and a large koi pond. There was a woman sitting at the koi pond feeding the fish.

"Hi!" Noah said, walking right up to her and extending his hand. "I'm Noah."

"Hi." The woman said, surprised. She looked at Noah with curiosity. He seemed familiar to her, but she didn't know why. She took his hand slowly and shook it.

Kelly looked at her with curiosity. She doesn't appear to be very old. I wonder what her story is.

"Are you new?" Noah asked standing too close to her wheelchair. The woman was visibly uncomfortable and wheeled herself back slightly.

"Yes, I'm new," the woman said smiling nervously.

"I'm not. I've been here for a long time. Since I was three. I love it here," Noah said happily. "But I live in a different part of the building. This part is for old people."

"Noah!" Kelly scolded. "Don't be rude."

"I'm sorry! I meant..." Noah was embarrassed. He usually had better manners than that.

"It's okay," the woman said graciously. "Why have you been here for so long?"

"My Mommy can't take care of me," Noah said sadly.

"Oh, I'm sorry." The woman said, immediately feeling bad for him.

"That's okay. I like it here," Noah repeated. "Do you have any kids?"

"I don't know. I don't think so," she said squirming in her chair. She wasn't used to such direct questions from a stranger. This one was young, and he wanted to know a lot. The only reason she was talking to him was that he seemed familiar.

Kelly watched Noah and the woman with deep interest. Aside

from their eye color, they had a strange strong physical resemblance and a few of the same mannerisms. *Am I crazy? Am I really seeing this? Who is this woman?*

"Why don't you know?" Noah asked the woman, not realizing that he was over stepping the line.

"Why do you ask so many questions?" the woman said, visibly annoyed.

Noah was sad. He didn't mean to make the nice lady mad at him. "I'm sorry. I just like to make new friends."

The woman looked at Noah. He was in his late teens, tall, with dark brown hair and beautiful green eyes. His eyes were a little too close together, but otherwise the woman thought he had a handsome face. She could tell that he was a nice boy, and she felt drawn to him in a strange way. But she was uncomfortable with the questions he asked. *Why does he want to know so much about me?*

"Well, you shouldn't ask people so many questions. It's rude," the woman said scolding him gently.

"I wasn't trying to be rude," he said his voice quiet. "I'm sorry if that I bothered you."

He turned around and started to walk away.

The woman realized that she didn't really want him to go.

"Wait, young man," she said, calling after him. "I don't want you to leave."

Noah turned around slowly. He looked at Kelly and she nodded at him, smiling. She could see why the woman was drawn to him. It was the same reason that everyone was drawn to him. His energy and enthusiasm made Noah hard to let go of.

"Okay!" Noah said brightly. He skipped back to the woman, happy that she changed her mind.

"Wheel me around," she ordered curtly.

Noah grabbed the handles of the wheelchair and pushed her slowly down the walkway.

Noah was careful not to talk. He figured she probably was tired of him asking questions. They walked on for a while in silence, with Kelly trailing behind them.

"Where did you come from, young man?" the woman asked.

"I used to live an hour from here, in a big house. But my Mommy couldn't take care of me," Noah said looking at the woman with serious brown eyes. "So I came to live here when I was three. They've taken care of me ever since I was little."

"So you like living here?" the woman asked, enjoying the sound of his voice.

"Yes. They give me ice cream, and we eat hot dogs. They are nice to me here. Especially Kelly." Noah said happily.

"That's good," the woman said smiling. "I like hot dogs."

"I think we can be friends," the woman said after they had walked on for a little while in silence. "But don't ask me a lot of questions. I don't know anything about myself."

"Nothing?" Noah asked, curious.

"Not much," the woman said, a trace of sadness in her voice.

"Why not?" Noah was hesitant, but he wanted to know why his new friend couldn't remember anything.

"I got hurt a long time ago, somehow. It hurt my brain, I think. And now I get headaches, and I can't sleep, and I can't remember anything."

"How did you get hurt?" Noah remembered the last time he got a boo-boo and he shuddered. He hated getting hurt.

"I don't know. I just know that my head got hurt. I think it shook my brain," the older woman laughed. "At least I know that I have one."

Noah smiled. "I have a brain, but it doesn't work good."

"What do you mean?" the woman asked puzzled.

"I'm not too smart." Noah said sadly. "Not like other boys my age."

"You seem smart to me," the woman said smiling at him for the first time. "You seem very smart."

Noah thought the woman was pretty when she smiled.

"Thank you," Noah said smiling back. Nobody had ever called him smart before. Especially not a new friend. "That's why my Mommy didn't want to take care of me. She didn't want a stupid kid."

"I'm sure that's not true at all," the woman said, patting his hand gently. She was enjoying their walk more than she thought she would.

Noah had a thought.

"What is your name? I know all of my friend's names. Andy, Steven, Kelly, Susan, Bob, Carol, Brian, Joe, Charlie..."

"My name is Carly," the woman said smiling at his long list. "Just call me Carly."

26

THE HANDSOME STRANGER

Brynn was on a mission to try to work a lot. Jane kept trying to send her home, but Brynn needed to do something.

"I haven't spent much time here, with the pregnancy and all, so it's time that I get caught up," she told Jane stubbornly.

"Yes, but that's why you pay me, and that's why you pay Lucia. We take care of all of these things for you." Jane was beside herself. After running the restaurant by herself for so long, Brynn was interrupting the flow.

"I know. But I have to do something." Brynn said, understanding what Jane was trying to say. "This is different than the first time that Adam left. I know he's not coming back. I know that I can't just lie in bed and lose myself as I did before. I have to work."

Brynn felt like she was going crazy. She couldn't stand to be home, staring at the empty rooms. She had cleaned most of them as the realtor came in and out with perspective buyers. The nursery was the first room to be boxed up with everything put away. The only livable rooms were the bedroom, the kitchen, and the sitting room. Otherwise, everything was in boxes, neatly lining the walls of the garage.

Maxie was beside himself locked in the back sunroom, but Brynn couldn't let him roam like he usually did. Brynn kept telling herself that it was temporary, and that it wouldn't last forever. *I have to get rid of the house. Every corner, every room reminds of him. Smells like him. I have to get out of this house!*

"You've been through a traumatic experience Brynn, both physically and emotionally. You need to make sure that you understand that and don't push it." Jane was concerned for her friend. At least this time, Brynn remained upright and functional every day. Jane was thankful for that.

"I know," Brynn said with a half-hearted smile. "That's why I'm here, to distract myself."

"Well, maybe you should stick to cooking or something else. You're driving Luis a little crazy," Jane said, smiling. Luis was the head prep cook, and he set the specials for the day. He was complaining to Jane about Brynn stepping on his toes, and it had only been a week.

Brynn was annoyed. If it weren't for her, Luis wouldn't even have a job. But part of her understood. She hadn't been hands-on in the kitchen for well over a year now, and Luis had been doing a very good job.

Brynn tried to smile. "I just need to do something."

"I know you do," Jane said hugging her friend. They had seen each other through a lot, and Jane wondered when Brynn was ever going to catch a break. "Why don't you come in tomorrow, get back into some of the book keeping, and work through breakfast?"

Brynn smiled gratefully. The restaurant and Maxie were all that she had now. Brynn had repeatedly tried calling Ellie, but she didn't return her calls. She knew that she shouldn't be disappointed, but she had been looking forward to possibly meeting her brother, after all.

After another sleepless night, Brynn came in the next morning at three a.m., and set to work. She was happy to let Jane have the day off to spend with the girls. The restaurant opened at six for breakfast and Brynn was surprised at how quickly the morning flew by. Lucia still worked a few mornings a week when she wasn't taking morning classes and was happy to see Brynn so early.

"How are you?" Lucia asked her beautiful cocoa brown eyes full of concern. Lucia knew what it was like to lose a child, only she had given hers up for adoption. There wasn't a day that went by that she didn't miss her and say a prayer for her baby.

"I'm okay," Brynn said attempting to put on a brave face. It had been a year since she lost Sophie and she still grieved, but losing Adam was still very fresh in her mind. "I miss them," she whispered.

"I know," Lucia said sympathetically. "I miss my baby, too."

They hugged each other and held each other for a long moment. Brynn pulled back first and wiped her eyes. She didn't want the employees to see her cry.

"I guess we should help the girls clean this mess up, huh?" she said, all business.

Lucia nodded her head, and they set to work getting ready for the lunch crowd.

The restaurant had cleared out after the breakfast rush, but there were still a few people coming and going throughout the morning. Most of the faces Brynn knew, but she was happy to see that there were many new ones.

As the door opened, Brynn looked up and felt her breath catch for a second. She turned away quickly, embarrassed.

It had been a long time since anyone had caught her off guard like that, nobody since Adam. Nobody ever, not since Adam. The man sat down at the small wooden breakfast counter and opened a menu.

Brynn was nervous. She looked around for Lucia or Gertie, but nobody was around. Crap. I'm going to have to go up to him. She paused for a moment, but nobody appeared to rescue her.

You're an idiot. It's just a man. No big deal. You talk to men every day. You can do this, Brynn. Brynn didn't know why this man made her so nervous. He was tall, with chestnut colored hair. And when he walked, Brynn could tell that he was sure of himself.

He probably knows how good looking he is, too. Brynn decided she didn't like him. He's probably arrogant.

He was looking around for someone to help him.

Crap, where are Lucia and Gertie?! Dammit!

Brynn walked over to him slowly. "Hi, would you like some coffee?"

He looked at her, his hazel eyes lighting up as he smiled. "Sure. Thank you."

He's nice. Dammit!

"Would you like to order?" Brynn asked using her most professional tone.

"Sure," he said looking down at the menu.

Brynn stood and waited as he read down through each page. *Why does the menu have to be four pages?*

"Okay. Got it," he said enthusiastically as he looked up at her. "Three eggs, over easy, wheat toast, hash browns, two sides of sausage, two sides of bacon, two buttermilk pancakes, and some corned beef hash."

"Wow!" Brynn said, in spite of herself.

The man laughed. "I know. I just flew in at two a.m., and there was nothing open, so I'm starving!"

"Well, I'll get that in for you right away, then," Brynn said, amused. He was built like he was athletic, but she hadn't expected him to order that much food.

Brynn rang in the order and a few seconds later, Lucia came out of the kitchen. "Is your guest count right on this, Brynn? Is this really for one person?"

Brynn looked over at the man sitting at the counter drinking his coffee.

"Oh my," Lucia whispered, following Brynn's gaze. "He's... he's...."

"I know," Brynn said quietly, trying not to stare.

Lucia smiled. She couldn't remember a time when Brynn ever looked at a man. Even though everyone knew that she loved Adam, Lucia also knew they had their problems. She wanted Brynn to be happy. Brynn was like a sister to her, and she couldn't remember ever seeing her completely happy. It was nice to see her mooning over a stranger.

"You should talk to him," Lucia said casually.

"No way!" Brynn said, her cheeks turning red. She had been working all morning after not getting any sleep, and wasn't feeling very attractive at the moment. "I look horrible."

"You look beautiful, like you always do," Lucia scolded her. "Turn around, he's calling for you."

Brynn turned around, and the handsome man was gesturing for her to come over. She smoothed her hair and tried to compose herself, feeling a strange nervousness in her belly.

"Did you need more coffee?" she asked politely.

"Yes. I mean no. I just wanted to know what there is to do in this city? I'm going to be here for a month or so for business, and I want to get my bearings. I'm assuming that you live here?" he smiled again, and Brynn felt a little out of sorts. "I'm Nicholas... Nick, by the way."

She sat and chatted with him and was surprised at how easy it was to talk to him. She tried to leave when his food came, but he insisted that she keep talking. Brynn forgot her nervousness and chatted away about all of the touristy things in the city that there were to do, until suddenly she realized that the lunch crowd had come in full force, and the restaurant was hopping.

"Oh, I'm sorry. I have to help out," she said jumping up and apologizing. She hadn't ever been that caught up in conversation that she didn't know what was going on around her. The hazel and gold in his eyes kept distracting her, as well as his laugh. She immediately felt guilty.

"I'm sorry," he said looking worried. "Will your boss be mad?"

Brynn laughed. "I'm the boss."

Nick was stunned and then he smiled a teasing smile. "So you mean, this whole time I was sitting here talking to the boss, and I didn't know it? Wow. Your employees must think you're pretty lazy."

"Yes. They hate me." Brynn smiled back. She couldn't remember having this much fun talking to someone in a long time.

"What are you doing tonight?" Nick asked, suddenly serious.

Brynn stood up. "Um, hanging out with my dog, watching Lifetime movies. He's a big fan."

"Why don't you hang out with me? I don't watch Lifetime movies, but I am fun to spend time with."

Brynn hesitated. *Why would he want to hang out with me? Who does he think that I am?*

"Don't say no. I'm going to the restroom, and I expect you to be here when I get back telling me what time to pick you up." As Nick stood up, Brynn realized that he was taller than she originally thought—at least six foot two. Brynn felt her breath catch again. He was casual in jeans and a t-shirt, but she liked the easy way that his body moved. Adam was the only man she had ever been interested in, and Nick definitely unnerved her.

I can't do this. I can't spend time with him. I don't know who he thinks I am, but I'm not someone who just hangs out.

Nick walked into the bathroom and washed his hands. He stared at himself in the mirror and tried to smile. *Damn, I've aged. I look like terrible.*

He thought about Brynn and smiled. She intrigued him. She was the first woman to catch his eye in a long time. *She's funny, but so tentative. She can turn it on and off in a blink.*

Nick thought about the past couple of years and how he needed to spend some time with someone who could make him laugh. He had spent time with a lot of women, but none he saw more than once. *This one, I would come back to see. This Brynn could be worth it.*

But when Nick got back from the bathroom, Brynn was nowhere to be found.

27

JESSIE'S LOVE

Jessie was in love with Adam. She knew it would happen even though she fought it. He was a mess, but she found herself in love with him anyway.

She knew he still loved Brynn, but she ignored it and pretended as though he were in love with her instead. Even when he cried Brynn's name out in the middle of the night, or called her "Brynn" when he was so drunk that he couldn't remember the next day, Jessie forgave him. *He's been through a lot.*

When he was sober, he was good to her, but he couldn't remain sober very long.

"Oh baby, I'm sorry," he said his blue eyes filling with tears.

"It's okay," Jessie said kissing his cheek. "I know you didn't mean to forget my birthday. You've been going through a lot."

"It's no excuse. We've been together for seven months, and I shouldn't have forgotten." Adam was angry with himself. He had never forgotten Brynn's birthday, and Jessie was so sweet to him. She was so good, and he had completely forgotten. He had gone to the bar right after work for Friday happy hour, and he didn't even know how he had gotten home.

Jessie was trying hard not to care.

"You shouldn't have forgotten. But you can make it up to me," she smiled that toothy smile at him.

"How? How can I make it up to you?" Adam was miserable. He was failing in every way, and he hated himself.

"You can take me out tonight," Jessie said brightly.

"I would love to. But I can't. My parents are in town." Adam was dreading dinner with his parents. They hadn't been close for a very long time, and he had been avoiding them for as long as he could.

Jessie moved a little closer to him. "Well... I could go with you," she said hesitantly. "That is, if you think it would be a good idea."

Adam stepped away. "Oh no. I don't think that would be a good idea at all. You wouldn't have fun. You would hate it!"

Jessie frowned. "Am I not good enough to meet your parents?"

"Of course, you are," Adam said quickly wishing he had a shot. "It's just them. They loved Brynn, and honestly, I just don't think that anyone will ever measure up for them. I don't think that they're ready."

Jessie was getting angry now. "All you do is talk about Brynn. But you left her, *twice!* And now, you have me, and you don't even care that you have me."

Shit! Adam was frustrated. *I wasn't ready for a relationship, and this is why. What am I doing?* "Baby, it's not about Brynn, or about you. It's about my parents being frustrated with me. Me! Please stop doing this."

"Stop doing what? Expecting, demanding, needing?" Jessie's arms were crossed and Adam thought she looked adorable.

"You look so hot when you're mad," he said grabbing her and kissing her neck. He felt her body loosen up a little, and Adam knew that she wasn't going to stay mad at him for long.

"Stop it," she said half-heartedly pushing him away.

"I can't," Adam mumbled grabbing her and pulling her toward him. "You just make me want you when you look like that."

Jessie tried to fight him off, but she knew that it just made things more exciting. She didn't really want him to go away, but she did want to meet his parents. "You just want me when you want sex."

"That's not true. But I do want you for sex. I want you for other things, too. Just don't push me baby." Adam was too busy with straps and pulling off clothes to continue arguing with her.

Jessie felt her body give into him as it usually did.

She loved him, and there was nothing that either of them could do about it.

28

CLARITY

Brynn knelt at the cold gravestone. Brynn was shivering because had forgotten her jacket. But she didn't care.

She tried to make it to visit Sophie as often as she could. She couldn't bear the thought of her being all alone, and Brynn needed to talk to her to help clear her head. She knew it was silly, but the shrink said that if it made her feel better, she should do it.

"I don't know why I just ran, but I couldn't help it." Brynn said, reflecting back on the day's events. "I haven't ever been with anyone since your daddy, and I just didn't know what to do."

She thought about Nick, the guy from the restaurant, who had looked at her in such a way that her insides felt like jelly. She hadn't felt like that since she was fifteen, and Adam was passing her notes in class. Even then, it had been different. Young, innocent. She had never had a stranger make her feel that way before.

"I know that I shouldn't have run away. I should have stayed. I should have made a new friend. The shrink says that I should be open to meeting new people, making new friends, blah, blah, blah." Brynn made a face as she pulled her dark hair back. She liked her shrink, but she was tired of seeing him every other week. *I've been in therapy all my life. When am I going to be normal? When can I stop?*

Brynn sat, caressing the smooth stone with her fingers. "Sophie, Sophie, Sophie. Why did you leave me? Why did you have to go so soon?" Brynn felt the pain welling up in her chest. *Just let it out, let it go. There's no one here to see. You can just cry.*

The tears fell silently down her cheeks, but Brynn refused to make a sound. *If I make a noise, I will scream. I will scream, and I will never stop screaming.*

The tears were so hot that Brynn thought she would see steam coming off her cold cheeks. She cursed herself for forgetting a jacket for the hundredth time. *I really need to start keeping one in my car.*

Brynn sat in silence for what felt like an hour. She didn't want to go back to the restaurant. She didn't want to go to the empty house that wasn't going to be hers anymore. She had nowhere to go and no one to see.

"I should be going home to you and to your Daddy," Brynn said softly. "But all that I have left now is Maxie. How did this become my life? How did I get to be so alone?"

The silence around her resonated, and Brynn felt the temperature dropping rapidly. She wanted to stay, but her fingers were turning numb. She stood up hating to leave. "I'll be back tomorrow, sweet girl. Mommy loves you." Brynn kissed her fingers and touched the smooth stone, imagining for one second that she was kissing Sophie's sweet face.

When she got in the car to warm up, she realized there was a message on her phone.

"Brynn-You left your purse at the restaurant. Again. XO, Jane"

"Damn." Brynn hated how forgetful she was becoming. She sighed and turned her car toward the restaurant.

When she walked in, Jane met her at the door.

"Look who came back," Jane said with a sly smile as she motioned toward one of the booths.

"Oh no," Brynn said, horrified.

Nick was sitting in the booth wearing a hunter green sweater and jeans. Brynn knew without getting close that the sweater would bring out the green in his eyes, and she felt her stomach flip flop without her permission.

"I've been at t-t-the..." Brynn stuttered.

"I know where you've been. You only go to two places and home. Here is your purse. Now go into your office and clean yourself up." Jane ordered.

Brynn looked at Jane helplessly. "I don't know how to do this."

Jane grabbed Brynn and pulled her into Brynn's office. "There is nothing to it. Just talk. Just be yourself. Don't you want to be happy?"

"He lives out of town. There's no point."

"Brynn, honey. You don't have to marry him. You don't have to sleep with him. Just talk to him. Make a new friend." Jane was smiling but Brynn could tell she was getting frustrated with her.

"I don't know if I can be happy. Look at my life. I don't even know if I want to be happy."

Jane pulled out a comb from Brynn's desk drawer, and started combing through Brynn's gnarled hair. "I don't even know what to say to that. If you want to be miserable all of your life, I can't make you do anything else. But Brynn, you have to start making some choices. Adam is gone for good. He is never coming back."

"I know," Brynn said wincing. "Stop combing my hair, I'm not five. I can do it!"

Jane smiled. "You have five minutes. He just ordered, and he's asked about you five times already. You should have seen his face when he came back from the bathroom and you were gone."

Brynn winced again. "I felt bad about that."

"You should have," Jane said as she headed toward the door. "Five minutes and then I'm coming in for you. And don't even think about sneaking out."

Brynn sighed. She went into the tiny bathroom and looked at herself in the mirror. *Bags! From crying, I knew it!*

She frantically pulled out her makeup bag and went to work.

After a couple of minutes, she looked into the mirror and smiled. *Well, better. But not great.* She looked at her long dark hair. It was in desperate need of a cut, and there wasn't much that could be done with it other than comb it and smooth it out a little. *Oh no, five minutes are up.*

Brynn walked into the hallway toward the dining room and took a deep breath. *Deep breaths, deep breaths.* She spotted the back of Nick's head and approached him slowly.

"Hey, there," Brynn said, trying to sound casual.

He looked up just as he was putting a huge bite of mashed potatoes in his mouth, and smiled.

"Oh, hi, Houdini," he said, smirking.

Brynn blushed. "I'm sorry."

Nick stood up, towering over her. Brynn forgot how tall he was. "Please, sit down."

Brynn looked around the dining room. The late dinner crowd was slower than usual, which Brynn was grateful for, because she knew that if it were busy that she wouldn't be able to relax.

She sat down, feeling awkward.

"We don't have to stay here if you don't want to," Nick said, as if he were reading her mind.

"Oh no. It's fine," Brynn said eyeing his plate. "Besides, you've hardly eaten anything."

Nick laughed, and Brynn thought for a second how much she liked his laugh.

"I've been eating here all day. I only left for a few hours, then I came back for lunch, and then I came back for dinner."

"I thought you had to work?" Brynn said, feeling very guilty.

"I had a meeting after lunch," Nick smiled. Brynn felt herself getting lost in his smile, and tried desperately to look away without being too obvious.

"Seriously, I'm stuffed. Let's go somewhere else," Nick said pulling out his wallet.

"Oh, no! I'll have Jane take care of your dinner. It's the least I can do since you are now a part of our frequent diner program," Brynn said putting her hand on his before she could stop herself, and then abruptly pulling it away.

"Thank you. I suppose it's the least you could do since you Houdini'd me earlier," Nick teased making Brynn blush again. "Well, where to?"

Brynn thought for a moment and her mind was blank. She rarely went out, and the first place that came to her mind was the restaurant where she and Adam had their last anniversary dinner, which felt like a century ago. Brynn shook her head trying to erase the memory.

"Are you okay?" Nick asked concerned.

"I'm fine. I just... don't know where to go," Brynn said embarrassed.

Nick stood up and disappeared for a moment. He came back and grabbed Brynn's hand pulling her from the seat. She was pleasantly surprised at the boldness of the gesture, and how it made her heart pound.

"Where are we going?" Brynn asked as he pulled her out of the door.

"That's for me to know and for you to find out," Nick said opening the door of his modest rental car.

The fall air was cool, and Brynn took a moment to breathe it in. This was her favorite time of the year with the crisp leaves and the closing of summer. The smell of the air made her wish for the thousandth time that life could just be simple, not that it ever was. She looked over at her new friend and wondered if it would ever be possible.

Nick caught her eye and gestured for her to get in. As he closed the door, Brynn felt her heart expand for a brief moment at the promise of the evening. She wasn't accustomed to feeling so hopeful, and it terrified her.

Nick got in swiftly beside her and buckled his seatbelt. He squeezed her hand quickly, and gave her a warm smile.

"Are you ready?" he asked sensing her nervousness.

"Yes," Brynn said smiling wide. "I believe that I am."

29

ELLIE'S DEMONS

Ellie was happy for how the world was evolving.

She no longer had to stick needles in her arms. She could just smoke her drugs, or snort them. It wasn't like the old days when she had to stick herself time and time again making her feel like a human pin cushion. But the drugs were a lot of the same with some wonderful new ones thrown in the mix, and she was thankful for that. She needed them, all of them.

She couldn't take the guilt anymore. First, it was Eva, then Jonas, Noah, and Dylan. Dylan who was sent to prison for kidnapping Noah, and then being killed right before his release. *Poor bastard didn't even know that Noah wasn't his.* Ellie thought about all of the people she had hurt in her life.

My Momma and Daddy were killed because of me. Jonas said so.

She knew that she had no proof, but in her heart, she knew that he was telling the truth. On his deathbed, there was no reason for him to lie to her. Not when the truth would hurt her so much. *Jonas loved to hurt me. He lived to hurt me. He showed his love for me by hurting me.*

After abandoning Eva, Ellie prayed for a long time for redemption. But she knew that she was never going to get it. *It's too late. There is no redemption now, no forgiveness. I don't know how I ever thought there would be.*

Ellie lit up.

She inhaled the stench, and she smiled. She didn't want to feel anything else, or think about anything else. She just wanted to be numb.

She took a sip of the vodka she had poured. It burned. Almost like rubbing alcohol. But she loved it. She loved how it felt running down the back of her throat. After a few minutes, she felt the familiar numbness starting to settle in. She smoked, she drank, she swallowed, she sipped, she inhaled, and then she swallowed again.

She slumped back into her big comfy chair, the one she liked to disappear into when she wanted to get lost. It was the one thing she had shipped from home to the apartment she was staying in while she tried to woo Brynn. It was her one comfort.

Ellie thought about Noah, his face swirling around in her hazy thoughts. *My sweet, sweet boy.*

She thought about when he was born, when the doctors realized that he was different. She hated herself for how her first thought was that she deserved better and should give him away. *What kind of awful, terrible person thinks that about their kid? I'm terrible and awful. I've done nothing worthwhile my entire life.*

Ellie thought about how she left him, like she had left Eva. *It was for the best. I would have been a terrible mother. I was a terrible mother. I had two children, and I abandoned them both.*

Ellie tried to get out of the chair, but her legs felt numb beneath her. She struggled and made it up, spilling her vodka all over her pretty lace nightgown. *Shit!*

She stumbled over to the bathroom and looked into the vanity at her reflection.

Old. You got old.

She pulled at her eyes and pinched the skin on her forearms. *Well, you still look pretty Damn good for what you've been through in life.*

Her eyes were bloodshot, and her brown hair was a tangled mess, but Ellie could still see traces of the fifteen-year-old girl she once was buried deep within. Her skin was not as tight and youthful as it once was, and all of the smoking and late nights were starting to show their wear and tear on her face, but men still looked, though not as hard and long as they once did. Ellie reluctantly had to admit that the quality of men that were looking at her now wasn't what it once was, either.

Ellie thought for a moment about her mother. She didn't think of her often, and when Amy's pretty face popped up in her head, she often pushed her away. But today would have been her birthday, and Ellie couldn't make her go away no matter how hard she tried.

Damn you, Momma. Why did you leave me alone? "Why did you leave me when I needed you the most?" Ellie cried out loud, her voice ragged, her words slurring together.

She had never admitted it out loud to anyone, but Ellie's heart broke sometimes from missing her Momma. Her relationship with Momma had always been complicated, but Ellie's heart couldn't deny that she still needed her. It felt like an unbelievable amount of time since she had seen her last.

"Why did you leave me? Momma, why did you abandon me? Oh Daddy, why? Why?" Ellie turned toward her comfy chair and tried to walk toward it, but the tears blinded her. The ground had started moving, and Ellie's stomach didn't feel very good. Ellie reached out to hold on to something to steady herself. She felt nothing but air around her. The ground came up fast and smacked her on the face, and Ellie realized that she was no longer standing. She tried to move to stand up, but realized that it wasn't so bad where she was.

The floor was cool on her cheek. "If I cou jus' ge'my... shit 'tgether, things cou be diffrnt," she mumbled to herself. "I cou do it. I cou take Noah, and we cou be together."

Ellie tried to pick up her head, but realized that it hurt too much to move. Her head felt wet, which didn't make sense. *Vo-ka?* She tried to lift her hand up but it felt like it weighed a thousand pounds. *Shit. Sticky. Sticky? Wha the hell iz so sticky?* Ellie saw a puddle surrounding her head, and Ellie was mesmerized at how pretty it looked on the wood floor. She finally moved her hand and touched it. Red. Ellie felt her eyes closing as she fought to keep them open.

Red. Ellie saw the pool widening around her and felt it reaching her cheek. She couldn't move her head away no matter how hard she tried. *So tired. I'll wake up tomorrow an' have someone clean thissup.* She was tired, and she felt herself starting to fade, she needed sleep.

I'll have someone clean thissup. I promiss. Ellie thought about how mad whoever found this mess was going to be.

And then she thought nothing.

30

BRYNN'S DATE

"Jane told me where to take you," Nick said to Brynn as they drove, destination unknown. "That is, after she made me give her my driver's license so she could make a copy and asked me every detail about my life. I believe she may have even Googled me while she was standing right in front of me."

"Oh God!" Brynn said, wishing she could crawl under a rock.

Nick laughed. "You can't be too careful these days. You're lucky you have such good friends. She really cares about you."

Brynn nodded uncomfortably. *What am I doing here? I don't even know him! What was I thinking?* After a few minutes, they pulled into a little local winery, one of Jane's favorite places.

"Oh, I should have known," Brynn said smiling.

"She said they have a wonderful Riesling, and to have you try it," Nick said knowingly.

They walked into the winery, and Brynn was impressed with how cozy it was with the nice leather chairs and the fireplace. It was a perfect night for a fire, and the winery was taking full advantage of it.

Nick chose a comfortable little table away from the crowd where they could sit and talk.

After they ordered a bottle of Riesling, they sat back in their chairs looking at one another. Brynn could feel the chemistry between them. She had felt it the moment she had met him, and it was electrifying, like a constant current was running between them.

With Adam, it had been more sweet and innocent. This felt more daring, more exciting, and completely different.

"What do you think?" Nick said, his warm voice interrupting her thoughts.

"I'm sorry, about what?" Brynn blushed, wondered if she had missed a part of the conversation.

"Of the winery. What do you think of the winery?" Nick asked, amused, his hazel eyes dancing from the light of the fireplace.

"Oh," Brynn was embarrassed. *He must think that I am a complete idiot!* "It's nice, cozy. I can see why Jane likes it so much."

"It's very nice," Nick said looking around appreciatively and then looking directly at Brynn. "So, tell me about yourself. You seem like you've had an interesting life."

Brynn was taken aback by his directness. She had never had anyone look right at her the way that he did, and it unnerved her.

"Um, I don't know about interesting. I, uh, well, I just…"

"Okay, I'll tell you about me first, and then you can talk if you want." Nick laughed in such a way that Brynn could tell that he wasn't laughing at her, and she appreciated his thoughtfulness.

Brynn was thankful for the wine in front of her. She held onto the glass like a security blanket and took big gulps trying to calm herself down as she listened to him talk. She liked the depth of his voice and how warm it made her feel when he spoke. His voice put her in a trance, and she felt as though she could listen to him talk all night. Her mind started drifting, and she realized that she wanted to listen to him talk to her all night, and then listen to him talk to her in the morning. She blushed, embarrassed, and hoped that he wouldn't notice.

"What's wrong?" he said pausing mid-sentence from what he had been saying.

"Why? Nothing is wrong. The um, wine is making me hot." Brynn knew that he didn't believe her and she tried focusing her thoughts on listening to him instead of allowing her mind to wander.

"Okay," he said smiling a different kind of smile than the one she had seen all night. This smile was sexier, more playful, and Brynn thought about how much she liked seeing that smile.

"So, you're divorced then?" Brynn asked trying to participate in the conversation. "Me, too. Just about a year, but he had left me before, and we were never the same after that. Then our baby died and..." Brynn paused. She was never good at talking about it, but for some reason she felt like she could talk to Nick. She could tell that he was really listening to her.

"I'm sorry," Nick said, his eyes looking at her with genuine sadness in them. "That had to have been difficult."

"You have no idea," Brynn said thinking back to the last two years and how everything had fallen apart with Sophie's death.

"I do," Nick said, his voice changing, suddenly very serious. "I lost my son, Teddy. He was three and a half, and he drowned in our pool. My wife... my ex-wife, was supposed to be watching him, but she fell asleep in the sun for just a few moments. And he was gone. She could never forgive herself for what happened, even though I forgave her. We tried therapy, church, retreats, everything that we could think of, but she just couldn't forgive herself for letting Teddy drown. I loved her, but... I couldn't watch her destroy herself any longer, and there was nothing I could do for her."

Brynn was silent, her eyes full of tears that refused to fall.

"Oh, I'm sorry. I'm a horrible date, aren't I?" Nick said his eyes wide as he looked at Brynn, half-expecting her to stand up and walk out.

"No, no," Brynn said quietly. "You're a lovely date. I'm glad you shared with me. I don't know why I feel that I can talk to you, but I just do. I haven't been able to talk to anyone like this in a long time."

"Me, neither," Nick said leaning forward and squeezing her hand.

Brynn felt her hand tingle from the warmth of his touch and was disappointed when he pulled his hand away.

Brynn told him about Sophie and how they lost her and how

Adam left her shortly after. "He was unable to forgive me like you forgave your wife. He felt as if I had cursed her somehow, and we were never the same after. He was the only man that I had ever loved."

Brynn barely noticed when the waitress dropped off the second bottle of wine, or when they called last call. Time seemed to stand still as they talked well into the night about every subject they could think of, hungry for the sound of one another's voice.

The winery was closing, and Nick stood up slowly and grabbed Brynn's hand, pulling her up and then refusing to let go. Brynn no longer felt awkward when he touched her. She felt herself leaning in toward him so that he could touch her, and he was happy to oblige.

"Well," he said smiling down at her.

Brynn liked how he made her feel protected, safe. "Well," she said smiling back as they walked toward his car.

"What do we do now?" He said stopping next to his rental car as he pushed her gently against it.

"What do you want to do?" Brynn teased lightly. The wine made her feel a little bit more comfortable, and she found that teasing came easier as well.

"I will tell you what I don't want to do. I don't want to say 'good night,'" Nick said, his eyes serious as they looked right into hers. "I'm not ready to let you go yet."

Brynn sighed. "I'm not ready to let you go yet, either," she said easily. Words had never been easy for her, but with him, she felt them flowing in a way that she had never experienced before.

"I have meetings tomorrow to wrap up and then I can be here for the rest of the week." Nick said looking hopeful, but vulnerable.

"I would love to spend as much time with you as I can," Brynn said feeling her heart opening up to him.

"Good, me too," he smiled pulling her close. He put his face close to hers and closed his eyes. Brynn couldn't explain it, but something hung heavy between them in the air, and she knew that they both felt it.

Brynn buried her head in his chest and held him tight. She could feel his heart beating in his chest, and she loved how his strong arms felt wrapped around her. The night was slowing down just for her, and she wanted to pour herself into it as much as she could.

"Do you want to come home with me?" Brynn said, her voice small, sounding unlike her own.

"I do," Brynn heard Nick's voice above her head. "But not for the reasons you may think."

Brynn pulled away. "What do you mean?"

"I mean, I just want to spend time with you. I've shut myself off from everything since Teddy's death, and I don't want to do that with you. I don't want you to feel like I'm trying to take advantage of you."

Brynn feigned disappointment. "Well, I was hoping that was all you were trying to do is take advantage of me."

Nick's eyes opened wide in shock as he took a step back from her.

"I'm kidding!" she said, pulling him back in close. "I just want to spend time with you, too."

Nick was happy and excited for the first time in a long time. Brynn made him laugh, and he hadn't laughed in a long time. But she was wounded, and he knew that he had to be careful with her. *Don't do what you usually do with women. Don't be an asshole. She's different. She's not a bat-shit crazy drunk like you're used to, so don't take your issues out on her like you usually do.* "Okay, good."

Brynn wanted him to kiss her, but the moment had passed. She couldn't remember ever wanting to kiss anyone as much as she wanted to kiss Nick. She thought about the house, and how it was a mess and that there was only one bed, and for once, she didn't care.

She just wanted be in his arms, listening to the sound of his voice, telling her that for once everything was going to be alright.

31

ADAM'S DISGRACE

"So you don't even talk to her anymore?" Adam's mom shrieked, her voice carrying in the quiet restaurant. With a great deal of effort, she lowered her voice while staring at Adam in disbelief. "How do you just walk out on someone you've loved all of your life?"

Hannah Michael realized with dismay that she didn't even recognize her son anymore.

"Hannah, calm down. Let the boy talk," Daniel knew that his wife was beyond upset. Adam was her pride and joy, all of her life wrapped up in his happiness. When they went on their two-year-long mission trip, everything had been going well. Their first grandchild was about to be born, Adam and Brynn had reconciled. But when they returned, everything was destroyed.

Hannah was heartbroken. "I don't understand how you just stopped trying, even after you went home. Don't you love Brynn anymore? She was like a daughter to us. Didn't you think about that?"

Adam couldn't believe his ears. "No, I didn't think about you! I was thinking about me! I was thinking about how I couldn't look at her face anymore without thinking about how she never wanted Sophie to begin with. I was thinking about how I had to convince her to have a family and a life with me. I was thinking about how selfish she's always been and how much I hated her for letting our baby die. And I was thinking about how I couldn't stand to look at her for the rest of my life!" He grabbed his full glass of bourbon and drank it down in one swallow.

"Who are you?" Hannah said, her blue eyes filling with tears. Adam was the spitting image of her, but his blue eyes had grown dark and empty and it frightened her. For a moment, she flashed back to when he was a boy, and she wanted to reach out and touch his hair, but she knew that he would never allow it. He was only a poor reflection of the man she once knew.

Daniel cleared his throat and pushed his glasses up on his nose. "We wanted to see Brynn. Do you think she would see us?" Daniel asked Adam calmly. "She is still our family, even if you aren't together anymore."

"I don't know, Dad. I just said that I don't talk to her anymore, so why don't you call her? I'm not her husband, so do whatever the hell you want." Adam's tone was angry. He knew that lashing out at his parents was wrong, but he couldn't stop himself. He knew that they would take Brynn's side.

Hannah looked around the restaurant and knew that everyone could hear them. She no longer had an appetite and stood up angrily. "I'm leaving, Daniel. I didn't come here to have my son talk to me this way."

Adam looked up at his mother. He had loved her all of his life, but even for her, he felt nothing right now. "You guys can just go. I'm staying."

Daniel held Hannah's arm. "Sweetheart, sit down. We can talk through this with him. We both know that he doesn't want to push us away like this."

"I do, actually. While you were gone on your 'mission trip', I could have used your help here. I didn't know what to do. So now, I've lost my baby, my wife, my house, and everything else. And you're just now showing up to help me. So, yeah you can go. I don't need you right now." Adam gestured for the server to bring him another drink.

"The drinking isn't going to help, Adam," Daniel said sadly. "It will make it worse."

"It can't get worse, Dad," Adam said leaning back in his chair.

Hannah looked at her son, trying to understand what she was seeing. He had lost at least twenty pounds, and his beautiful blue eyes were streaked with red. He didn't look like he had slept in ages, and his clothes were wrinkled. But what disturbed her most was that he was an empty vessel—this man who had once been so beautiful and giving.

The food arrived and they sat in silence, Hannah and Daniel picking at their food while Adam simply drank.

Hannah spoke up, breaking the awkward silence. "Why didn't you call for us, honey? We would have come home. We didn't know you needed us so badly."

Adam shrugged. "What would you have done, Mom? There was nothing that you could do."

Hannah sighed, trying to hold in her tears. *What will become of my sweet boy now?* She knew that Adam loved Brynn, he always had. She never imagined him with anyone else, even when he separated from her the last time. But this was divorce. This was permanent.

Daniel leaned over. "It'll be okay sweetheart. He's a man, and he will figure it out."

Hannah smiled and kissed him on the cheek. She loved how Daniel always knew what she was thinking. Not a day went by that she didn't thank God for him and his love. She had hoped that Adam would find the same love with Brynn.

"Yes, Parents. I will figure it out." Adam was sufficiently drunk, and Hannah eyed her son distastefully. She wasn't opposed to a glass of wine on occasion, but this was unacceptable.

They asked for the check, and Daniel decided it was best to drive Adam home.

"Home... oh you mean my crappy little apartment, sssssuuuuure, you can drive me there," Adam slurred.

Hannah was happy when he passed out in the back seat.

"He's disgusting and a mess. And he smells," She whispered to Daniel, wrinkling her nose. "What is he thinking?"

"He's thinking that he's in pain, honey. Don't be so hard on him. It's just a phase he has to go through. You went through that once, don't you remember?" Daniel loved Hannah, but her memory could sometimes run short.

Hannah was silent for a while, listening to Adam snore in the back seat. She looked back at her son and smiled thoughtfully. "You're right, Daniel. As always, you are right."

Daniel knew just how to soften her up, which is why she had chosen him over the man she had been engaged to when they met. She had been a mess for a while, but he had gotten her through. He needed her to remember that, for Adam's sake.

They pulled up in front of the apartment and plotted how they were going to get him in.

"Oh my God, this was so much easier when he was five," Hannah grunted as they hoisted his arms around their shoulders and tried to maneuver him in.

"Y-y-ep," Daniel groaned. "At least he's on the first floor."

They half-dragged, half-carried him to Apartment 110.

"Keys, do you know where his keys are?" Hannah asked, feeling the sweat prickling on her forehead.

"Probably in his pocket," Daniel said reaching into his son's pocket to try to find keys.

Just then, the apartment door opened, startling both of them.

"Can I help... Oh, Adam!" the pretty redhead exclaimed, and looked surprised. "Um, you must be Adam's parents."

Hannah looked at the girl in shock. She can't be more than twenty-two years old, and where are her clothes?

Jessie looked down at herself and realized that she was only wearing one of Adam's t-shirts and no shorts. "Oh my God," I'm so sorry. I thought... I mean I didn't realize... I just..." Jessie flew out of the room leaving the door to the apartment wide open.

Daniel looked at Hannah and shrugged. "Okay, well let's get this boy in."

Adam was dead weight, and when they got to the couch, they let him go and he fell in face first.

"Should we go, or should we stay?" Daniel whispered.

"Oh, we are definitely staying," Hannah said smoothing her hair. "We need to get to the bottom of this."

"Bottom of what?" Daniel asked, annoyed. "Hannah, he's a grown man. We don't know everything that has happened. This girl could be..."

"Twenty-one? She's a baby and..."

"Actually, I'm twenty-two."

Daniel and Hannah turned around and realized that the girl had come back into the room, this time fully clothed in yoga pants and a bra under her shirt.

"Well, you look like a baby," Hannah said unapologetically.

Daniel cleared his throat. "Um, so we're Adam's parents, Daniel and Hannah."

"I'm Jessie," Jessie said feeling her cheeks burning. "I'm Adam's... uh, friend."

"Well Adam never mentioned you. Do you know about Brynn?" Hannah was staring Jessie down. Daniel was horrified. He had never seen this side of his sweet wife before.

Jessie seemed to shrink down a little bit. "I did... I mean I do know about Brynn. Not a lot. Just that they were high school sweethearts and now they are divorced."

"Well, they were together half of their lives, so don't rush into anything," Hannah warned.

"Okay, well we should be going now," Daniel said embarrassed. "I'm sorry to be so abrupt. Adam didn't tell us about you, that's all. It caught us off guard. I'm sure you're a very nice young lady."

"It's okay, really," Jessie said her face still red from the earlier embarrassment. "I understand."

Daniel was pushing Hannah out the door before she could say anything else.

Jessie locked the door behind them and stood over Adam, tears burning in her bright green eyes. "How could you do this to me?" she said knowing that he couldn't hear her. "After all I have done for you, how could you humiliate me?"

Adam lay face down on the couch, not moving. She knew that he was out for the count until he woke up with a vicious hangover. *He won't even miss me. He won't even know I'm gone.*

Jessie went into the bedroom and packed her bags. She knew that it would come to this one day, but she hoped that it wouldn't.

That's okay. It's better this way. She thought moving her hand to her belly. It's better if he doesn't even know about the baby. We don't need him in our lives when he doesn't love us.

Jessie found a notepad and left him a note:

Adam,

I met your parents while I was in my underwear. It was humiliating and horrifying. I know now that you don't love me and that you never will. I wish you the best always and wish that it could have been different for us.

I will always love you and remember the time we had together. Don't call me or contact me. I never want to see you again.

J~

32

BRYNN'S NIGHTMARE

Nick awoke to screaming.

"What the...." He jumped out of bed and realized that he wasn't in his own bedroom. He was half-asleep and confused. "Where am I?"

Oh, that's right. Brynn!

"Brynn! Brynn!" Nick looked around the bedroom and realized that it was empty. He followed the sound of the screaming, his heart pounding in his chest.

"No! No! Don't hurt me. Please stop hurting me! I'll be good, I'll be good!" Brynn's voice was sobbing and screaming, getting louder as he got closer to the kitchen.

He opened the door and saw Brynn crouched on the floor, tight up against the cabinets, her arms shielding her face. She was thrashing around desperately trying to cover her body up and protect herself from an unknown threat that seemed to be right above her. Maxie sat a few feet away whimpering.

Nick had never seen anything like it.

"Brynn, Brynn!" he was next to her in a split second, grabbing her tight with his strong arms. "Brynn, you're okay. I'm here. It's Nick."

Brynn kept thrashing, her hair flying as she tried to break out of his grip. "Don't hurt me! Don't hurt me! I'm sorry, I'm sorry! Pleeeeease stop!"

Nick looked into her eyes, which were wild with fear. Her eyes were even bigger than normal, and they were staring but not seeing. "BRYNN!" Nick screamed grabbing her face with his hands. "BRYNN, WAKE UP. WAKE UP!"

Brynn stopped thrashing immediately, her eyes still wide. Nick saw her trying to focus on his face, and he watched as the realization hit her and her body slumped to the ground.

"Oh my God, I'm so sorry, Nick," Brynn said lying on the floor, her long dark hair covering her face.

Nick got close to her and pulled her hair away, gently caressing her cheek. "It's okay, it's okay," he said trying to soothe her. His heart was starting to beat normally. He felt like his body was on fire from the adrenaline, and he scooped her up in his arms and held her close. "What were you dreaming about?"

Brynn was silent as she curled up as close to him as she could get trying to get control of herself. She wanted to hide from the humiliation of her dream. This is what she had been afraid of when Nick told her that he could push back his return home and stay for the week. She was afraid of the dreams, but somehow being with him, had kept them at bay, until now. "I was dreaming about my father. The one who adopted me, the one who used to hurt me."

She could hear Nick suck in his breath. *This is far more than he ever bargained for*, she thought bitterly. She knew that once he was gone, she wouldn't hear from him again after this.

"I'm sorry. I didn't know," Nick said holding her as tight as he could. He couldn't imagine anyone ever hurting Brynn.

"I know," Brynn said tearfully. "There's no way you would have. I wish you hadn't seen this."

"Why?" Nick asked pulling away and as he made her look him in the eyes.

Brynn looked down. She was mortified that he had seen her nightmares. They got better, and then they got worse. The shrink said she might never get a handle on them. Most nights she took the sleeping pills he gave her to knock herself out, but she didn't take them when Nick was there.

"It's embarassing. I'm sorry," Brynn said, so quietly that Nick could barely hear her.

"I'm sorry you had to go through that. You should never be embarrassed, not ever. Not around me."

Brynn sighed, the emotions still swirling around her. She didn't want to cry in front of him, but she didn't know how she couldn't. She closed her eyes tight and tried to breathe, but she still felt the wave of tears threatening to overcome her.

"Oh baby, you can cry. Don't hold it in," Nick whispered in her ear. Brynn felt the flood coming and for the first time, she let it out, sobbing freely in his arms. Nick held her close, feeling protective. He didn't want anything to hurt her and wanted to look out for her every chance he got. She was healing him from the inside out, and he wanted to do the same for her.

They clung to each other on the kitchen floor for a long time. Nick wanted so badly to protect her. He had gotten to know her so well in their short time together that he couldn't imagine being without her.

Brynn looked up at him, grateful to have him holding her close, sheltering her. She kissed his neck softly, surprising herself. They had been affectionate, but her kiss told him everything that he needed to know. She wanted to be as close to him as she possibly could. She had only given herself to Adam, but she wanted Nick more than she had ever wanted anyone.

"We said we were taking it slow," Nick whispered in her ear as he felt her hands all over him.

"I know, but I changed my mind," Brynn said panting as she pulled him into her. Nick had no choice but to give in. She was more than he ever imagined she would be, and he was drawn to her in such a way that he couldn't deny. He wanted all of her, even if it was only for a brief time. He wanted as much of her as he could have. He needed her.

Brynn made him feel as if everything were right in the world. The feel of her soft skin on his, the curve of her back, and the touch of her fingertips. Nick knew there was nowhere else he wanted to be but with her, close to her, filling his whole world up with only her and letting the rest of it all fall away.

They fell asleep, clothes strewn all over the kitchen floor. Brynn reveled in the deliciousness of lying half-naked on the cool tile of the kitchen floor. She was close to being as free as she could be, yet careful to hide her scars. He had seen enough for one day. She sighed happily, and lay as close to Nick as she could, falling quickly into a deep sleep.

Nick woke with a start.

He hadn't even checked the clock when he ran downstairs, and he was surprised to see the sun coming up through the kitchen windows.

He held onto Brynn, but strained his neck to see what time it was on the microwave clock.

Oh, Shit! I have to leave in thirty minutes to catch my plane! Nick tensed up without realizing it.

"Are you okay?" Brynn said wiping the sleep out of her eyes.

"Yeah," Nick said looking away. She was already good at being able to tell when he wasn't being honest.

"Seriously, what's wrong?" Brynn said grabbing his chin and turning it toward her.

"My plane. It leaves in two hours. I have to leave soon." Nick said apologetically.

"Oh, is it that time, already?" Brynn asked, gathering herself and extracting her body from his grip. She didn't realize that it was so early in the morning.

"It is." Nick hated to leave. He had already extended his trip by a day, but he had to get back home. He had to get back to the office. Then he had to try to figure out when he could get back to Brynn.

Brynn looked at him, her eyes sad. He thought she had sad eyes anyway, but looking into them was heart wrenching even for him.

"Will you be back?" Brynn asked shyly.

"Yes, I will. Definitely. I just don't know when. It's Maryland to

Ohio, and I have to try to figure out a schedule so that I can get to you soon and often," Nick said looking straight at her.

Brynn knew that she looked terrible from crying so much, but somehow it didn't seem to matter. When Nick looked at her, she felt beautiful. She knew that she would miss him, even though they just met, the connection between them strong and palpable.. She never imagined she would connect with someone after Adam, but Nick was so much different than Adam and made her feel things she never imagined she could.

Even still Adam had been her first love, and as hard as she tried, she often missed him and found her thoughts drifting to him throughout the day. She wondered if that would ever change for her and hoped that it would. For the first time in her life, she felt truly hopeful.

"Don't look so sad. We'll Skype, and we'll stay in touch. It'll be okay." Nick held her close and breathed in her clean scent. He loved how she smelled and willed it to stay with him for as long as it could.

"I know. I just..." Brynn couldn't continue. She didn't want to define anything yet. *For all I know, he will walk out my door and he won't come back. I may never hear from him again.* "I just want you to have a safe flight."

"It'll be fine," Nick said trying to be cheerful. He got up and took her hand as he walked into the bedroom to pack. Brynn took him in, enjoying watching him move.

He packed quickly, and Brynn sat on the edge of the bed waiting for the inevitable.

"Okay, so this is it," Nick said throwing his arms in the air.

"Okay. Well, have a safe trip and text me when you get back," Brynn said smiling up at him.

"I will. And I'll be back to see you soon. Or you can come see me," Nick said smoothing her hair.

"Okay," Brynn said feeling the awkwardness of the moment approaching.

Nick leaned over and kissed her, and Brynn was lost in time, enjoying the feel of his lips on hers with nothing else to think about.

They pulled away from each other, both of them gasping for air.

"I really need to leave or I'm going to miss my plane," Nick said smiling, his hair tousled from Brynn's hands. She liked how unguarded he looked, and she wished she could take a picture of him at that moment.

"Let me know when you get home safely," Brynn said smiling.

"I will. And I *will* see you soon." Nick said kissing her one last time. He picked up his bag and walked out of the bedroom, looking behind at her as he left.

Brynn flopped down on the bed, her body aching in all of the right places.

She was already replaying the week in her mind. The late night talks, the intimate details about their marriages, their divorces, the deaths of their children. For the first time in a long time, she felt like she could really talk to somebody other than Jane. She tried unsuccessfully to push down the excitement in her chest, even though her head kept telling her not to trust it. She had been so hurt, but Nick was making her feel as though there were possibilities.

She hadn't told him everything about Thomas, or about when she used to cut herself to ease the pain, but she figured those conversations would have to come at a later time.

There's a connection, a real connection. I'm not imagining it; I know that I'm not.

Brynn closed her eyes and let herself get lost in her bliss, thinking about nothing but Nick.

She heard an odd sound, a buzz, and she looked around for the source. She didn't recognize it, and then she realized it was her cell phone, put away in a drawer.

Brynn's heart leapt to see she had a text.

He's texting me already!

She opened it up:

Brynn~ Need to talk ASAP. Adam.

33

JOHN'S LOOSE ENDS

John Palmer loved his job, but there were parts of it that he didn't like. Specifically, the parts that involved dealing with Ellie Harper.

He knew that he had people to do that for him, but he had made a promise to her deceased father long ago that he would always help take care of the Harper family. He planned to keep that promise no matter what.

And now she was dead.

John was secretly relieved that she was finally gone for good. He had seen the blood soaked body for himself, and was thankful that this time he wouldn't be in store for another surprise return. The coroner said that Ellie overdosed, and then had bashed her head on the floor as she was falling. She had no chance. John knew that it was only a matter of time. On the outside, he played the part of the grieving family friend, but on the inside, he finally felt that he could breathe a little easier.

But there were loose ends to tie up now. Noah. Brynn Michael. He knew that Ellie was going to tell Brynn about Noah, but he wasn't sure if she actually ever did.

He thought that if he took Tricia with him that Brynn might be open to him. He had done his research on her, and he knew that she was a closed book, and that it took a while for her to open up to people. John needed her to be willing to be Noah's guardian, for Noah's sake. He no longer had anyone to count on, and as his half-sister, John wasn't sure if Brynn would be willing to take on that job. John didn't think that if it were he, that he would do it. But Brynn would have every resource available to her that she could think of, and John wanted her to know that.

He pulled up through the gates of the home where Noah had been staying since he was three. He was dreading telling him about Ellie, and he wasn't sure if Ellie ever told him about Brynn. He needed to see for himself. This was James Harper's family, and he needed to make sure that everything was taken care of as though it were his own. He owed James that much and more.

"Noah Harper," he said to the front desk clerk as he entered the building. John had turned into a very no-nonsense type of person, drastically different from the young man that James had mentored in his earlier years. James straightened his wire-rimmed glasses on his face, and pulled the collar out on his nicely pressed linen shirt. He didn't know how Noah was going to react to the news of his mother and it made him nervous.

He was relieved to see that Kelly, the pretty attendant that Noah liked so much, accompanied Noah to greet John. Kelly's grandparents had founded the home, and Kelly worked there because she wanted to, not because she had to. She was a caregiver by nature, and John trusted her completely with Noah.

"Hi, John," Noah said smiling broadly as he ran up to John and gave him a bear hug. He liked John. John always brought him candy and army men, and today was no different as John handed him a bag full of lots of goodies. "Thanks, John! You're the best!"

"You're welcome, Noah." John said smiling at him. He's gotten big. Really tall. What a sweet kid! He followed Kelly to a common area where John sat down next to Noah and watched him play with his new army men.

"John, do you know where my mommy is? I haven't seen her in a very long time," Noah asked after a few minutes of making shooting and bombing sounds as he pretended his army men were at war with each other.

Kelly looked at John, her face full of concern. John had called and had prepared her for the worst.

"Well, Noah. Your mommy won't be coming to visit you anymore," John said slowly. "She died last week, and she won't be able to come here now."

Noah sat and played with his army men as he had been when they sat down, and John wasn't sure if he heard him. "Noah, did you hear me?"

"Yes, John. Mommy died. She won't be here anymore."

"Do you understand what that means, Sweetie?" Kelly asked Noah putting her hand on his shoulder.

"Yes!" Noah's voice was starting to show signs of irritation. "I'm not stupid! I know what it means when you die."

"Well, um, how do you feel about it?" Kelly asked tentatively.

"I'm fine," Noah said quickly pretending to blow up the plastic tank that sat on the table in front of him, shooting it across the room.

Kelly and John looked at each other carefully.

"If you want to talk about anything, we can do that," Kelly said patiently.

"No. I know what happens when you die. They take your sheets off your bed, and then you don't sleep there anymore. That's what happens here all the time to my friends, and you don't get to see them anymore," *Noah was tired of feeling like they thought he was an idiot, he just wanted to see his mommy.*

"Well, I have a new friend now. I don't need Mommy anymore," Noah announced, busying himself with his toys.

"Oh, do you now?" John asked amused at Noah's independence. He thought back to visits when Noah wouldn't leave Ellie's side, not even to let her use the restroom. It was nice to see him more independent now.

"Yes!" Noah was agitated, and John thought that it was best to let him express himself. He had prepared himself for the worst, and he was still holding his breath and waiting for it to happen. "Do you want to meet her?"

"Uh, sure," John said hesitating. "There's something else I have to tell you, Noah."

"I know. Mommy's dead. She's not coming back. I won't see her again. I know," Noah's voice was rising, and his face was getting red as he concentrated on his army men.

"No, that's not it," John cleared his throat. "Noah, you have a sister."

Noah stopped playing with his army men. *He had always wanted a sister or a brother. He had begged Mommy for one lot of times, but she just ignored him and said she didn't want any more kids. It always made him sad.*

"A sister?" John could tell that Noah was very interested, even though Noah still refused to look at him.

"Yes. Her name is Brynn. She was El- your mommy's daughter before you. She's older," John said trying to keep it simple.

"Is she nice?" Noah asked quietly, keeping his head down.

"Um... yes, she's nice," John said carefully.

They sat in silence for a while, Noah looking at his army men while John and Kelly watched him, waiting for more of a reaction.

Noah jumped up suddenly, "Do you want to meet my friend?"

"Sure," John said standing up. *How am I going to get Brynn here to meet Noah? Or should I bring Noah to Brynn?*

Noah led John and Kelly through the grounds of the home. They walked for a long time. John kept looking at his watch. *It's a long drive back, and I want to be home for dinner.*

Suddenly Noah stopped. "There she is!"

John looked over at the woman sitting in the wheelchair. *Something struck him. God, I know her!*

As they approached, the woman looked up at them, a sweet smile coming across her face as she saw Noah. She reached out her hand for him, and he took it.

John felt his face getting hot as he broke out into a cold sweat. "It can't be..." He whispered to himself as he slowed his gait.

Kelly looked at him, concern written all over her face. "Are you okay?"

John stepped backward, nearly falling over his own feet. The woman looked up at him puzzled.

"W-w-what's your name?" John asked, trying to make his voice sound as normal as possible.

"Carly," the woman answered scowling at him. She didn't like how he was looking at her, and it made her uncomfortable. She tried not to shift in her seat but she couldn't help it, her eyes looking around at everything but the strange man who wouldn't take his eyes off of her.

"Are you sure?" John asked trying not to sound as though he didn't believe her.

"No. But that's what they've been calling me."

"Who?" John asked, curious.

"The people here. My friends, my husband." Carly said, annoyed with all of the questions that the strange man was asking her.

"Your *husband*?" John felt his heart beating wildly in his chest. "Who is your husband?"

"I think he's my husband... I get confused," Carly said rubbing her head. "Petey... his name is Petey. He's my husband."

John was silent for a moment. It was all too much. He looked at Noah and looked at Carly, and the resemblance was uncanny. He looked at Kelly and could tell from the look on her face that she saw it, too.

"Why are you looking at me that way?" Carly asked John, her voice tight and angry.

"Because I know you," John said looking her right in the eyes. "I know you very well."

"How?" Carly asked, her voice slightly quivering. Her expression told John that she didn't want to believe him.

"I know you, and I know your husband. Only your husband's name isn't Petey."

"Who am I then?" Carly asked, quietly. This man looked at her and spoke to her as though he really knew her, and she was intrigued.

"You're Amy. Amy Harper, and your husband is James Harper."

34

NICK'S HOMECOMING

Nick was dreading the plane ride home.

He didn't want to leave Brynn. Spending time with her was the first time that he had felt alive and happy in years. He sat on the plane and thought about what it was like to hold her in his arms. He thought about how she smelled clean, like soap—and how her skin tasted, salty and sweet at the same time.

He sat back in the seat and closed his eyes. *I wish the flight were longer, I need time to regroup.*

The week hadn't been nearly long enough, and he wished he had more time with Brynn. He knew that she was special from the moment he met her. He just hadn't realized how special she was. He had met a lot of women over the years on his trips, trying to forget, trying to ease the pain of his life. But none had affected him like Brynn. None of them had taken away the loneliness and despair like Brynn.

What am I doing? What have I done? What is wrong with me? Nick felt his heart racing in his chest, and he gestured for the flight attendant to bring him some water.

"Are you okay, sir?" she asked leaning over him and putting her hand on his shoulder.

"I'm fine," Nick said, taking a big drink of his water. "I'll be okay."

The flight attendant walked away, giving him a backward glance. He smiled weakly.

There is a special place in Hell for someone like me. Nick thought wryly.

He hadn't lied, completely. He had merely reshaped the truth a bit, though he knew that Brynn would never see it that way. But he knew that if he told her everything that she would never have agreed to spend time with him. Especially now, after everything that he knew about her.

She can never find out what I've done. She can never know that I didn't tell her everything.

Nick thought back to the last few years of his life and how miserable they had been. He had been a coward though, and hadn't been honest with himself.

I need to be honest with myself. I need to start over clean, for myself. For Brynn. I need to figure out what I'm doing and just do it.

They were safely in the air, and Nick turned his phone back on. It vibrated immediately with a text:

Are you in the air? Are you safe? I can't wait to see you! XO

Nick slammed his head back against the seat. *Shit!*

He spent the rest of the flight with his eyes closed, picturing Brynn in his mind. Her long dark hair flowing down her naked back, her big brown eyes staring up at him, wanting him. Her voice telling him about her sadness and her horror, making him want to hold her forever.

Nick brushed back his dark hair and thought about her hands touching him.

It was clear that he wasn't going to be able to stop thinking about her easily.

Nick felt his chest squeezing tight as the plane started to descend. He didn't know how he was going to get through the next couple of days.

Take deep breaths, it's going to be okay. You're going to be okay.

Nick smoothed out his shirt and ran his hands through his hair again. He was actually nervous!

He grabbed his carry on and pulled it down, letting everyone pass in front of him. He wanted to be the last one off the plane.

He walked off the plane slowly. He didn't have any luggage, and he walked to the gate, dragging his feet. He was dreading what was going to happen when he got to the other side of the gate.

Oh, shit! He thought, quickly reaching into this duffel bag and rummaging around. There! He pulled out the cool piece of metal that had been buried in the bottom of his bag for the entire week. He slipped it on his finger, immediately squirming. It felt like a noose around his finger, choking the life out of it.

He glanced at his hand one last time and walked slowly to the gate entrance.

"There you are!" he heard a familiar voice say, excitedly.

He felt his stomach flip as he turned around. There she was, standing in front of him, small, blonde, and frail as ever. He couldn't remember the last time that he looked at her and felt any love or passion.

"Hi," Nick said bending down and hugging her stiffly, feeling her bones through her shirt.

"I missed you," she said trying to kiss him, but only getting his cheek.

"It's good to see you," Nick mumbled, kissing her quickly on the forehead.

"Is that all you took with you?" the woman said pointing to his bag.

"Yeah. It wasn't supposed to be a long trip, but it just ended up being that way," Nick said absently as he looked away. "So, did you eat while I was away?"

The woman looked at him, annoyance crossing her face. "You just got back. Why are you asking me if I ate?"

"I just want to know if you ate. It doesn't look like you ate; that's all." Nick said defensively.

"Yes, I ate. I ate every day, at least once. Sometimes twice." The woman said stubbornly.

They walked in silence. "Do you need to stop somewhere before we go home? Did you eat?"

"No. I just want to go home and go to sleep. I'm really tired," Nick said avoiding her eyes. He didn't want her to pick him up from the airport. He had asked her not to pick him up, but he knew that she probably would anyway.

Even though he had told her that he wanted a divorce before he left on his trip, she did what she always did and ignored him.

"Okay. Well that's good. I can drive home then," the woman said grabbing his arm.

Nick pulled away, more violently than he meant to. She looked hurt and he felt terrible.

"Mel, please," he said trying to make his voice gentle as though he were talking to a wounded animal.

"Nicky, you don't want to divorce me. You were just upset when you left. But I'm eating now, and I'm taking my medicine. I'm not drinking much at all. I'll be good, I promise!" Melanie was crying, her tiny frame shaking uncontrollably.

Nick looked around and saw people looking at him in disgust, assuming, as always, that he was the one to blame. "Melanie, please stop. Don't do this here." Nick felt like an animal. He shouldn't have told her like he did. He shouldn't have told her right before his trip. Melanie's doctor had told him to be careful, but Nick didn't listen.

Melanie was drunk when he left. She was drunk more than she was sober, and Nick was disgusted by her.

He told her that he was getting a lawyer, and then he left, just like that. He hoped that she would believe him this time. He had come so close to doing it before, he had warned her before. But she never accepted it. He shouldn't have expected anything different this time.

"Melanie, please. Just sit." Nick walked her over to the black lobby chairs. "We aren't the same. Don't you get that? You're a freaking train wreck. You're an addict and an alcoholic. I just can't do this with you anymore, Mel! You're destroying yourself, and you're taking me with you. "

People were staring at them, giving Nick dirty looks, but Nick didn't care any longer. He had told her the same thing a thousand times, but then she cried and Nick gave in in. He had loved her since they were six years old in the first grade. But he was finally realizing that there was nothing that he could do to help her anymore. She had been teetering on the brink of stability for most of her life, but losing Teddy had put her firmly over the edge.

"Nicky, you can't leave me. I need you," Melanie pouted, her baby blue eyes appearing larger than usual, long lashes holding her tears captive.

"I can't stay and watch you do this to yourself anymore. It's killing me."

"I know. I know. I'll get help. I promise," Melanie's words rang hollow on Nick's ears, and he felt as detached from her as he had been feeling for so long.

"Mel, *I* lost a son, too," Nick said his voice flat. He looked at her long blonde hair, her beautiful small face, and her arms that were nothing but sticks crossed over her small breasts. He closed his eyes for a moment and thought about how beautiful and healthy she had once been, his chest tightening as he did so. *God, I miss her. I miss my wife.*

Without warning, Brynn's face flashed before his eyes. He thought about how she had made him forget about Mel, and about his pain. He thought about how it felt to lie in Brynn's arms and just feel content and happy, even if it was short lived.

"I know," Mel's voice brought him back to her. "Please, just let's go home. Just go home with me, and we can talk about it tomorrow."

Nick sighed. He was tired. He needed to rest. He needed to sleep.

He followed Mel out of the terminal, letting her weave her arm through his this time.

He was too exhausted to fight her tonight and knew that he would need to figure things out once he was rested.

35

REUNITED

Brynn froze as she re-read the text over and over.

Brynn~ Need to talk ASAP. Adam.
  Brynn~ Need to talk ASAP. Adam.
  Brynn~ Need to talk ASAP. Adam.

Why now? Why does he want to talk to me now?

Brynn felt herself breaking into a cold sweat as she forgot completely about Nick. She stood up and paced. *Oh My God, what do I do? What do I do?*

She started to text him back, but her fingers were shaking too hard for her to be able to type the words in. She threw her phone down on the floor, thankful that it landed on the soft area rug and not the hardwood floor.

She looked around at the empty house and she cursed.

Her phone buzzed again.

Brynn~ Are you there? Adam

Brynn felt infuriated. *How dare he text me now and then expect me to just drop everything and answer him? Who does he think he is?*

Brynn walked out of the room, Maxie trailing behind her, his nails clicking on the floors. "Maxie, sit!" Brynn said, irritated. Maxie put his ears back and looked at her, tilting his big soft head in curiosity. "I know, I know. It's just that... Daddy Adam is texting me. What do I do? Do I answer?"

Brynn sank to the floor next to Maxie and looked at him, wishing he could answer.

Brynn picked up the phone and stared at it.

She typed quickly and paused before hitting send.

What am I doing? Brynn sat on the floor and rocked herself back and forth while absently petting Maxie. His soft fur soothed her. He laid his big head on her legs and gave her a funny look. "I know, I know. I'm freaking out right now," she said looking him in the eyes.

She sat on the floor and time seemed to stop. She had no idea how long she sat there.

The doorbell rang and Brynn jumped. Maxie scuttled up quickly and ran to the door barking. Brynn chased after him and could tell that Maxie was happy to see whoever was on the other side of the door. She felt her heart beating wildly in her chest, and she paused for a moment, trying to catch her breath.

She opened the door slowly and there he was.

"Hi," Adam said shyly looking Brynn up and down, taking her in as he used to so long ago. Brynn felt her body shudder, and she suddenly felt extremely awkward.

"Hi," she said, the word barely coming out.

They stood at the door staring at one another. It had been over a year since they had seen each other last, both stunned with how drawn they felt to each other despite how much time had lapsed. The last time they had been together was in court. Brynn shuddered when she thought of that day.

"Um, do you want to come in?" Brynn asked slowly opening the door a little wider.

"Sure," Adam said looking around as he stepped through. He looked wounded as he took in the empty shelves and the empty rooms. The "For Sale" sign outside now said "Pending," but he wasn't prepared for the hollowness that he felt in his heart.

Brynn watched Adam carefully, her heart going out to him. She had imagined this moment, or a similar one for a long time, but in her mind, it had never been this way. She thought she would be angry, or that he would be angry. She envisioned ugly words, screaming, yelling. She expected the continuation of the war that was going on inside of them to spill out in their hatred, for the loss of Sophie and of their life together. But she hadn't expected this reverence and sadness.

Adam touched the walls that he had painted, and the woodwork that he had sanded, closing his eyes for a brief moment. He looked at each room from top to bottom as Brynn followed him around like a ghost.

When he got to the bedroom, he paused.

He turned to Brynn and looked at her, his eyes sadder than they had ever looked before.

Brynn could smell the whiskey on him. It was an old familiar smell that used to fill her with panic. But Adam had finally convinced her that he would never hurt her, and she wasn't afraid of him now.

"You look terrible," Brynn said, her voice cracking. She didn't like the scraggly beard he was wearing or his unkempt hair. She thought he looked dirty and terrible.

"I know," Adam said wryly. He couldn't remember the last time that he looked in a mirror, but he knew that he looked bad. His pants were falling off him, and his shirt was wrinkled and stained. "I'm sorry."

"Don't be sorry, you just need to clean up. Do you want to clean up here?" Brynn said walking toward the master bathroom.

"No, I mean, I'm sorry. I'm sorry for what I've done to you," Adam's voice was low, but Brynn heard every word. "I left you. I know it wasn't your fault, but I had to blame someone for losing Sophie."

"I know," Brynn said, feeling hot tears stinging her eyes without warning. "We can talk about this later. You need a hot shower right now."

Brynn steered him toward the bathroom. She reached into the closet and grabbed a nice big towel. As she stood closer to Adam, she couldn't believe how bad he smelled. Like whiskey and a combination of odors that she didn't want to recognize. She ran a nice hot bath and started to walk out of the bathroom.

"Wait, stay," Adam said stumbling a little as he turned around. Brynn grabbed his arm and caught him. "Help me."

Brynn suddenly felt bashful, her cheeks turning red and hot.

Adam chuckled. Brynn's breath caught. She had forgotten how much she loved the easy richness of Adam's voice. He had always gotten to her that way, and she tried desperately to block it out.

"Why are you laughing at me?" she said, her brown eyes angrily at him.

"I'm not laughing at you," Adam said quickly, immediately flashing his best puppy dog look. Brynn smiled in spite of herself. She tried to look away from him, but his deep blue eyes were drawing her in.

She thought for a second about how different Nick's eyes were, and she caught herself. She had never had feelings for more than one man before, and it felt oddly exhilarating.

"Stay, Brynn. You've seen me naked a thousand times. I just want you to stay," Adam struggled with his clothes, finally dropping them in a dirty pile on the floor. Brynn could see the steam rising up from the tub and worried that it may be too hot. But Adam sank right into it, immersing himself for a minute until he came up soggy, but slightly revived.

Brynn sat on the edge of the large tub, careful to sit as far from him as she could.

"What?" Adam asked, looking at her with an amused smile on his face.

"Well... um... Why, I mean why are you here?" Brynn asked trying to avoid his gaze.

"I'm here to redeem myself," Adam said matter-of-factly. "With you, with anyone who will listen."

Brynn stared at him.

"Brynn, in case you didn't know, I was a jerk. I had a wonderful life, a wonderful home, a beautiful wife who I've loved since I was fifteen. And I gave you up. I let you go. Not just once, but twice! Twice! What kind of fucking idiot does that?" Adam's voice was full of torment. "I'm willing to make amends. I'll do whatever it takes for as long as it takes."

Maxie grunted from the corner of the bathroom, making Brynn and Adam both jump. They had forgotten about him.

"I don't know what that means. I don't know what you are saying." Brynn's mind was racing and her legs felt weak.

Adam was running his soapy hands through his dark brown hair and Brynn found herself getting lost in the gesture, remembering running her own hands through his thick hair. She could still remember the feel of it between her fingers.

"Brynn, I've been drunk for a year. For over a year, really. For as long as we have been apart. I don't know how it happened, but I just started drinking and then I didn't stop. The drinking helped me stop thinking about you and what I did to you. And I hated myself for drinking, and I thought a thousand times over how you would hate me, too. Especially, with your bastard father drinking and hurting you..." Adam's voice was low, confessional.

Brynn couldn't stop listening even though she wanted to. She had been through so much with him, and she thought that she was done worrying about him and trying to figure him out.

"What do you want me to say?" Brynn asked searching his face for a clue.

"I don't know," Adam said shaking his head slowly. "I don't know what I expect you to say. If I were you, I would hate me. But I don't want you to hate me. I don't want you to hate me at all. I hate myself enough for both of us. I want you to forgive me, but I don't deserve it. I didn't deserve it the first time, and I don't deserve it now."

Brynn had already been through the period when she hated

Adam. While it only lasted for a brief time, she had felt it as true and real as anything she had ever felt before. But now she was done being angry with him, she just couldn't do it anymore. And part of her understood him better than she understood herself, so she couldn't blame him for leaving again.

"I don't hate you," Brynn said carefully. "I wish I could, but I don't."

Adam looked relieved, his face relaxing a little. Brynn couldn't believe how much he had aged in a year. He looked tense and worn, and part of her ached for him and the pain that he was going through.

"Thank you," he said gratefully, grabbing her hand. "Thank you. You just don't understand how much that means to me. You can't possibly understand."

Brynn felt electricity surging from his touch. She locked eyes with him and felt herself moving toward him.

Before she knew it, his lips were on hers. She barely felt the water drenching her as he pulled her into the tub. She barely felt anything, but his lips and his skin. She vaguely realized that he was taking her clothes off. All she could feel was his hands on her naked body, familiar and exciting, touching her in all of the places he knew that she liked. She felt a groan escape from her throat.

Brynn was lost once again in her Adam, and she didn't want to be anywhere else.

36

THE HARPER HOUSE

Tricia Palmer had never known her husband to joke with her. He was earnest and sincere in everything that he did.

When he called to tell her that he found Amy Harper, she thought that he was either joking or that he had lost his mind.

"How? Are you sure?" John could see Tricia's blonde head bobbing back and forth the way that it did when it was animated, even though they were only speaking on the phone. He knew her so well, and wished that she were with him at the home.

"Yes, I'm positive. It looks exactly like her, only older. Trish, she looks exactly the same! It sounds like her. It is her even though she doesn't realize it." John was talking quickly. He didn't want to let Amy out of his sight for very long. "She thinks her name is Carly."

"Where has she been?" Tricia said barely able to speak. "Where has she been all this time? Does she know about Ellie? About Eva?"

"She's been living in a small town called Sullivan. A few hours south of home. Honey, she doesn't even know who she is. She has no idea." John was desperately rubbing his temple in that way that he did when he was baffled by something.

"What are you going to do?" Tricia asked, her voice stunned and shaking.

"I'm already on it with lawyers and with everyone else," John said matter-of-factly.

Tricia's heart warmed. She knew that her husband would have already gotten the ball rolling. He amazed her with his efficiency.

"Can you bring her home?" Tricia asked. "Is she in good shape?"

"She looks great. But she's older and she can't remember anything. She has no idea who I am, and she doesn't remember what happened to James. She doesn't even remember James." John was trying to disguise the frustration in his voice. He was happy that he found her, but wished more than anything that she could remember what happened to his mentor and his friend.

John hung up the phone and felt better. The sound of Tricia's voice always soothed him. Sometimes she didn't even need to say anything; he just needed her to listen. He turned around, and he walked back to Noah and Amy.

He already had people working on getting her and Noah released from the home. The arrangements were being made to have the Harper House cleaned up and prepared for Noah and Amy to return. And he was working on getting Kelly hired on at the Harper House full time. Three short conversations had gotten the ball rolling, and John felt himself breathing easier.

Now he had to convince Noah and Amy to return with him.

He made the short walk back to Noah and Amy, and sat down on a bench next to Noah. Noah and Amy were engrossed in a competitive game of checkers. John could tell that Noah was concentrating so he waited patiently, pretending to be engrossed in the game.

"Yes!" Noah jumped up, raising both hands in the air in victory.

John high fived him and jumped up and down with him.

Noah was basking in the glory of his win as he sat back down. Amy was smiling, happy for Noah's win. He had been trying to beat her for a week, and it was well deserved.

"Well done, young man!" Amy said pretending to curtsy to him, as she sat in her wheelchair.

"Thank you for teaching me how to play." Noah said happily.

John looked at both them, surprised by their bond. "I have a proposal."

"A proposal?!" Amy said suspiciously.

"What's a proposal?" Noah asked, curious.

Kelly stared at John, fearful. Noah was unpredictable, and with the news about his mother, Kelly wasn't sure how he was going to react.

"A proposal is when I ask you a question and you have to answer 'yes' or 'no'," John said, clearing his throat. *Maybe I should wait. Maybe they aren't ready yet. Maybe I should just hold off on this.*

Noah and Amy looked at John, waiting for him to talk.

"I would like you to come live in the Harper House," John said, getting to the point quickly.

Noah looked at him, waiting for him to say more. "What is the Harper House?" Noah said finally.

"It's a big house where your mommy lived when she was a girl. And..." he said looking at Amy, "You lived there, too."

"I don't remember, and I'm not going anywhere," Amy said stubbornly.

"Don't say 'no' yet," John said quickly. "Maybe you could come see it and then you'll remember.

Amy looked at John angrily, as she backed her wheelchair away from him as quickly as she could, knocking over the checkerboard. "I don't know you. I'm not going anywhere with you!"

Amy started to wheel herself away and stopped suddenly.

"Carly!" John looked past the wheelchair, and he saw a man and a woman coming toward Amy. He immediately noticed how massive the man was—his chest large and shoulders wide with gigantic hands. The kind of hands that could squeeze a man's head in, John thought uneasily.

John, Kelly, and Noah were all frozen where Amy had left them, checkers strewn all over the pavement and the grass. Noah was visibly upset by Amy's sudden departure, and he looked up to Kelly helplessly.

The man and woman froze realizing that they had an audience.

"Carly, don't leave!" Noah said suddenly, jumping up. Amy looked at the man and woman and looked back at Noah, confusion written all over her still-very pretty face.

"Lily, Petey. I want you to meet my friends," she said gesturing to the man and the woman who looked like they wanted to do anything but.

They walked slowly toward her wheelchair and, at her urging, turned her around and pushed her toward the little group.

"I would like you to meet my friends," Amy said, pointedly to Noah. "This is Lily and Petey."

"Hi," Noah mumbled, not hiding his jealousy. He wanted Carly all to himself. He didn't care who these stupid people were.

"...and these," Amy said to Lily and Petey "...are my friends, Noah and Kelly."

John noticed that she intentionally omitted him out of the introductions.

"Hi," he said stepping forward and offering his hand. "I'm John Palmer. I actually am her friend. I've been her friend for a long time."

The big man looked worried, his big feet shuffling back and forth.

"What do you mean, a long time?" the woman asked calmly, staring at John with even gray eyes. John looked at her for a long moment before he spoke. She seemed genuinely concerned about Amy, and her tone even seemed protective.

"I mean, I know her as someone other than Carly. I know her as Amy. Amy Harper," John searched her face for a hint of recognition, as she continued to stare at him evenly. He could see out of the corner of his eye that the big man was backing away slowly.

Suddenly, there was a thunderous sound of feet running on the pavement, and within a second, Lily and the big man were face down on the ground. Men were flashing badges, and there was the audible sound of handcuffs clicking closed. Noah looked on in awe, his big green eyes wide as he clung tight to Kelly.

"Lily! Petey!" Amy was beside herself, wheeling herself as close to them as she could. "Where are you taking them? Petey. Petey! Where are you taking my husband?"

John ran to Petey and grabbed his collar as hard as he could.

"What did you do to him? Where is James? What did you do?"

The officer shoved John aside. "Sir, we'll take care of it. We'll find out what happened. Back off!"

John was desperate. Once he realized who Amy was, one of the phone calls he made was to the police. He knew that somehow the people who kidnapped her were bound to show up. They wouldn't have put her in a place like this if they didn't care about her. And if they cared about her, he figured they would come to see her. He just didn't realize it would happen so quickly.

The big man looked down at John, unfazed by John's sudden outburst. John was surprised by the sadness in the big man's eyes as he gestured for him to come closer. John immediately felt foolish, realizing that there was nothing about him that would intimidate this giant. He walked close to him slowly, feeling sheepish.

"Please," the big man said his voice low and gentle. "Please take care of her. I never hurt her. I would never hurt her. Please, make sure that she is happy." The officers jerked him away and they were gone as quickly as they had arrived, leaving the little group to themselves.

John was stunned. It was clear that Petey loved Amy. He looked back at Amy, her eyes following Petey until he disappeared, tears flowing uncontrollably down her cheeks.

"Sir," an older officer stood next to John and tapped him on the shoulder, startling him. John was caught up and didn't realize that there was anyone standing next to him. "We will need to talk to her. When you are settled down, and can make arrangements, I will need her. Sooner rather than later."

John nodded, not taking his eyes off Amy. She looked broken and sad, and it broke his heart. What have they done to her? Did they brainwash her?

John looked over at Noah and Kelly, who were stunned by the sudden turn of events that had just taken place. "Are you okay?"

They nodded without speaking.

"Are you still taking me? To the big house?" Noah asked after a few minutes, breaking the silence.

"Yes," John said, putting his hand on his shoulder. "Yes, I am."

37

INTRUDER

Adam woke up, his head splitting, his body aching. It was a familiar feeling, but something was different. The bed he was laying on was comfortable, soft. He closed his eyes and sunk into it. He knew this bed so well. It was his and Brynn's bed. He had missed it.

His head was fuzzy as he tried to remember every detail from the night before. His mind flashed images of Brynn in the bathtub with him, her clothes coming off easily, piece by piece. She was soaked, and she didn't care. He had never seen her so free in her nakedness before. She excited him in a way that he couldn't remember her exciting him before. They couldn't get close enough to one another, both of them clinging desperately, breathlessly, intensely.

He had missed the softness of her skin, and running his fingers up and down the bumpiness of her scars. He loved her scars as much as he loved her; they were a part of her that he couldn't deny.

Where is she? He wondered, realizing that she wasn't lying next to him.

He stood up uneasily, waiting for the throbbing in his head to intensify as the blood started to flow. He took a deep breath and started to walk around the house. He caught his reflection in the mirror, his dark thick hair standing up in messy waves. He grinned, his dark blue eyes lighting up. He was home.

He wandered around the house aimlessly looking for Brynn, looking in all of the usual spots. He didn't see Maxie anywhere either, but wherever Brynn was he would surely find Maxie. That dog loved Brynn, and rightfully so. She was good to Maxie. She had been good to Adam, too. But Adam had left her twice now. *How will she ever take me back?*

Brynn, Brynn, Brynn. He walked up and down the halls all over the house. *She's gone!*

He sat on the steps, his heart sinking.

Adam decided that he wasn't leaving. He wasn't going anywhere ever again. Living without her wasn't living, and he was tired of being miserable, tired of the constant shifting of his heart. Even Jessie knew that his heart wasn't complete without Brynn, and she had grown tired of it. Adam couldn't blame her. *I tried, Jessie. Honest to God, I tried.*

I'll call the realtor, and I'll call off the sale. I'll tell them that we are keeping the house, and we are going to live here forever. I'll tell them that it was an awful mistake. Adam needed aspirin. He padded around the house getting water, aspirin, looking out the windows. *Where did she go? She didn't even leave a note! I hope she is okay.*

Adam was getting worried. She probably just went to the restaurant.

He was hungry. *I'll text her and see where she is.*

B~Where are you?

Adam waited, but Brynn didn't answer. After an hour, he gave up and made a bowl of cereal. *Maybe she's freaked out. Maybe she hates me, and she is waiting for me to leave.*

The house was quiet, too quiet. He hated it. He walked around the house and pictured it the way it used to be. He remembered painting the walls with Brynn, laying the flooring with his own hands. He remembered the first fight they got into about the color of the sitting room, and how she thought the house was too big the first time she saw it. He remembered walking out of it the first time, believing he would never return. And then he remembered coming back and planning to have a baby with her, painting the baby's room, and watching Brynn's belly grow.

The nightmares. The terrible nightmares. He thought about finding Brynn hiding under the bed, in the closet, behind doors, and locked in the bathroom. Night terrors from Thomas and from when she was abandoned. Adam lay awake almost every night, the guilt tearing at him, knowing that Brynn was probably having another night terror and that he wasn't there to help her, to soothe her. He hated himself.

His parents weren't talking to him, and Adam was completely alone. Even Jessie had abandoned him, all because they knew what he had been refusing to acknowledge. Adam loved Brynn. Adam belonged with Brynn.

Adam walked up to the room he had been avoiding. The room with the door closed, that neither of them talked about. Sophie's room.

He opened the door and sucked his breath in. The room was untouched. It looked as it did the day they finished it. The walls were a pale pink, with delicate white butterflies painted whimsically all around the room. The crib sat quiet and isolated, white and pink and pretty. Adam looked around, breathing in the smell of talcum powder. He sat down in the rocking chair and imagined that Brynn often did the same, rocking and remembering the last time they held their tiny baby.

Adam choked back tears.

He remembered standing in this very room drunk and screaming at Brynn who cowered before him. "It's your fault Sophie is gone. You never wanted to be a mother! You never wanted to have children! You're a damaged, broken, useless bitch, and I hate you!"

Adam sunk to the floor from the chair and huddled in the fetal position, the shame, and the guilt washing over him in waves. *How could I? How? I am a disgusting person.* Adam held himself to the floor as tight as he could. He wanted to sink into it, to disappear. The carpet was soft, barely touched, and he never wanted to leave this room.

I need a drink. I need a fucking drink.

Adam hated the thought that crept into his mind a hundred times a day. He never used to drink because he hated what Thomas' drinking did to Brynn. But when they lost Sophie, something inside of him snapped, and he started drinking every day, all day. And now that little voice was telling him he needed a drink, even when he would already be drinking. He wanted to kill that little voice.

I'm not drinking again! I'm not! Not here, not ever. He felt like he had violated Sophie's room just by thinking about it. Her room felt like a sanctuary to him.

How can I ever leave this house again? How can I ever walk away from it? This is Sophie's room, her home, and Brynn's home.

Adam didn't realize that Brynn wasn't in the house. He stopped searching for her, lost in his thoughts as he lay on the floor of Sophie's room.

Brynn had gotten out of the house as quickly as she could in the morning, and drove around searching for clarity. She had never been with another man besides Adam, and despite the night before, all she could think about was Nick. It was strange how spending the night with Adam brought her a sense of closure. Brynn finally felt as though she could move on.

She realized that the only thing she wanted was to talk to Nick. Brynn fumbled for her cell phone and called him. She knew that it was early, but she decided that he would understand once she told him that she needed to hear his voice and to hear his laugh. She couldn't wait to talk to him, couldn't wait to make plans to see him again.

"Hello?" a female voice said sleepily.

"Hello?" Brynn said before she could stop herself. She pulled the phone away from her ear to see if had dialed the right number. His picture danced in front of her face, and she knew that it was no mistake.

"Who is this?" the female voice said, suddenly sounding very awake.

"Um, who is this?" Brynn said suddenly feeling on guard, the hairs on the back of her neck standing up. Who is answering Nick's phone this early in the morning?

"This is his wife!" The voice said swearing at Brynn.

Brynn didn't continue to listen; she simply hung up the phone and sat stunned.

She didn't need Adam. She didn't need anyone. Everyone in Brynn's life who was meant to protect, watch over, love, and listen to her had abandoned her. She couldn't believe that she ever imagined Nick to be any different.

Brynn looked sadly at Maxie who had been sitting quietly in the back seat. You're the only one who loves me. You're the only who has ever been true, who has loved me unconditionally. Maxie leapt up and licked her face and the tears that were starting to fall.

Brynn was embarrassed, she felt stupid. His wife! Brynn couldn't believe it.

Brynn sped home as quickly as she could with a sudden need to be completely alone. She needed Adam to leave. When she walked in the house, it was quiet, too quiet. Maxie's nails clicked on the floor behind her as Brynn started searching the rooms for Adam. He was nowhere to be found, but she knew that he was still there. She saw his wallet and keys on the side table when she came in.

She walked up to the room where she always kept the door closed and realized that it was wide open. She saw Adam lying in the middle of the floor, a silent trespasser. Brynn never went into that room. She wanted it to remain untainted, untouched. She couldn't bear the thought of anyone disturbing anything.

Adam didn't hear the footsteps walking into the bedroom.

Brynn's voice was low. He could barely hear it. "What are you doing in here?"

Adam jumped, "Brynn!"

"What are you doing in Sophie's room?" Brynn's voice was louder, and Adam realized that she didn't sound happy.

"I-I-I just wanted to see it." Adam suddenly felt as if he were trespassing.

"I don't want you in here. Get out!" Brynn's voice was rising. Her face was contorted in anger as she pointed to the door. "Get out! You have no right to be in here."

"No right? How can I not have a right to be here?" Brynn had touched a nerve with Adam.

"This isn't your home any longer. You didn't want to live here. You don't have a right to be here. Get out!" Adam had never heard Brynn's voice sound like this before. It was high, and shrill, and had a hysterical edge to it. He stared at her in disbelief.

"I'm not leaving. I'm not going anywhere. This is my house. I love you. I want to come back to you. I was a fool to leave. And I know you love me. If you didn't love me, you never would have been with me last night." Adam was pleading. He knew that he was begging, but he didn't care. He would give anything not to leave again.

Brynn stood in the room, her feet planted. She was confused about many things, but she wasn't confused about wanting Adam to leave.

As she stared at Adam in disbelief upon him violating Sophie's room, Brynn felt something break inside of her and she was furious —beyond furious. *Why is he here? What does he want from me?*

"GET OUT!" She screamed at Adam, lunging at him. "I need you to leave RIGHT NOW!"

She grabbed his shirt and started to drag him out of Sophie's room. Adam was taken off guard and was stunned by how strong her tiny body was. The anger was resonating from her, palpable and dark. He had never seen her like this before and he struggled against her, trying to stand his ground.

"BRYNN! Stop! Stop and calm down!" He tried to hold her tightly, tried to soothe her, but she refused to let him. She fought violently against him until Adam put his hands in the air, "I'll leave. God, I'm sorry, I'll leave."

Adam hurried down the stairs with her right behind him.

"You never should have gone into Sophie's room. You never should have come back here. Don't ever come back here again, Adam!" she hissed. "I don't need you, and I don't want you. All you've done is hurt me, and I am done with you. I don't want you in my life anymore!"

Adam was standing outside before he realized it, Maxie staring at him from the other side of the window.

"Brynn, Brynn..." Adam heard the click of the lock and the curtain close on the window.

Adam stared at the front door in disbelief.

It was over. After all of their years together, after he had returned, he would leave again. After last night, Adam finally knew that his life with Brynn was gone for good. And this time Adam knew that it was forever.

38

BRYNN AND JOHN

Brynn found out that Ellie died when a man named John Palmer called and asked if he could meet with her. They met face to face at a little coffee shop, and in spite of herself, Brynn liked him immediately. He felt almost like she imagined family should feel. Though she was usually distrustful, John made it easy for her. She liked that he was direct and to the point, and she trusted that about him. He seemed to have no interest other than protecting the family name and assets, and she admired his loyalty to her grandfather and to the family. John talked about James Harper fondly, and Brynn knew that he had meant a great deal to him.

He wasn't sure how Brynn would take Ellie's death, which is why he asked to meet with her in person.

"I hate to be the bearer of bad news, but your birth mother, Elizabeth Harper, overdosed and has died," John said hesitantly.

He wasn't sure how Brynn would react, and was intrigued to find that she barely had a reaction at all. She simply sighed, and said, "Is that all you wanted to tell me?"

Brynn knew that she should feel something about Ellie's death, but she simply felt relief. She never wanted to have a relationship with her. She simply wanted to confront her about why Ellie abandoned her the way she had. Now that Brynn had done that, she realized she didn't need anything from Ellie anymore, or even had any feelings about or for her, good or bad. And now that Ellie was gone, she was shocked to discover that she hadn't thought about Ellie much at all anymore.

Ellie had not been one of John's favorite people, and he was glad to not have to deal with her any longer, even though he struggled with the guilt of feeling that way. He knew that James loved Ellie more than anything, and John felt that he had failed them both by not being able to prevent her death. But he realized there was nothing else he could have done to save her.

He was hoping that Brynn would be very different from her birth mother. He wasn't sure what to expect when he met her, but had done extensive research on her background. He was prepared to hard sell her on being involved with the Harper Family, but he was taken off guard by how much he liked her. He could see a lot of James in her. James had been his mentor, and had taught him everything he knew. John had admired James' focus, his ability to get what he wanted easily. He saw the same focus and strength in Brynn, and he was careful not to underestimate her, but he found that he enjoyed their conversation and felt almost paternal toward her right away.

When he told her about the Harper House and that he wanted her to move in, he could tell right away that she didn't like the idea. She couldn't imagine that she would ever be comfortable in a home so big.

"I can't live in that big house!" she protested, her head still spinning about the inheritance. "That's ridiculous! I'll just buy a little bungalow by the restaurant and call it a day!"

"You can't just go off and live in a bungalow and ignore everything else." John said, and Brynn got the sense that he was a little annoyed. "There's more than the inheritance to consider."

"More?" Brynn's mind was already reeling. He had just told her that Ellie was dead. Then he told Brynn that she was inheriting the Harper fortune, which reached numbers that she had never imagined in her wildest dreams. "How is there possibly more?"

He explained about Noah, and Brynn fought the initial urge to run. Ellie had told her about Noah, but Brynn didn't anticipate that she was ever going to have to be his guardian and take care of him for the rest of his life. She didn't know if she would be able to do what John was asking of her, or even if she wanted to. She wasn't ready to take care of a younger brother she didn't know. Especially not one who needed so much. "Just meet him," John urged. "You'll fall in love with him, I promise."

Reluctantly, Brynn allowed John to set up a meeting between them a week later.

John had started hiring staff for the Harper House, and had the driver, Tony, take them to the home where Noah had spent most of his life. The drive up was pleasant, and John told Brynn a little bit about her family history. He was evasive when she asked about her grandmother, but she was so distracted with the thought of meeting Noah that she hadn't noticed. Brynn was impressed when they drove up. It didn't look like anything she had expected. It looked like an expensive resort, but Brynn was still saddened by the fact that Noah had to live here.

Noah had been waiting for them, and had started jumping up and down when he saw the car pull up. He came bounding up to the car, army men in hand, ready to introduce himself to his new sister. He introduced her to Kelly, telling Brynn that she was his "best girl." Kelly smiled graciously, and Brynn decided that she liked her immediately. Noah was clearly excited as he took her hand and showed her around his home, introducing her to all of his friends, except for his new best friend, Carly, who was in for her morning nap.

"I can't wait for you to meet Carly," he said, talking so quickly she had to concentrate to keep up. "She's great at checkers!"

Despite herself, Brynn did fall in love with Noah—at first sight, actually. He was sweet, vivacious, and energetic, and his adventurous spirit caught her off guard. She knew that she would never be able to leave him behind now, which is what she figured John was banking on. She realized that in Noah, she now had family. When Sophie died and Adam left her, she felt as though her chance at ever having a family were gone forever. Brynn was overwhelmed with the feeling that now she had a brother, and she knew that there would be no going back. She would now have a brother—forever.

A few days after she met Noah, John asked to meet with her again at the coffee shop where she met him the first time. Brynn was suspicious that he was inviting her to have coffee for the second time in a week.

"What do you mean, I have a grandmother?" Brynn was shocked and almost spit coffee out all over him. The look in her eyes told him that she wasn't up for any more surprises, and he almost felt guilty for keeping Amy from her. But he couldn't take the chance that Brynn would reject her. He wanted her to be hooked on Noah first. He knew that if she were, there would be no problem with introducing her to Amy. He also didn't want to overwhelm Brynn with too much at once.

When she got over her initial surprise, and John assured her that there wasn't anything else he was keeping from her, Brynn responded exactly how he hoped she would.

"I want to meet her as soon as possible!" she exclaimed, her eyes glistening with excitement. "I just don't understand how she could be alive this long, and how nobody knew about her."

John explained what he had gotten from Petey and Lily, before they had gone to prison. He knew the whole story now, and went through it with Brynn. Brynn cried as she imagined her grandmother alone, losing her memory, her past, her husband, and her life. She wanted to meet the woman who had adored her so much as a child. John showed her pictures of the two of them together, and the love in Amy's eyes was obvious.

But Brynn agreed to wait until John could bring her home, and the months felt like years.

John finally convinced her that moving into the Harper Home was the best thing for everyone. Brynn was in awe of the beauty of the old house, and she busied herself by setting up rooms and suites and updating the big house so that it didn't feel so empty and lonely.

She planned each room carefully and meticulously based on their needs and the feedback that John gave her. She called Kelly for advice on Noah's room, and since she was also coming to live with them, she talked to her about how she would like her room set up, as well.

The hardest room for Brynn to set up was the nursery. She had set it up with Adam in the Victorian, but she never wanted to do it alone. Sadly, now she realized that she had no choice. She was going to have to do it by herself, whether she wanted to or not.

39

BRYNN'S DISCOVERY

The memory of that day, and discovering that she was pregnant was hard for Brynn to revisit. It had been a hard day for her, and a hard moment for her to make it through. Brynn had sat in the yellow bathroom of the Victorian with Maxie lying loyally by her side on the cool tile. Brynn prayed.

She stared at the stick that sat on the edge of the bathroom sink as though it were a snake, and then stared at her watch. *One minute.*

She couldn't understand why time moved so slowly during the most painful or crucial moments of her life, yet the good ones flew by.

Two minutes.

She took a deep breath and looked at the stick. There was a plus. *Plus? Plus? What is a plus? Pregnant? Not pregnant? Pregnant? Oh no! Pregnant!*

Brynn sat down on the toilet, nearly falling in. She swore and flipped the cover down, and then sank to the floor hugging Maxie tight. *I can't be pregnant! This can't be!*

After Sophie's death, she realized that she wanted to be a mother. But she had never thought that she would do it alone. She thought about Adam, and she thought about Nick, and she realized that either of them could be the father. But neither of them were father material now. Adam, with his drinking and constant abandonment of her, and Nick with his wife. Brynn was disgusted with herself and disgusted with both of them. It had been a few months since she had last spoken to either of them, and she had no desire to have them in her life.

She desperately wanted to cry, but couldn't find the tears.

But now that she had come to terms with it, she was nervous and excited at the same time. She had lived through a lot of horrible things in her life, but bringing life into the world was beautiful, and Brynn felt thankful that she would have another chance to be a mother. Even if it meant she wouldn't get to share it with the man she loved.

Brynn enjoyed watching her belly grow little by little. She looked at herself in the mirror every day, dismayed that the scars from her early years of cutting to escape Thomas' abuse were still visible. She wished that they would fade away so that she never had to see them again, but they remained like the scars that resurfaced in her dreams. She decided that she was happy about being pregnant, and she pushed aside the feelings that Nick or Adam wouldn't be so happy.

Setting up the nursery in the Harper House was turning out to be fun. Jane was helping her, and had convinced Brynn to indulge a little since she now had the resources to do so. Brynn wasn't used to having an unlimited amount of money, and it made her uncomfortable. But Jane kept telling her that it was okay, and that spending money on the baby was a wonderful thing.

Brynn was thankful she had Jane, even though Jane asked her the hard questions that she sometimes didn't want to answer.

"So you are definitely going to do this alone? No Nick, No Adam?" Jane asked while they shopped.

"No, I'm not alone," Brynn smiled weakly, "I have you."

Jane shook her head and hugged her friend. She wondered when Brynn was ever going to allow herself to be happy, to let go and allow someone to love her. Even if she didn't know who the father of her baby was, Jane had hoped she would figure it out so that everyone would be happy. From what Brynn had told her, she knew that both Adam and Nick would be thrilled with the prospect of being a father again. But Brynn was stubborn, and she knew that it would be difficult to change her mind. She just wanted her friend to be happy. Right now, Brynn's happiness was wrapped up in finishing the house and having it ready for her new family.

The nursery was the last room to be renovated, and then the Harper House was complete.

Moving day for Amy and Noah had finally come. John Palmer had wished for it to happen much sooner, but there were many details to wrap up. Finally, he could breathe a sigh of relief knowing that his plans were coming to fruition.

Noah was sad to leave his friends, and the only home he had ever really known. He was happy that Kelly was going to be coming with him. It was the only consolation that he had. Noah had met Brynn a few times. She seemed nice enough, but they weren't quite friends yet. She was pretty, but Noah saw her make sad faces a lot and that made him sad, too. *Brynn reminded him of Mommy, and that made him really sad.*

Noah did like Maxie a lot. He always wanted a dog, but Mommy wouldn't let him have one. Brynn told him that Maxie could be his dog, too, and that made Noah very happy. *He liked throwing Maxie the ball because he liked to fetch, and Maxie liked to give kisses, which made Noah laugh.*

He didn't have a lot to take with him from the home. Just some army men, some clothes, and a few pictures. One of the pictures was of him and Ellie. *He could hardly remember her now, but he missed her and it made him upset to think of her. So he didn't.*

He was happy that his friend Carly was moving with him, too. But he didn't understand that John kept calling her 'Amy'. Noah tried calling her by the 'Amy' name, but he kept forgetting and it came out as 'C-amy'. Carly said he could call her whatever he wanted to. Everyone seemed happy that Noah and Amy were such good friends. *Noah didn't understand why everyone cared so much, he just wanted to keep seeing his friend and playing checkers with her.*

But Carly seemed sad, too. Carly and Brynn were sad women, and it made Noah sad sometimes to look at them. He tried to do funny things to make them laugh, and it did. But then they would look sad again. It didn't make sense to Noah.

Kelly was the only woman in his life who seemed really happy. Noah thought she was so pretty, and he thought he might want to marry her one day. But Kelly said, even though she was flattered, that she had a boyfriend. Noah said that he would keep asking, but Kelly said that he should find a nice girl his own age. He knew he wouldn't. *He thought Kelly was the prettiest woman he had ever met, with her silky blonde hair and bright blue eyes.*

Noah was excited about going to the "Big House," like everyone was calling it. John said he was going to have a big room where he could fit all of his army guys. John said that he would get him a lot more army guys to play with. John said that he could have anything he wanted, but he didn't want much. He just wanted his army guys and a soft bed. He didn't really like his bed at the home, but John said he would love his bed at the new house.

Kelly helped him pack his stuff, and then they went over to Carly's room to see how she was doing.

"C-Amy, are you ready yet?" Noah asked, bouncing on her bed.

"Not yet," Amy said shaking her head. "I don't know where I put my suitcase."

"I packed it for you already," Kelly said putting her hand on Amy's shoulder. "You're all ready to go now."

Amy looked around the room sadly. "I don't know where I'm going."

"You're going to the house you lived in a long time ago," Kelly said gently. "Your old house. The 'Harper House'. Do you remember?"

"No. I don't remember. I only remember living with Lily and Petey. I miss Lily and Petey. They loved me. They were my friends." Amy looked at Kelly, tears brimming in her beautiful brown eyes. "I don't know where I'm going."

Kelly smiled patiently. She had been having this conversation with Amy for weeks, and she hoped that when Amy got to the house it would be different and that she would remember. Kelly hoped that she would at least feel at home there.

"It'll be okay, Amy. Don't worry." Kelly gave her a quick hug. "I'll be there with you. Don't worry."

Amy nodded, trying to smile.

"Do you know what happened to Petey? Do you know what happened to my husband?" Amy was wringing her hands together faster and faster, her voice worried. "Nobody will tell me where my husband is. When he comes back to get me, I won't be here. How will he find me? How will he know where I am?"

Kelly frowned. She hated lying to Amy, but knew that she couldn't tell her the truth. She would never understand that Petey and Lily were gone, to prison, for a long time. She knew that it would only break Amy's fragile heart to know the truth. She grabbed Amy's hands to stop her from wringing them together, and she held onto them tight. "Amy, Petey has gone away, and he's not coming for back for a long time. He said to leave, and he will find you. He said not to worry, and that he wants you to go to the Big House. He said that you would be safe and happy there. Now, we have to get ready to go. The car is coming to get us very soon."

Amy looked around the room sadly. She didn't want to leave. She thought of her big husband, and how sweet he was to her, and it made her miss him even more. *How will he find me when he comes back? How can he think that I will be happy without him?*

"Come on C-Amy! Let's go see our new big house!" Noah was excited, and he couldn't wait to see his new house and his new room. Brynn had been getting the house ready for them and he couldn't wait to see his room.

Kelly's phone buzzed, and she checked it quickly. "Okay, folks," she said a little too brightly. "It's time to hit the road to the Harper House."

Noah jumped up and down in excitement. Amy looked at him, annoyed with Noah for the first time. She wasn't ready to go yet, but before she could protest, Kelly was wheeling her chair out of the room toward the elevator.

Amy watched her room disappear when the elevator doors closed, her stomach feeling sick suddenly. She hoped the feeling would go away, but the nauseousness was coming more and more lately, and it seemed like she never went too long without it.

All three stopped when they got out the front door. The big, sleek truck in front of them was mesmerizing. A sharply dressed middle-aged man in a black suit appeared out of nowhere. "Hi, I'm Tony. I'll be your driver today. Please, get in," he said gesturing to the open door. Noah and Kelly got in promptly, but Amy sat there waiting for Tony to help her, which he quickly obliged.

He expertly folded the wheelchair up and put it in the back of the truck. "When we get to the Big House, Miss, you'll have an electric cart to take you around in. You'll be able to go all over the grounds." He smiled at Amy and tipped his hat.

Kelly wondered briefly if Tony had been at the Harper House when Amy lived there, but that would have been over thirty years ago. Unless Tony was five or ten when he lived there, Kelly doubted it. She was trying to make a connection between the house and Amy. She knew that it would make Amy feel better about the move.

The drive to the House was quiet and seemed to take a long time. Kelly could feel the nervous energy in the car, and she tried to steady her nerves. She didn't know why she was so nervous; after all, this was a short stay for her. Kelly was getting married next year, and declined the servant quarters for a quiet home a few miles away. She wanted to be close, but still have a life of her own.

The car suddenly slowed and turned into a long driveway lined by magnificent pine trees that were hundreds of feet tall. They all peered out the window in awe, Noah's face pressed tight up against the glass, smearing it with breath and spit.

The driveway was long and pulled into a large roundabout. All three stared at the house in amazement. It definitely lived up to the name "The Big House."

Amy looked at the front entrance and felt a strange familiarity tickling at her. She knew that she had been here before, many times. She was eager to get out of the car.

They pulled to a stop before the front steps. Amy noticed that there was a wheelchair ramp that looked new, to the left of the stairs. A petite, dark haired woman was standing in front of the house. Amy thought that she was beautiful and hauntingly familiar.

Tony opened the door, and Noah exploded out of the car like a bullet. Kelly got out and held her hand out to Amy who grabbed it tightly. Tony and Kelly got Amy situated in the wheelchair and Amy took a breath and inhaled deeply through her nose. *I know the smell of this place! I've been here before!* Amy suddenly got a picture of a handsome dark haired man smiling at her. *James!*

Tears pricked at her eyes. *Where have I been? Where did I go?*

The woman standing at the steps looked at Amy, concerned. After she had hugged Noah and Kelly, Amy noticed that the woman didn't move. She just stared at Amy, with curiosity. The woman looked familiar to Amy, but she didn't know who she was. Amy never knew who anyone was anymore.

But this woman was different.

Suddenly the woman started walking toward Amy. She walked as Ellie used to walk and she reminded her of Ellie.

The woman opened her mouth to speak, and Amy thought it was Ellie speaking. The woman's voice had the same earthy tone to it, and Amy closed her eyes for just a second. She opened them quickly, her eyes wide in recognition.

She grabbed the younger woman and pulled her as close as she could, with a strength that she thought disappeared a long time ago.

40

HOME AT LAST

Everyone held their breath as they watched Amy grab Brynn and hold her tight.

"Eva! Eva! Oh my Eva! I thought that I would never see you again!" Amy cried.

Brynn stared into Amy's big brown eyes, the same brown eyes as her own.

She searched Amy's face, a face so much like the one she stared at in the mirror every day, only older. And if possible, sadder. She knew Amy's face, she felt as though she somehow remembered her face. Brynn saw glimpses of a younger face smiling at her with perfect white teeth, almost like an angel.

In all of her life, Brynn couldn't remember ever letting anyone hold her so closely and so soon, without wanting to pull away. Not even Adam. But Amy felt familiar in a way that Brynn couldn't explain.

Amy felt like home.

Brynn saw tears falling down Amy's cheeks and felt warm tears on her own cheeks. The two women hadn't even had a conversation, but Brynn knew that they didn't need words. There had always been something special between them. This had been the bond that Brynn had been missing; not Ellie, not Adam, not even Nick. All along, she had been waiting for Amy. Amy and Noah. They were her family now, and Brynn knew it just as certain as she had ever known anything. With the growing child inside of her, Brynn was struck with the realization that she was finally going to have the life that she had longed for, prayed for, even as a child. She was going to have a home with people who loved her.

Brynn had a family.

There was something about Amy and Noah that felt as familiar to her as anything had ever felt. She had always felt out of place in the world, but now she not only had a physical home, but people who felt like home to her.

Time stood still as Amy and Brynn held onto each other. Brynn closed her eyes, and she felt like a little girl, and imagined Amy holding her as a child. When they pulled away from one another, they smiled the same smile.

Brynn had wanted to meet Amy before. She had begged John. But Amy hadn't been doing well, and John felt it was best to wait.

Kelly watched from a distance and was amazed at how much they looked alike, the resemblance uncanny. She could see the resemblance in Noah, and she was happy that they had found one another. Something felt complete, and Kelly was happy to be a part of it. It had been hard for her to leave the home that her grandparents had built. But Kelly was drawn to Noah and Amy, and when John asked her to take care of them, she didn't hesitate. She didn't need the money that he offered her, but she did it so she could remain a part of them. They were special and she couldn't part with them as she had done with so many of the other residents.

Brynn ushered everyone into the house and had the help show them around. The house was full with the entire staff. Brynn wanted them there for the homecoming so they could all meet and work out their schedules. She was managing the house as she managed the restaurant, quickly and efficiently, giving everyone a role and sending them off to do it.

Noah had noticed her growing belly on his last visit before moving into the Big House.

"Brynn, you're getting fat." He said pointing to her stomach. "Are you eating too much food?"

"No," Brynn smiled, ruffling his hair. "There's a baby growing in there."

"There is?" Noah smiled. "I like babies!"

Brynn smiled back at him. "You're going to be an uncle!"

Noah jumped up and down in excitement. "I'm going to be an uncle! I'm going to be an uncle!"

He stopped suddenly, a worried look coming across his face. "What's an uncle? I don't know how to be an uncle!"

"You will be a wonderful uncle!" Brynn smiled at him, ruffling his hair. She tried to hide her fear from him and from everyone else.

"Who is the baby's daddy? My daddy is dead." Noah asked and stated all at once.

Brynn wasn't sure how to answer him, so she didn't. She didn't want to tell him that she wasn't sure who the father was. Adam, who was no longer in her life, or Nick who she was trying desperately to ignore.

The last time Brynn talked to Nick was before she knew that she was pregnant. She had refused to answer the phone, but he kept calling and texting.

She finally picked up the phone one last time to tell him to stop calling her. "I don't want to talk to you," Brynn yelled at him on the phone.

"Brynn! Brynn! Please, hear me out!" Nick was begging, and Brynn admitted to herself that she loved the sound of his voice. "I'm done, I've moved out. The divorce is almost final. Please, let me visit you. Let me explain it to you. I've been a horrible person, but I never meant to hurt you. I was trying to protect her, take care of things so that she would be okay. I'm so sorry for hurting you."

"I can't!" Brynn said gripping the phone in her hand. "I can't trust you anymore." She wanted to trust him. She wanted to give him a chance. But she couldn't. She couldn't stop thinking about Nick. She couldn't stop lying awake in bed at night remembering his lips on hers, or the sound of his voice in her ears. But she couldn't allow him to hurt her again.

"I can't talk to you anymore, Nick. Please." Brynn was crying, her sobs crushing him. He never wanted to hurt her. After he caught Mel answering his phone, he finally found the courage to leave her. He knew at that moment that he only wanted Brynn. He hadn't loved Mel for a long time, her boozy anger and mismanaged mental illness had slowly destroyed him, wearing him down.

Nick realized that in a few short days, Brynn had begun to heal him, connecting with him in their mutual pain, and that all he wanted was a chance to be with her. He just wanted to be able to show her that even though he lied, his feelings for her were real.

"Please don't call me again." Brynn said, her voice barely audible, and then she hung up, refusing to pick up the phone again when he called.

41

FAMILY

Brynn's life was so different than it had been a year ago. Jane managed the restaurant solely now, and Brynn had given her full partnership. Brynn was barely involved and trusted Jane completely. Her days were full with Noah and Amy, and as her pregnancy progressed, she found herself more fatigued.

Brynn found that she loved the house and rarely found excuses to leave. She was proud of the work she had done and how it had been beautifully restored under her supervision, years of neglect stripped away. She tried to imagine what it looked like when she was a baby, being carried into the house for the first time. But that had been so long ago and nothing that happened after was happy. Brynn wanted her baby to come into a happy home, and she wanted the home to be filled with love and laughter. With Amy, Noah, Kelly, and the staff, she was finding that there was plenty of love and laughter to go around.

Even though she hadn't had the ultrasound yet, Brynn knew that her baby was a girl. She talked to her baby girl every day, apologizing for her own shortcomings, explaining her decisions when she talked to her baby, she didn't feel so alone.

Walking into the home for the first time with her grandmother,

Brynn had been a little afraid. John had assured her that she had done a beautiful job and that the house was beautiful. But she was afraid that she had changed it too much, and that Amy wouldn't recognize it. John warned her that Amy might not recognize it anyway.

Amy looked around in awe as Brynn wheeled her through the gigantic foyer in front of the winding double staircase. "I lived here?"

"Yes," Brynn said softly. "You lived here, for a long time."

"It's beautiful," Amy breathed. "Did it look like this when I lived here?"

"It looked a lot like this, but I made some changes." Brynn said smiling.

Amy patted her hand. "Good girl. It's gorgeous." Brynn couldn't help but beam. Her heart was bursting with pride that Amy liked it. The hard part was over now, and she could get everyone settled in.

John smiled as he watched them move through the home. He had spent his entire life trying to restore the Harper legacy, and now it was finally coming together. He breathed a sigh of relief, happy to see the Big House restored and lived in again. He knew that James, his good friend and mentor, would be proud of him.

The next few months were a blur as everyone settled into normal life. Brynn's belly got rounder, and she and Amy were inseparable. In a lot of ways, Amy was the mother that Brynn longed for all of her life.

Amy's memory came back in flashes, but it didn't matter anymore. She felt at home with Brynn, and she didn't miss Petey, or his sister, Lily, as much, when she was with her granddaughter. She didn't remember baby Eva, but something about Brynn's big brown eyes gave her comfort. She knew Brynn by her eyes. She was the only person she was completely comfortable with...

Brynn and Kelly became close, almost as close as sisters.

Besides Jane, Brynn never had another female friend as an adult. She had never allowed herself to get close to anyone before, but Kelly was different, and for some reason, Brynn trusted her right away. She was helpful with Noah, but it was more than that. She seemed to understand Brynn, and she was a true caregiver. Kelly was smart, organized, and thoughtful. Brynn liked having her around. Kelly noticed that Noah was happier and calmer. The house had a soothing effect on him, and he spent hours pretending that he was an explorer as he discovered every nook and cranny of his new home. Much to everyone's surprise, he was even cooperative with his new tutor, Trina. Kelly took care of more than just Noah and Amy. Even though Brynn didn't realize it, Kelly was taking care of her, too.

"How are you feeling?" Kelly asked Brynn, as she neared her seventh month.

"Tired!" Brynn exclaimed smiling weakly. Brynn rubbed her belly absently. "This little girl is wearing me out."

"I hear it only gets worse," Kelly said smiling wryly.

"Yeah, thanks!" Brynn said sticking out her tongue.

"Oh, wait," Kelly disappeared from the kitchen. She arrived carrying a large bouquet. "These are for you."

Brynn frowned, her face growing dark. Kelly pulled out the card. "Shall I?"

Brynn was quiet.

Kelly pulled the card out slowly waiting for Brynn to protest. "Brynn..." she read slowly.

Brynn was still.

"I miss you."

There was no reaction.

"I need you in my life. You've restored me. Please."

Brynn's eyes filled with tears.

Kelly hesitated, and read on.

"Please," she repeated. "Talk to me. Give me a chance. Let me show you. Love, Nick"

Brynn stared at the beautiful assembly of mixed flowers and smiled. She'd heard it all before. He had been emailing, texting, and instant messaging her for months, but she had ignored him. He didn't know that she was pregnant, and she had no intention of telling him. He didn't know anything. Brynn wondered what he would say if he knew. She imagined that he would be happy. But they barely knew each other. How could they start a relationship with a child?

And then there was Adam. Adam who had just spent a month in rehab. Adam, who wouldn't take "no" for an answer. Adam who kept calling, texting, stopping by unannounced. She had managed to avoid him, until a couple of months ago when he arrived unexpectedly on the porch of the Harper House.

"You're pregnant?!" He was stunned. "You're pregnant, and you didn't tell me? How could you not tell me?"

Brynn tried to ignore the hurt in his voice. She avoided looking into his blue eyes because she was afraid that they would still turn her inside out.

"I didn't tell you because it's none of your business anymore," she said, her tone sharper than she meant it to be.

"My child is my business!" he said bitterly, pacing back and forth in front of her.

"Who said it was yours?" Brynn said angrily.

The tension between them was thick. Adam looked at Brynn in disbelief, trying to find his Brynn in the woman she had become. His Brynn would never sleep with someone else. His Brynn loved him and would never glare at him with those dark angry eyes—eyes that belonged to a stranger. His Brynn would never keep her pregnancy from him.

"Leave!" Brynn said, opening the front door.

"So we're not going to talk about this? How do I know if that is my baby?" Adam couldn't believe she was walking away.

"You don't. And it's not." Brynn walked through the front door and closed it behind her, locking it. Adam always had a way of showing up in her life, but she had spent a lot of time over the years locking him out. Nobody had hurt her the way that Adam had, deep and to the core. She convinced herself that she hated him, and this baby wasn't going to give him a reason to hurt her again. The fifteen-year-old kids that fell in love, so very long ago, were gone forever.

Brynn's phone buzzed.

"Did you get the flowers? I'm in town. I want to see you. Please meet me at the winery. 5 p.m. Don't say NO!"

Brynn shook her head and laughed. *The winery! What will he say when he sees me, and he realizes that I can't drink wine?*

She showed Kelly the text, and Kelly's eyes grew big. "What are you going to do?"

"I don't know. I don't know. I think..." Brynn was hesitant. "I think... that I should go see him and talk in person. I think that I should just do it."

Brynn had spent months convincing herself that she didn't love him. She thought that it was insane to love someone that she had only spent a week with, but she couldn't stop thinking about him no matter how hard she tried. Even if it didn't work out, Brynn knew that she had to at least talk to him. She couldn't go the rest of her life not knowing what it would have been like to at least give him a chance. Brynn had spent her entire life afraid of something or someone. She was tired of being afraid, and of living in fear.

She had given a lot of thought to what she would do if Nick ever came to see her. And now, he was here, and he wanted to see her. She didn't want to live her life regretting her chance, to see what he would say about the baby. At least then, she would know whether her feelings for Nick were true or fleeting.

"Are you going to respond?" Kelly asked, curious to see if Brynn was serious.

"No, I think I'll just show up. That way, if I change my mind, he will never know."

"Brynn!" Kelly scolded.

"I'm going! I know I'll go. He came all this way to see me. I have to," Brynn sighed, already second guessing herself.

Kelly smiled. *It's about time!*

42

BRYNN'S HAPPINESS

Kelly wanted Brynn to be happy. She had grown to love Brynn and to admire her strength. She could tell that Brynn had scars that she desperately tried to hide, but they surfaced when Brynn's guard was down. Kelly watched her with Amy and with Noah, and even though they were still working through the ebb and flow of their relationships, they were a solid family now. Amy was doing better than Kelly had ever imagined and Noah was thriving every day.

But Brynn's pain was far beyond the simple sadness of most people. It was desolate, devastating sadness, the heartbreaking kind. Brynn didn't talk about it, but Kelly recognized it from her years working at the home and seeing it in the faces of the residents. It was deep, true, pain—the kind that is masked, but never goes away.

"You need to figure out what you are wearing." Kelly said affectionately.

"I don't think it will matter," Brynn said rubbing her stomach. "Once he sees this, I could be wearing a prom dress, and I don't think it would matter!"

She had been so angry with Nick, for lying, and for not being truthful in the first place. She just wasn't sure. And she realized how hypocritical it seemed, considering the fact that she wasn't being honest with him. He didn't know she was pregnant. And he didn't know that it might be his. She had never been with anyone other than Adam. To be with two men during the same time period threw her. She didn't know what to do.

She went upstairs and went through her closet, dreading her meeting with Nick, but looking forward to it at the same time.

She had thought about him so much, imagined what it would be like to see him again. She tried to forget about their week together, but no matter what she did, she couldn't get him out of her mind. She couldn't make herself forget. It was the way he looked at her, the way he touched her. But most of all, it was the connection that she couldn't forget.

She paced her room.

Amy's voice startled her. She hadn't heard her wheel herself in. "Are you okay?"

"Yes!" Brynn said jumping a little. "I'm fine."

"Why are you pacing then?"

Brynn looked at Amy. She was looking frailer by the day. The doctor assured Brynn that she was well, but Brynn was constantly worried. She had just found her and didn't want to lose her so quickly.

"I'm fine, Grandma," Brynn smiled and leaned over to give her a hug. "Don't worry."

"I just want you to be happy," Amy said looking at her evenly. "I don't know that you have ever been happy. You deserve to be."

Brynn felt tears springing up in her eyes without her permission. She hadn't ever been happy. But when she was with Amy, she was happy because she knew that she was truly loved. It was the only time she had ever felt that way.

"I will be, Grandma. I'm always happy when I'm with you." Brynn hugged her gently again.

"Peanut!" Amy said suddenly.

Brynn looked at her, puzzled. "Peanut?"

"I used to call you Peanut when you were little. I had forgotten all about that." Amy said, her eyes looking past Brynn.

Brynn was used to these moments, as Amy seemed to have them more often with some memories resurfacing. Brynn smiled. "Peanut. I love it," she rubbed her stomach. "That's what we can call your great granddaughter."

"Yes," Amy said rubbing Brynn's stomach, affectionately. She was the only one Brynn would allow to touch her like that. "Well, I'll leave you to whatever you were doing."

"I'm trying to figure out what to wear to meet an old, um, friend." Brynn said glancing at her closet in dread.

"Whatever you choose won't matter," Amy said cupping Brynn's face. "You will be beautiful no matter what."

Brynn closed her eyes, cherishing the feel of Amy's soft hand on her cheek. She wished for the thousandth time that she had been with Amy all of her life. "Thanks, Grandma," she whispered.

"You're welcome, Peanut." Amy wheeled herself out of the room, and Brynn was left alone to face her closet.

After an hour, she finally picked out a maternity dress that was both fashionable and functional. Her baby belly was obvious, but it also accented her pretty legs. *It doesn't matter what I wear. The first thing that he is going to see is my stomach. There is no getting around it. Literally!*

She checked the clock. *It was already four-fifteen! Where did the time go?*

She grabbed her purse and moved as fast as she could. She didn't want to be late! She was afraid that he would think she wasn't coming and leave, and the winery was at least forty minutes away!

"Whoa! Where are you going so fast?" Nina, the housekeeper said flustered, as Brynn flew by her.

"I'm late!" Brynn said, trying not to sound panicked.

"You should have Tony drive you." Nina said, concerned about how nervous Brynn looked.

"No! I don't have time for that. I'm ready to go now and I can't wait for him." Brynn said, blindly digging around in her purse for keys.

She finally located them, feeling victorious, and got to her car as quickly as she could. She set her GPS just in case she couldn't remember how to get there, after all she had only been there once, and it had been from the restaurant. She wasn't sure that she would know how to get there from the Harper Home.

As she drove, she felt herself calming down.

What will I say to him? How will he look? What if he leaves the second he sees that I am pregnant?

She felt a little nauseous and fought the urge to turn around and go back home. *It'll be okay. It'll be okay. It'll be okay.*

She tried to take a deep breath and clear her mind. She wanted to be calm when she saw him. She wanted to tell him that she couldn't stop thinking about him, and that she wanted to give him a chance. She wanted him to know that she could see herself with him for a long time, and that he was the only one she had ever felt like she could be completely herself.

She was wrapped up in her thoughts, the pleasant voice on the GPS steering her way.

Brynn didn't see the F150 in the oncoming lane swerving in front of her. She didn't see the intoxicated driver with his eyes closed as he sped toward her, completely overtaking her lane. She didn't see anything until she heard the horrible sound of metal crunching, glass breaking, and then felt her body fly forward forcibly through the windshield. She suddenly felt the pain of a thousand knives slicing through her face and through her body.

And then, Brynn didn't feel anything.

FINISH EVA'S STORY IN THIS BRILLIANT FINALE

Get your today at your favorite ebook retailer.

"My god this book. Once again this author knows exactly how to use her words to grab my heartstrings and rip them right out! I couldn't have asked for a better conclusion."-Brienna Shacklock

"The plot is unpredictable, the characters compelling, and the karma is almost instant ... there are a lot of sub-stories that the reader really needs to pay attention. This is not a mindless read, this is the creator of book hang-overs....the reason that no book after this one will compare....it's just a lot. This book has all of the feels and it takes no prisoners."-Stephenee

EPILOGUE

The young woman sat at her vanity slowly brushing her long, dark hair. She stared at her reflection in the mirror, seeing a mixture of excitement and sadness on her pretty face.

She tried to hold the tears back, but she couldn't, no matter how hard she tried. This is a happy day!

She kept reminding herself that it was a joyous day. Sadness didn't belong in the day; although, she knew that it would be there no matter how hard she tried to fight it off. It had been there all of her life. It was there on her first day of school, when she got her first bra, when she left for her first date, at her senior prom, at both of her graduations, and it was here now. The sadness was a part of her no matter where she went or what she did. She knew that it would be here today of all days, alive and as palpable as ever.

Will it ever go away? She sighed.

She had asked to be alone right now. Too many people were milling about, in and out of her room, trying to be too helpful. There was too much noise, and no time to think. She needed to think. She needed to reflect. She needed to feel her, here.

She knew that she couldn't do that through all of the noise.

She walked to her window and looked out into the garden. There were a lot of people there, some his and some hers. She held her breath. She knew that there would be. So many people! *I just want to get through this without crying, without ruining my makeup.*

There was a gentle knock on the door.

"Eva, Are you ready?"

"Almost," she said straightening up. She reached up and felt her floral headband to make sure that it was still firmly in place. She took a deep breath and opened the door.

It was Aunt Jane. Jane's eyes immediately filled. "Oh sweetheart, you look so...so...."

"It's okay, Aunt Jane," Eva smiled. She knew what she was going to say, she was thinking it, too. "I look like my mother."

Jane nodded, choking back the tears. "Yes."

"Shall we?" Eva said motioning toward the staircase.

"Oh, yes," Jane said trying to compose herself. "I told myself that I wouldn't cry, but I just couldn't help myself."

"It's okay," Eva hugged the older woman who had been so much like a mother to her. Eva had begged her father from the time she could remember, to let go and find another wife. She desperately wanted to have a mother, but he refused. Now he just said that he was too old, even though he wasn't. She just wanted to see him happy once in her life.

They started down the long winding staircase. Daddy was standing at the bottom of the stairs waiting for her.

"Oh, Eva," he whispered. He was seeing what she had seen in the mirror. Except for the color of her eyes, she was nearly the spitting image of her Mom. "You're a vision, you know that, right?"

Eva nodded. *I wish she were here with me!*

Eva had never known her mother, but she longed for her every day. She had been taken from her in a violent car accident, with a drunk driver. It had been a horrific accident, and her mother had been kept alive for a couple of months after the accident in order to preserve Eva's life that still needed time to grow inside of her. Eva had heard the story a thousand times of how she easily could have died, too. There were days when she wished she had known her. Nobody understood the emptiness she felt without her.

"It was a miracle they were able to save you," Daddy had told her for as long as she could remember. He wanted her to understand how lucky she was. He wanted her to live her life to the fullest and appreciate every moment. The mangled picture of her mom's car was burned into her brain. The twisted blue metal, the shattered windshield, the bloodstains. They stayed with her like a vision, reminding her that she got to live.

Nobody understood the emptiness she felt without her mother. She loved her daddy, but living with him was like living with a ghost. She grew up in the big empty house virtually alone, with Daddy, and for a short time, Uncle Noah.

She loved Uncle Noah, but they said that he died so that he could be with Grandma Amy, who had died of a broken heart. She hadn't known Grandma Amy, but Eva hoped wherever they were that they were there together. She hoped that they weren't lonely like she used to be.

But now that she had Chris, she wasn't as lonely anymore.

"Are you ready to do this?" Eva said looking at her dad.

"I'm ready," he said smiling at her. He had aged. Eva had seen pictures of him from his younger years, and he had been so handsome. But he was a sad shadow of that young man now, his hair white and his eyes permanently sad. She thought of him as Eeyore from her Winnie the Pooh stories, perpetually sad and mopey. She had inherited his beautiful blue eyes, but she tried hard to not let them betray her.

The walk down the aisle was breathtaking. The backyard of the Harper House had been transformed into a beautiful scene for their wedding. She felt beautiful, like a princess, with her handsome prince waiting for her at the end. Chris was wonderful to her, and she knew that her mother would approve. She often talked to her, telling her all about him. Eva didn't know if she could hear her, but she told her anyway.

The moment that Eva had met Chris, she felt her loneliness start to disappear. He was larger than life, and filled her days and nights with laughter and happiness. She couldn't believe how lucky she was to meet him. She hoped that their child growing inside of her would have her blue eyes and his beautiful blonde hair. She envisioned a house full of tow-headed children running around creating chaos and joy, finally bringing the Harper House to life.

The ceremony was beautiful. Their kiss was full of affection and passion, and everyone in attendance stood up and cheered as they walked down the aisle Mr. & Mrs.

Before they prepared for the reception, Eva held Chris' hand and told him that she needed to make a stop.

"I'll be quick," she said kissing him sweetly on the cheek.

He nodded at his beautiful bride knowingly. "Do you want me to come?"

"No, later," she said kissing him, once more.

Eva walked down the quiet hallway to the room at the end.

She opened the door and peered in. Kelly looked up at her and smiled. "Are you married now?"

Eva nodded and Kelly hugged her tight. "Congratulations! I would have felt guilty leaving her all alone."

"I know." Eva smiled. Kelly had been there nearly every day of her life. She had her own family now, but she was still devoted to theirs. Kelly had loved her mom. "How is she today?"

Kelly looked down at the bed. She shrugged.

"She's the same as every day," she said sadly.

Eva sat on the side of the bed. She kissed Brynn's scarred cheek as she held her lifeless hand. "I did it, Mom. Chris and I are married now. The ceremony was beautiful. I wish you could have been there and seen it."

Brynn's body was still, except for the up and down of her chest rising from the breathing machine. Eva hated that she had to live like this, but Daddy refused to let her go. Brynn had never changed him from being her Power of Attorney when they divorced, and he always had the final say. Eva couldn't imagine that she would want to live this way, or that anyone would want to live this way. She had never known her, but she knew enough about her to know that she would hate this! Aunt Kelly and Aunt Jane had told her that she would have rather died, but neither of them could convince Daddy to let her go.

"She's a shell, Daddy! She shouldn't have to live like this. Why can't you just let her go?" Eva had begged him time and time again.

"I can't let her go! I need her. I can't let her go!" Adam argued with her and anyone else who fought him. "She could come back, it happens! There's activity on the brain monitor from time to time. I've abandoned her before, and I'm not going to do it again!"

They had nearly lost her on countless occasions, but Adam always made them bring her back, hoping she would fully return to him, but she never did.

Brynn's body lay small and motionless on the bed, her muscles deteriorated, and her scarred face sunken in and barely recognizable. She was full of tubes for feeding and monitoring, the big machine next to the bed taking every breath for her.

Eva had been coming to her room, talking to her, nearly every day of her life. But she knew that it wasn't really her mom lying there. Brynn's body was simply an empty shell, a faded vision of the beauty that she once was. Eva was ashamed to admit that all of her life, part of her wished that Brynn had just been taken away permanently when the truck hit her car. Watching Brynn lying in the bed, wasting away and helpless was sometimes more than she could bear. It was torture to have her mother there beside her, but not with her.

"I wish that he would have just let her go," she muttered to herself sadly.

"I know. I do, too," Kelly said a trace of anger in her voice.

The monitor hooked to Brynn's brain blipped, and they both looked at the same time.

"That's why," Kelly said shaking her head. "He thinks she is still in there somewhere."

"What do you think?" Eva asked, even though she knew the answer.

"She's been gone since the moment that truck hit her."

They sat in silence, the world outside of the doorway moving rapidly without them, preparing for the large reception.

"Don't you have to get to your celebration?" Kelly asked finally.

"Yes," Eva said slowly getting up. It made her feel morbid, but she liked sitting here. She liked hiding with her mom. She sighed, hating to leave. "I suppose that I should."

"Bye, Mom. I'm going to my reception now. I'll stop back and visit before we leave for Europe. We'll be gone for two weeks," Eva said, bending over to kiss Brynn's forehead. She smoothed her brown hair across her forehead.

She hesitated. She hated leaving her like this, but she knew that she had to. She had been leaving Brynn all of her life, but this time when she left, she knew that it would be for good.

She walked slowly toward the door and opened it.

"I love you, Mom," Eva said trying to make her voice sound happy. If there is a chance she can hear me, I want her to know that I am happy.

She closed the door behind her and leaned against it for a moment.

She heard the music playing down the hall, and knew that her guests would be waiting for her. She didn't want to keep them waiting. She felt guilty walking away from the room, as she always did. But she forced herself to do it anyway.

She had always longed for her mom, and hated that she was right in front of her but wasn't really there. She had lost her a long time ago. She turned back toward the door and stared at it, wishing that Brynn would walk right out.

But she didn't and she never would.

Eva turned around and walked toward her new groom, her own life, and her own happiness. She knew that was what Brynn would have wanted.

Kelly watched the door close behind her and sighed. She loved Eva, almost as much as she loved her own children. It was sad watching her grow up without her mother, but she had tried to help as much as she could. She could have left a long time ago, but she couldn't leave Brynn. She spent hours with Brynn, talking to her, reading to her, watching the lines on the monitor, and praying for a miracle. But she had given up on miracles a long time ago.

She stood up and cracked her back. The room was too dark and she walked over to the curtain to let some light in. "Well, Brynn, your baby is married. You should be very proud," she said staring out the window wishing her friend understood what she was saying.

Suddenly, Kelly froze.

Someone was in the room with them, she could tell. She could feel it.

The hairs went up on the back of her neck, and she turned around slowly. She scanned the room, feeling as though someone were watching her. She stood stock still, not daring to move. Time passed slowly, and the sensation eventually disappeared.

She chuckled at herself for her foolishness and sat back down in the chair next to Brynn's bed. This house is getting old. I'm getting old.

"Brynn. We're getting old, girl," she said glancing over at the lifeless body of her friend, knowing that she wasn't going to answer. She looked at Brynn not believing what she was seeing.

"Oh my God, it can't be!" she whispered, jumping up out of her chair, her heart beating wildly in her chest.

When Kelly looked at Brynn, all she could see were her huge brown eyes staring right back at her.

AFTERWORD

Thank you so much for reading Losing Eva.

Please help others to find my book by leaving an honest review on Goodreads and Amazon!

Reviews don't have to be long or detailed. They can be one or two lines that simply state how you felt about the book! It helps readers want to take a chance on a new-to-them author and we appreciate it so very much!

If you'd like to keep up with me, please join my email list and you'll receive a free eCopy of The Good One, the first book in the Happy Endings Resort Series, as well as updates and news about my author journey.

Thank you so much for reading!

X,

Jennifer

ALSO BY JENNIFER SIVEC

Leaving Eva

Losing Eva

Saving Eva

The Eva Series; the Complete Collection

I Run to You

The Forgotten

The Other Half of Me

The Good One, Part One

The Good One, Part Two

Grey's Harbor Series:

Grey's Landing (Book One)-Lark Griffing

The Grey's Harbor Anthology (Book Two)-JC Wing, Piper Malone, Carol Cassada, Lark Griffing, Jennifer Sivec

Hope Adrift (Book Three)-Lark Griffing

Harbor Tides (Book Four)-Lark Griffing

Perfect Seas (Book Five)-Jennifer Sivec

(Harbor Song (Book Six)-JC Wing)

A Grey's Harbor Christmas Anthology (Book Seven)-JC Wing, Lark Griffing, Piper Malone, Jennifer Sivec

ACKNOWLEDGMENTS

The sequel to Leaving Eva flowed quite a bit faster than the original. Even when I began, I had no idea where or how it would end, and may not have gotten there if it weren't for a few key people.

My family, as always, gives me encouragement and support, but at the same time they completely ground me. As I can have a bit of an obsessive personality, I sometimes become completely consumed by a story when I am writing. They remind me that my true life's story is about them, and not about my characters. I love them for that.

My in-laws, John and Andrea, have been wonderfully encouraging in this writing process from the moment I shared it with them. They are truly Mom and Dad, and I am thankful for them every day.

I've had the wonderful good fortune to work with some incredibly talented women who have worked on the Eva Series, from the beginning and have helped to make it what it is today: Rogena Mitchell-Jones, Brenda Gonet, JC Wing, Samantha March, Sarah Strawinski, and Margery Walshaw. Through each version, these women have believed in and encouraged me and I am grateful that I know them.

If not for Rick and Kim Miller, I don't know that *Losing Eva* would have come to such a riveting conclusion. Rick gave me some great feedback along the way and challenged me to think carefully about the direction of the story. They have been stalwart supporters through *Leaving Eva*, and I am so grateful for the time they take to read my work and to give me feedback.

And last, but not least, I want to thank my cousin, Lara Robins. From our childhood days of dress up and singing along to Madonna, she has always known me so well. Giving her *Losing Eva* to read, and to give feedback on, was one of the best things I could have done. She has an amazing eye for detail and, as an avid reader, always asks the questions that the reader would want to know. I loved hearing her thoughts on a character or a scene, and having her help really enhanced the story.

Since the release of *Leaving Eva*, I've met and have been able to interact with so many wonderful people. I want to thank anyone who has ever read my work! I am still overwhelmed and amazed that people take a chance on my books. I love the opportunity to share my writing and am so grateful anytime anyone finds it worthwhile. I look forward to growing in my continued journey with all of you.

ABOUT THE AUTHOR

Jennifer Sivec writes beautifully broken stories with heart.

She is attracted to and writes stories with characters that are complicated, flawed and completely imperfect. Her books are often a reflection of life, encompassing difficult subjects such as cancer, addiction, abandonment, and abuse. She writes with a raw, complex, yet hopeful approach often weaving tragic stories with honesty and grace, creating unforgettable characters.

Jennifer 's passion for reading and sharing stories gives her perspective and peace of mind.

She lives in Ohio with her husband, two boys, and herd of dogs who create balance and levity for her. She loves her crazy life and wonderful readers, and is grateful for all of it, every day.

For more information about Jennifer:
www.jennifersivec.com
jennifersivec@yahoo.com